THE HOUSE AT THE END OF THE WORLD

OF THE WORLD

By Madeleine Marsh

THE HOUSE AT THE END OF THE WORLD
by Madeleine Marsh

ISBN-13: 978-1482569070
ISBN-10: 1482569078

Thank you

Without my beloved husband, Simon Marsh, I never would have done this. He's a constant source of inspiration and encouragement, endless patience and boundless enthusiasm. Thank you, Simon, for supporting me in this crazy endeavour.

I owe my two proof readers a huge debt. Sue Wadsworth-Ladkin and Linda Wilson were wonderfully frank, honest and saved me from making some terrible and embarrassing mistakes! Any errors that remain are my own.

Thank you too to my oldest and best friend, Toria Nelson, for her advice, her in-depth knowledge of the English language and her knitting skills.

My incredible cover illustration artist is Vongue, who is a joy to collaborate with and made everything seem suddenly very real. Her work can be found here at www.vongue.daportfolio.com

Finally a mention for my Mum, Rosamond, because she's my Mum, she's hugely excited about this and I hope I don't let her down.

No one does something like this alone. It's those who take the trip with you who make it all possible and worthwhile.

Further information about me, the author, as well as free short stories featuring the characters in this book, can be found at www.madeleine-marsh.com

Acknowledgements

The following films, shows, novels and songs are mentioned in the book.

Coma written by Robin Cook

Ghostbusters written by Dan Aykroyd and Harold Ramis

Inspector Gadget created by Andy Heyward, Jean Chalopin and Bruno Bianchi

What Hurts the Most written by Jeffrey Steele and Steve Robson

Dawn of the Dead, *Day of the Dead*, *Diary of the Dead* written by George A. Romero

Scooby Doo copyright Hanna-Barbera Productions

Avengers copyright Stan Lee and Marvel Entertainment

James Bond created by Ian Fleming

Contents

BOOK ONE ~ THE UNUSUAL SUSPECTS

An electrical storm rages overhead; bright and loud and violent. It tears the night apart, ripping across the inky sky, leaving white trails on the black canvas. It's as beautiful as it is terrifying. Nature's fierce malevolence on display, as if all of Heaven is showing off. Perhaps they are. They might have reason to.

'That's some celebration.' Rick's East Coast accent is coloured by sarcasm. He sounds tired; 'seen it, done it' kind of tired. His bottom lip's bleeding and he wants a cigarette. The sleeves of his grey shirt are torn at the cuffs and red blood stains streak the front of it in sticky red and dry brown. He lets the heavy tyre iron he's been clutching like a lifeline fall from his aching fingers and it vanishes before it hits the ground. He doesn't notice. He's too busy scowling up at the sky, at the storm that might as well be hundreds of thousands of dollars' worth of fireworks the way the other three are staring, wide-eyed and open-mouthed, at the spectacle.

He glances at Gabe standing next to him and watches as he takes a pack of cigarettes and a lighter from an inside pocket of his long black winter coat. He, his coat and his expensive blue Italian suit are covered in dirt and blood but he either hasn't realised or no longer cares. Rick watches as he taps out a cigarette from one of the many packets he stowed about his person before they left the diner. He's seen Gabe squirrel away more packets into more pockets in more liquor stores than he can recall. He really wants a cigarette.

'Did you steal that coat from Inspector Gadget?'

'Nope.' Gabe holds up his index finger, unlit cigarette hanging from sticky lips, and fumbles for something in an outside pocket, eventually holding up a black leather wallet and opening it. 'From... Detective John Hammond, Second Grade, LAPD.' Grinning, he goes to sling the gold shield before thinking better of it and slipping it away again. Rick has no idea why. It's not as if anyone they've run into recently has had even the slightest respect for authority.

Rick nudges him and, reluctant as always, Gabe offers the pack and holds the flame of the disposable lighter steady. Rick closes his eyes as he sucks the smoke deep into his lungs, nicotine seeping into his blood stream. He doesn't smoke as a rule, although he's developed something dangerously close to a habit over the last few weeks. He's surprised the others haven't too. It's comforting somehow, the illusion it gives him of some measure of control over his own mortality. As he lifts the cigarette from his lips he opens his eyes and peers at the scorched tip. It's burning red, not orange, which is curious, and turning his hand to bring it closer he sees something moving in the glowing ashes, something he can't quite make out. He lifts the cigarette to eye level, certain he can see things shifting in the smouldering embers. He's right. It's impossible, but there are little people dancing... no, not dancing. Writhing. He looks deeper, picking out details: the fire on their skin, the pain in their tiny faces—

'Jesus!' He drops the cigarette, belatedly searching for it against the dark spread of dead leaves under his feet to stamp it out.

'Hey!'

Guiltily he glances at Gabe, shrugging apologetically. 'Sorry.' He doesn't offer an explanation. He doesn't have one to offer because despite everything they've seen this is his first hallucination. He shrugs and Gabe scowls but they've been through too much to fight over a paper stick of nicotine, no matter how rare they're quickly becoming.

As Gabe smokes he thrusts his free hand into the pocket of his coat and pulls it closer around him, shivering. It worries Rick because he isn't cold at all, quite warm and toasty in fact despite the wind and spots of rain that are starting to fall. On his left, Emilie tugs her ratty grey cardigan around her narrow shoulders so that it pulls tight over her small, denim-clad bottom. He can't remember what happened to the last in the long line of jackets she's stolen. Each one seems to have met a different fate.

'It's not as if they don't have anything to celebrate,' she points out.

'If we won,' Rick qualifies. The idea of Heaven celebrating irks him.

Joe too, apparently, because he hunches forward, shoves his hands into the shallow pockets of his heavy brown biker's jacket, the one he's managed to hold on to no matter what, and grumbles, 'Yeah. So where's our champagne?'

Gabe takes the cigarette from his mouth (Rick purposely doesn't look at the glowing tip) and casually blows out smoke as if this is the end of just another brawl. He points back over his shoulder. 'There could be some in the house.'

It's then that Rick realises they're no longer in the park. They're somewhere else; somewhere new. He turns to look, Emilie shuffling round in a tight circle next to him, and sees that they're standing in the yard of a once proud, Georgian-style, two-storey house. The walls are white-washed, specked with spots of black mildew and mould. The grey drain pipes are broken and there's water dripping from the slate roof where every other tile is missing. Steep, stone steps lead up to the splintering front door. The windows on either side are broken, leaving the ground floor of the house exposed to the elements. There's a turret room, with a steeply slanted roof, above the entrance.

The large front yard is lined with the skeletons of trees holding the remains of long-abandoned birds' nests up to the sky like sacrificial offerings. Two paths vanish around either side of the building and Rick's seen enough houses like this to imagine the rusted wreck of an old car in the gloom out back, with holes in the floor, the guts of the engine ripped out and rats living in the chewed up seats. He knows the type of people who live like this; hoarders who cling to the past and worry about the future. He grew up around them. Until not too long ago, he made his living preying on them.

The weather, which hasn't been kind to the outside, will have wrought the same havoc inside and he can imagine how bad the interior's going to look, feel and smell. But it's starting to rain and many things are better than standing out getting drenched. Of course, many things aren't.

They've stayed in worse places, making the best out of very, very bad situations. It amuses him that the others are all looking around as if something better is about to miraculously appear, momentarily resembling a small family of meerkats. But there's nothing else for miles, even in the dark he can see that, and a cold, damp, derelict house is better than no house at all in the storm that's gathering strength and pace.

It looks like it's been empty for far longer than most places they've sought shelter in but they know from experience that it pays to be sure. It's Joe who makes the first move, but then it usually is while the rest stand rooted to the spot. Joe isn't scared of death; he's made that perfectly clear. So he's the first into any new place, the first to see the damage, while the rest of them wait, tensing for whatever new horror could be about to confront them. They watch him climb the steps to the front door, nimble for a man in his late fifties and the strongest of them in every respect. Rick guesses they might have to jemmy the door open but Joe applies pressure to the handle and it swings inwards without so much as a squeak. He glances back at them before stepping cautiously into the dark. Rick has a brief flashback to the house in Morgan Hill, the one that looked so welcoming until Joe took that first step inside and vanished straight through the floor, the boards having been eaten away by the slow leak of bodily fluids from the dead stock-piled in the hallway. So Rick's holding his breath until light floods the doorway and he sees Joe standing there safely, waving them all inside.

He's not about to wait. Only a few of the places they've taken refuge in over recent weeks have revealed such gruesome surprises as Morgan

Hill. More often than not they've just been homes abandoned in the midst of life. Often that's been more harrowing to see than a pile of dead bodies or an overfed thing lying bloated in the hall. So if there are a couple of corpses in the bedroom or a plate of severed limbs in the kitchen, a bathroom painted in blood or dead animals in the pantry, he's okay with that. He doesn't think he should be, but he is.

Gabe and Emilie are hot on his heels, more than happy to be inside and out of the cold. The moment they're all in it starts to rain in biblical style. Rick expects to hear dripping water, to feel and smell the damp in the house, but he doesn't and when he looks around he's pleasantly surprised. They're standing in a large, hexagonal hall with a staircase to their left, winding up around the walls in three staggered dog-legs to a mezzanine-style first floor that's surrounded by a bronze rail and overlooks the hall. Hanging directly above them from the first floor ceiling there's a stunning crystal chandelier. The walls are split by a dado rail, dark wainscoting on the bottom half, ornate paper on top; a bold, gold fleur-de-lis pattern on a background of blues. The hall seems to be the heart of the house, everything else branching off or away from it. There's a huge, creepy fireplace at the back, big enough that if the mood took them they could all stand in it with only a slight bend in their backs, and Emilie could stand up straight. There's an overstuffed brown leather couch squatting in front of the grate, again in better shape than he would have expected in a leaky old house. A bookcase leans against the wall to the right of the fireplace, tall and narrow with glass doors, and an antique grandfather clock stands beside the front door, hands stopped at five minutes to one. There's a closed door to their right, which Joe tries but it's locked, and an open one to their left through which Rick can see a large kitchen.

At least there are no immediate nasty surprises, although it is strange that the house bears no resemblance on the inside to how the outside suggests it should look. There are cobwebs in the corners but no dust, no sign of damp, and the strangest thing of all is that the windows aren't broken in here. It's the best place Rick's set foot in since he left Friendly Hills six weeks ago and that includes the diner at the gas station where they've been laying low for the last five days.

They all stand in the hall and look at one another until Emilie breaks the silence.

'Where are we?' No one answers and chances are she isn't expecting anyone to. 'Okay. How about, how did we get here?' They exchange glances. 'What do you think happened to Luke and Matt?'

9

Joe responds to that one. 'They were alive at the end. I saw them at the top of the hill. They were together.' He squeezes her shoulder, reassuring her, something Rick's never been good at doing with any kind of genuine feeling. 'Could be they just didn't come with us... wherever we are.'

Rick doesn't think she's the crying type but he doesn't want to be around if she does shed a few tears. He's rubbish with emotional women. Rubbish with emotions full stop. He moves away from the group, approaching the fireplace and crouching down in front of the hearth for a better look. There's an etching in the soot-black stone at the back, two angels with horns held high in exultation, their wings spread. It's supposedly meant to be a comforting sight but it isn't. He becomes gradually aware of vague sounds right at the edge of his hearing, sounds he can't quite place, but as he turns around to look back into the room they fade to nothing and he isn't sure they were ever there. There is the possibility that there are more people here, upstairs or in the other rooms, alive or dead or somewhere in between.

'Is everyone okay?'

Rick looks up at Joe and confirms that he is. He sees the others check themselves for wounds. He can't feel any injuries other than his split lips. They all sound off, they're all fine. There isn't anything worse than a couple of cuts and bruises amongst them and that's a miracle because they were all in quite a desperate state at the end.

He hears Gabe ask, 'What's with the windows? Weren't they broken when we were outside?'

At the same time as the unlikely words, 'I'll take a look upstairs,' fall from his own mouth. All three turn to look at him. He's surprised himself. It's unusual for him to volunteer to do anything even a little bit risky.

'Are you sure?'

Rick nods at Joe. 'I'm sure.' It even sounds convincing as he lifts an iron poker from the fireplace. They're used to having access to a wide range of weapons, thanks to Matt and Luke, but it's the only thing to hand unless he wants to go back outside to look for the tyre iron he dropped, which he doesn't. He's usually the one who will wait for others to act first but he's got a genuinely uncomfortable feeling and he wants to look around.

He cautiously starts up the stairs. There are five steps to the first dog-leg, eight to the next and six to the top, to the first floor. Up here the walls are decorated with similar paper to downstairs but in greens rather than blues and there are the same dark floorboards on to which the chandelier is casting glittering sparkles of coloured light. Close to the top of the main stairs there's a second staircase, this one a tight spiral leading up, presumably to the turret room they saw from the yard. It's a strange-looking construction. The steps are narrow with empty space between them and there's a flat iron banister that follows the twist on the left hand side. All he can see when he peers up into the darkness is a door at the top, set back from the stairs.

There are five rooms off the mezzanine, all with their doors standing open. Four are bedrooms, each one looking as welcoming as a five-star hotel, with four poster beds and neat, clean sheets. He checks and finds that two are en-suite. The fifth room, the farthest from the top of the stairs, is a large opulent bathroom with a free-standing claw-footed bath and a showerhead the size of a dinner plate. The bronze fixtures and fittings are polished to a high shine. The floor is tiled. This is nothing like the places they've been camping out in or the dumps he was bedding down in before he met up with the others. This is luxury and that raises his suspicions.

Four bedrooms, one for each of them if Matt and Luke don't show. That's some coincidence. He considers whether or not it would be safe for them all to sleep at the same time, without a look-out. He lingers in a bedroom doorway and stares longingly at the bed. But tempting as it is to lie down and close his eyes for a couple of minutes, he is hungry. He's hopeful there's food somewhere, even if it's just in tins. There's only one more room to check so he climbs the narrow spiral steps carefully, the poker held at the ready. He puts his left hand on the iron banister, feels a texture to it, and when he looks closer he sees there's a snake-skin pattern etched into the surface of the metal. He follows it up and when he reaches the top his fingers slide over a bulge on the stair post. The end of the banister is shaped like the head of a snake, with its mouth open and forked tongue flicking out, captured and frozen. It looks so incredibly real that he snatches his hand away.

He's on a square landing just big enough for one person, standing in front of an exquisitely carved wooden door. He's never been particularly appreciative of art, except for acknowledging its monetary worth, but even he can see the craftsmanship and dedication that went into creating this. What he can see of the detail in the dim light is astounding and he runs his fingers over what looks like a battle scene, with fierce dogs on the attack, arrows flying and corpses in gruesome piles on the ground. He tries the door, quietly turning the smooth metal knob, but it's locked. He considers knocking but doesn't, just turns his head and leans in close enough to put his ear to the wood.

There's no sound, not for a long time, but finally he thinks he can hear soft snoring. He hopes that if there is someone behind the solid door it's Matt and Luke, and not just for the obvious reason that he really isn't up to getting into another fight right now. He hopes it's them because they saved his ass, because Emilie has been head-over-heels for Luke from the moment she set eyes on him, even though she doesn't stand a chance. And well, because he likes them. They're good guys with specialised skills, like the ability to fatally maim any and all manner of creatures, to pump gas when there's no power, and to find a beer in the most hostile or simply unlikely of places. He's learnt a lot from them, he can only hope he has a future in which to forget it all.

~..~

Leaving Gabe to start a fire, Joe shrugs off his jacket and hangs it on one of the hooks next to the front door before heading into the kitchen. He finds the light switch on the wall just inside, a tiny metal flicker that he pushes upwards to turn on a naked bulb hanging on a short flex in the centre of the off-white ceiling. It's a huge room, wood-stained cabinets lining the walls, floor-standing and wall-mounted, under and over a black granite worktop. A large, bare window looks out over the front yard, two Belfast sinks set into the surface under it. A solid oak kitchen table stands just off-centre of the room, with a metal grill suspended over it, pots and pans hanging from heavy metal hooks. There's no dust or damp in here either and like in the hall the window isn't broken.

Joe's wife, Babs, used to admire other people's kitchens while he was more inclined to appreciate a well stocked tool shed or a properly maintained garage. But even he can tell that it's a good, functional room. At home, back when his life held some semblance of normality and most days made sense, Babs did the cooking. It wasn't that he couldn't cook, just that he worked and she didn't, so he never had to wait for his supper to be on the table when he got home and how fucking antiquated did that sound? He would cook when tradition demanded it; Christmas and Thanksgiving, when there was a bird the size of a house to deal with. Only after Babs died did he have to learn how to look after himself and as it turns out he's more than capable.

He walks over to where a heavy kettle sits on a hob over the oven and experimentally he tries the gas. It takes a couple of seconds before he can smell it, but it's definitely on. It's the same with the water when he turns the faucet over one of the sinks. Somewhere above him he can hear the pipes, banging and groaning like the un-dead, but a splash of surprisingly clear, cold water is finally coughed out followed a moment later by not so much a stream but definitely a constant dribble. Letting it run, he starts opening cupboards. His first discovery is a jar of coffee. It's not freshly ground, so it won't make their resident coffee addicts happy, but it'll do for starters. There are packets of custard, sugar and dried soup, beans in tomato sauce, tinned vegetables and fruits in syrup. There are even stews although from the pictures on the front of the cans they do not look appetising.

There's a white door on the other side of the kitchen and, curious as always, he has to open it. It's his curiosity that landed him here in the first place, opening doors he should have left well alone. But once he started it just wasn't in him to quit and even though this door just leads to a pantry it's still a discovery. Luckily, not one of the nasty ones.

In Wallace, seriously hungry, he and Gabe had opened up the pantry of a house whose dead occupants were still in the kitchen, only to find something had eaten everything in sight and was lying distended on the floor of the cramped room surrounded by empty packaging and half-regurgitated, unidentifiable bits of food. There was nothing left but then, after seeing that, they really weren't hungry anymore.

In this pantry there's fresh food: cakes and biscuits, fruit and veg. It isn't right, it shouldn't be here, but there's enough food to feed them all for at least a couple of months and none of it is rotting or mouldy like half of everything else they've tried to eat recently. Somehow, someone must have stocked this place not much later than yesterday, if not for the long haul then definitely for an extended stay. But whoever did that, they're gone now. At least, he hopes they're gone. They've all had enough surprises for one lifetime, they deserve a break. They deserve some good cooking too. But first things first. Closing the pantry door and spying the free-standing fridge against the opposite wall, he calls out into the hall,

'Anyone for coffee?'

~..~

Despite his addiction – he craves coffee more than he needs to smoke – in all honesty, right now, Gabe would prefer an ice cold beer in a frosted glass with condensation running down the sides. Matt and Luke have an uncanny knack of finding beer, but most of it has been warm and although he's never once complained he yearns for the cold fizzy stuff he used to drink back home. Not that he likes to remember the past, even the recent past, because it makes him ever so slightly suicidal. It isn't because he misses anything or anyone in particular. He isn't married; he's never met that one *special* person. He doesn't have close family or friends to mourn. But he was living the good life when everything went crazy. He was having fun and it upsets him in a very shallow way to think that he'll never have it that easy ever again.

He lived in the San Pedro area of Los Angeles before the madness started. He drank in a basement bar where everyone knew everyone else. Although he wouldn't have referred to any of his fellow drinkers as 'friends', he did know several of them by their first names and he enjoyed the many nights he spent there, sinking a couple of cold ones after work. Maggie, the girl who worked behind the bar, knew him, knew his poison and his usual food order. He liked her right up until the moment he watched her rip a man's arms off for complaining that his beer had too much head. Gabe's own joke, that it wasn't possible for a man to have too much head, unfortunately left his mouth a moment before the arm ripping incident and almost cost him his own limbs. He narrowly escaped the bar before the blood bath that ensued. It was the start of the carnage that had torn his little slice of ideal life apart.

He misses the little things, the clack of pool balls on green baize, hearing Rascal Flatts playing on a jukebox. While he's been on the road with Matt and Luke, as part of their little posse, they've spent a few nights in roadhouses even if they've had to step over the remains of previous patrons to reach the bar and serve themselves. Matt's a demon with a cue. He and Luke make money hustling unsuspecting players. It never seemed much, not the games Gabe saw anyway, but it was often enough to buy essentials so they didn't need to steal absolutely everything. And he did hear *What Hurts The Most* on the radio in the jeep one afternoon before the last of the local stations stopped broadcasting. Still, he mourns his old life. He was good at what he did, selling extravagant sports cars to anyone who could afford one and, on a particularly memorable and celebrated occasion, more than one. He led a mostly meaningless life for which he's never felt the need to apologise. He drove a different car home every night.

Everyone loves an expensive sports car. They're sleek, sexy and fast. They're the ultimate status symbol, a suggestion of power, a very blatant display of wealth. They make women, and men, of a certain persuasion go weak at the knees. He used his access to the cars mercilessly to get laid, happily swinging either way, and it was a lifestyle he sold to everyone who stood undecided in the showroom worrying about balancing their company's accounts at the end of the year or explaining the dent in the trust fund.

Not everyone needed persuading, of course. But Gabe's strength was being able to sell to anyone he approached. His bosses loved him and rewarded him well for his high sales figures which meant he could afford life's little luxuries. He treated every one of his dates like royalty, men and women alike. He took them to dine in restaurants where well-known chefs cooked only the most exquisite food, where tables were scarce and securing one required a Gold Card. He booked only four-figure suites in five-star hotels with Egyptian cotton sheets and discreet room service. He lived by just one rule; he never took anyone back to his home. That was a different life, a different side of him. San Pedro, Maggie's Bar, the deli he frequented on Sunday mornings, that was the Gabriel his mother brought up. The city, the extravagant food, the great sex in impersonal hotels, that was the Gabe who emerged from Business School with the hope of finding a job that didn't involve so much hard work.

The bar is almost certainly gone now. Maggie and his fellow drinkers are undoubtedly dead. The last time he saw them was the night before he saw the devil, before he left town, leaving a two hundred thousand dollar car on his driveway. That was eight weeks ago, so it's little wonder the thought of a cold beer is making him salivate. There have been so many times since that night when a warm beer has tasted like the finest wine, when any liquor, the stronger the better, has done the trick and enabled him to sleep. Some might even ask, when his story is eventually told, how he made it through without turning into a habitual alcoholic. Gut-wrenching terror is the best hangover cure there is. He's poured everything from neat vodka to low calorie Coors down his throat in the last two months, yet in all that time he hasn't wrapped his hands around a cold beer. Most bars were looted empty, cold stores left open and power disconnected. The chances of there being beer, never mind cold beer, in this house are minimal to none because it looks – at least on the outside – as if it was abandoned months ago.

Not so much on the inside, which is a little disconcerting, but then again he's been living with disconcerting since late July.

He's built a fire in the grate with the kindling and logs stacked either side of it. It takes a while with a disposable lighter to get a flame to catch but eventually it blazes up. He sits back, pleased with his efforts, listening to the pop and crackle of the dry wood. There are other sounds too, coming from the kitchen; the unmistakable clatter of a man inside a fridge. Then he hears Joe call out again,

'Or a beer? Anyone for a cold beer?'

~..~

Emilie crawls forward and kisses Gabe on the cheek, eternally grateful as she sits herself down in front of the fire, knees bent, hugging them to her while she warms up. She glances up at Rick as he steps away and heads for the closed door across from the kitchen, poker still in his hand. He's complaining that it's already too warm in the house. He's insane. She's freezing. More often than not over the last few weeks she's been in someone else's coat; sometimes Gabe's when he's let her borrow it because a suitable alternative hasn't been available. She stole a fleece from a man in Mina, but some asshole demon got blood and guts on it in Middle Gate so she had to dump it. After that she picked up a biker's jacket in Stillwater, managing to hold on to it for a week before one of the un-dead went for her heart, literally, during a fight in Susanville. In the ensuing struggle the jacket got filthy from the mud on the ground. Finally, after a succession of coats, jackets and the odd fleece, she stole a beautiful black leather number from a smashed store front in Plymouth only to have some living bastard steal it from the back of her seat in a bar in Pioneer. Every neighbourhood has fallen apart. The state, possibly the whole country and maybe even the world, has gone to Hell. She misses the Malibu sunshine.

As a trauma intern at the Inter-Community hospital she saw some terrible things. She was in her ninth month of working there. She's certain she'll never go back. Up until six weeks ago she thought she'd seen the worst damage one human being could inflict on another: the carnage caused to the human body by a bullet, the chaos wrought by a knife blade, the wreckage left by the impact of a car. She was wrong. There are much worse things. She isn't squeamish, wasn't even as a child, but she had imagined that when faced with living, breathing people rather than med school cadavers she would feel something for them: sorrow, sadness, worry, pity. Anything. Working at the hospital just didn't affect her that way. She's certain that when they first laid eyes on her four weeks ago, Matt, Gabe and Joe wanted to leave her behind, despite the shotgun in her hands and the group of expired un-dead at her feet. Luke vouched for her but chances are the others saw her as a potential burden not an asset, a girl forced to grow up into a woman real quick. She knew her own worth and all she could do was prove it over the weeks that followed. She knows how to kill with a multitude of household objects but that doesn't make her a tracker like Luke and Matt.

The same way the injuries she saw as an intern never bothered her, watching one guy rip the guts from another and stuff them into his mouth like premium steak didn't either. She half-thinks there's something not right with that but she's too exhausted and too relieved to care. She made it through; she's alive when so many others aren't. At least, she hopes she is.

Joe leans across her with a stemmed glass and she stares at it.

'Wine?'

He sounds smug, like he's made it himself and for all she knows he has, because why would there be wine in the house when the world's gone crazy? Never mind what looks and smells like a very nice, cold Californian Chardonnay. Still, she takes it, smiles a 'thank you' and watches as he hands Gabe a glass of cold lager. The gratitude on Gabe's face is palpable and for a second Emilie thinks he's going to throw his arms around Joe and hug him. He doesn't though, just takes a gulp of the fizzy stuff and closes his eyes in bliss.

She's seen them hug before. There's no false bravado between the men, they've been through too much for that. It's likely they saw the comfort Luke and Matt were to one another every single minute of every hour of every day and wanted to feel it too. There have been hugs and not all of them involved her. There have been tears and not all of them came from her. They've experienced horror in all its forms but it looks as if they've struck lucky for once with this place. She can only hope it is luck and not something else.

For the last week they've been living in a diner at a gas station out on I5, just outside Five Points, to the east of the Diablo Mountain Range. They stopped there because Matt said they needed to. They found the diner empty and well stocked and stayed for five days. There was fuel in the pumps and they filled up the cars; the jeep that the four of them travelled in, along with Luke and Matt's Mustang. They filled themselves up too, Matt proving a dab hand at the diner's griddle, making pancakes for breakfast and burgers for dinner. They slept to recharge, stretched along the PVC seats in the booths at the back, and took it in turns to keep watch in pairs: Luke and Matt, Joe and Gabe, she and Rick. They didn't talk much while they were there but there was only one real topic of conversation and it wasn't something they wanted or needed to discuss. She thought they would rest for a few days, a week at most, then get back on the road and head north. She was wrong.

~..~

With the fire lit and the perfect beer in his hand, Gabe watches Rick try the locked door across the hall again with no luck. He half-expects him to kick it in like they've kicked in so many other doors lately but he doesn't seem inclined to and instead he goes into the kitchen. Gabe hears him say a few words to Joe then hears drawers being opened and rifled through and he gets that Rick's trying to find a key. The house seems secure, they don't have weapons but they do have drinks, and Joe's cooking up something in the kitchen using culinary skills that haven't been in evidence during their week's stay at the diner or indeed at any other time. It means that the important stuff is under control so when Rick comes back with a bunch of keys to try, Gabe goes into the kitchen. For a minute he just stands in the doorway and watches Joe work. He considers the guy a friend and while he doesn't know very much about his life before they met, he doubts cooking has ever been one of his fortes. Now, though, he's working the kitchen like a man possessed, which Gabe can only hope he isn't. While he's no idea what Joe's cooking up, it's starting to smell great, like the best thing he'll have ever eaten, although a McDonalds cheeseburger would possibly taste heavenly right about now.

'What are you making, Chef?'

Joe looks up and smiles. 'Garlic Chicken with crunchy fries.' He beams proudly for all of two seconds before it starts to slip. 'Don't look at me like that.'

'I'm just amazed you found chicken!'

'You're not the only one.'

'Are you sure it's safe? I mean... we've no idea what this place is.'

"Honestly, I don't know. But it was in the fridge, it smelt fine and I'll charcoal it to make sure anything that was living in it isn't by the time we eat it. We've eaten riskier things, I promise you. As to this place... I'm actually too tired to care what it is or even how we got here. Until something tries to oust us, I don't see why we shouldn't take advantage.'

Gabe drinks his beer. He isn't certain he agrees with Joe's philosophy but short of leaving he doesn't have all that many options. 'Was your wife a good cook?'

Joe nods. 'She wasn't Carla Hall but she never let me go hungry.'

He suspects that Joe, like Em and perhaps even Rick, has built strong defences up around his grief, defences which will soon crumble if it turns out they are safe, if it becomes obvious that it really is all over. But for now they're holding firm.

'I used to dabble, that's all. When she died I looked after myself, I didn't starve, so I know my way around a kitchen. You can stop acting so surprised.'

Gabe shrugs, raising his hands in mock-surrender. 'Hey, in the diner—'

'In the diner Matt was happy, having fun. I don't think that kid's had much fun in his life. Best to let him enjoy himself while he could.'

Nodding his understanding, Gabe moves further into the room, brushing his hand over the rough surface of the table before lifting himself back and up to sit on it.

'How did you get involved, Joe?' he asks, and it's a question that's been a very long time coming. They haven't really talked about their origins before, there have always been other more important topics: the immediate threat, the enemy just defeated, the horror left behind. But he feels like he can ask here, now. This house feels safer than anywhere they've holed up before and that last fight felt like it could have been the final one. 'How did you meet up with them?' Them. Matt and Luke. The two guys they owe their lives to. The reason they're all here.

Joe's got his head stuck in a cupboard and Gabe doesn't think he's going to answer. But once he's fetched out four plates and dumped them on the worktop, he closes the cupboard door, straightens up and leans back against it, folding his arms.

'I lived in Alpine, a little town east of San Diego. I worked as a car mechanic at a small independent garage, Mick's Motors, owned by this guy Mick Franks who took it over from his Pop years before. He was a good guy, Mick, a guy you could enjoy a beer and a game with. One of our regulars was an old man, Mr Jacobs, in his seventies, retired. He owned this beautiful silver 1953 Porsche 550. It was his pride and joy. He brought it in for servicing every six months without fail, left it with us overnight and picked it up the next day. He loved that car. Two months ago he brought it in and I did the work, but when he didn't come to pick it up the next day I thought something must have happened, thought he might have had a fall or a heart attack or something.'

The timer pings. It's one of those old fashioned egg-shaped ones in faded blue. Gabe stares at it as Joe checks on the chicken in the oven, the strong aroma of garlic hitting them as soon as the door is opened. 'You actually seasoned it?'

Joe shoots him a warning glance over his shoulder and Gabe lets it go. The egg timer has put him in mind of his Ma. She used to have one exactly like it in their kitchen at home in Phoenix, the same duck-egg blue with a slightly off-white face and a crescent handle in the centre to set the required time. He's only seen one since, in a kitchen in a house where they sought shelter from a pack of rabid dogs a couple of weeks back. Odd that this place should have one too. His Ma died peacefully eighteen months ago and he's glad of it now, she wouldn't have wanted to be around for everything that's happened.

'Gabe?' He blinks and looks at Joe, who's obviously been trying to get his attention. 'You listening or what?'

'Yeah, sorry. Go on.'

Joe nods once and continues his story. 'So I looked up Mr Jacobs' address in the files and went round to his house. He lived on Main Street, in a bungalow set back from the road. It was a state. The front gate was broken, hanging from its hinges. There were weeds in the front yard taller than me. The house was in real need of a lick of paint and a whole load of work to the guttering, the windows, the roof.... It struck me how much he must really love that car to take such good care of it when everything else around him was going to shit. I leaned across the porch because I wasn't sure it would hold my weight, knocked on the front door for a good few minutes. I started to feel like maybe I was trespassing, sticking my nose in where it wasn't wanted. But when no one answered I went around back. The garden was the same state as the yard, with grass up to my knees and plants running amuck. The back door was open and I thought about calling the cops but then if he'd just fallen he'd be more in need of an ambulance so I went inside.'

Gabe knows what's coming next. He's heard it from others caught up in the mayhem, the same story over and over. He doesn't want to hear it again but he's going to listen because the way Joe is looking at him, he knows that Gabe knows and there's an apology in his eyes.

'Mr Jacobs was lying in his kitchen in a pool of his own blood. Back then I had no idea the human body held so much of the stuff. He'd been... split, straight down the middle from chin to testicles, sliced straight through his clothes and opened up. All his organs were gone, he was just... empty. Not even staring 'cause his eyes were gone too. I turned and ran. It had been a long time since I ran like that and my muscles were screaming by the time I reached the garage. I called the cops from there. Mick overheard me, looked at me like I'd lost my mind but I knew what I'd seen, won't ever forget it. Mr Jacobs was the first. But it was that call to the cops that really scared me. It was a local station, local sheriff. I knew most of the officers who worked there because we were the only place in town and we had a small contract to service the cop cars. I got through to Dave Reese – Officer Reese – and when I told him what I'd seen I heard him muffle the phone and shout across to someone else, 'We've got another one'. Sent shivers down my spine when I heard that. When I hung up, I took the keys to Mr Jacobs' Porsche and told Mick to get the Hell out of Dodge, that something was happening, something was coming. I could feel it. I drove home to grab some clothes and left Alpine. I haven't been back since. I feel guilty about that. I should have tried to do something, tried to alert the rest of the town, but I was so damn scared. I didn't want to start a panic for my own selfish sake. I wanted a clear road.'

There's so much Gabe can say and before he met them he probably would have said it all. But he's learnt that words are inadequate comfort. They've all done things that under normal circumstances would be considered morally wrong and legally questionable. Desperate times really do call for some hideously desperate measures.

Despite the subject, despite the raw memories, the chicken smells good and his stomach's grumbling as if it hasn't had food in weeks. 'How did you meet Matt and Luke?'

Joe shifts from one foot to the other, just making himself comfortable. 'I was headed north out of state. I knew there was something going on and it was extending much further than Alpine. I kept switching between local radio stations as I drove and while some of them sounded shocked at a first brutal death, others were closer to 'state of emergency' type panic. In hindsight the Porsche wasn't the best car to choose, it drank gas and I was filling up every hundred and fifty miles. Two days out of Alpine I stopped in this place called Coaldale, a two-bit town with a motel, a bar and nothing much else. It was late. I decided to get a room and head off again in the morning. The bar was right across the street, a real dive but they served cold beer and warm Scotch so I pulled up a stool and ordered a couple of rounds. About an hour after I arrived there was a ruckus at the pool table; one guy accusing another guy of hustling. I didn't pay it much attention and the bartender eventually threw them out. I assumed they settled it out in the parking lot then took off; they weren't there when I left. But I've thought about it since and although I've never asked them I think it might have been Matt and Luke. We've both seen them do it, hustling for money to buy food and fuel when we still had to pay for those things.'

When there were still people around who ran businesses. When people still cared about currency and ownership. Good times.

'I went back to the motel and went to bed, slept 'til around three when I got woken by this screaming, so shrill it sounded like it could break glass. Didn't sound human. I ran outside and it was obvious which room it had come from. One of the doors was open, there was light spilling out and as I got closer I could see a dead guy, or a dead something, just inside the room and two living guys standing by the bed in their underwear holding shotguns.'

Gabe smiles. 'Matt and Luke.'

Joe nods. 'Matt and Luke. They looked as surprised as I felt, though I got the feeling it was me who'd surprised them and not the dead thing on their floor. Without me uttering a single word, Matt started to explain that it had broken into their room brandishing knives. I didn't see any but after what had happened back in Alpine, everything I'd heard on the radio and the fact they weren't making a move to shoot me too, I just went with it. By the time they'd done with that short explanation, they were dressed, packed and ready to leave. I grabbed my stuff too, in case anyone had seen us and linked me to them, and I was all ready to follow them out of the parking lot and straight out of town, until they both saw the car I was driving and laughed themselves stupid. I took offence of course but Luke told me to get in the back of the Mustang, that having to stop every few hours for gas was gonna hold them up. I did what he said without question, abandoned the Porsche in the motel parking lot and went with them. You know, to this day I've no idea why. Kid's got to be twenty years younger than me.'

'People do what they say, follow their orders even when they're not orders. It's why those people stay alive. I've never given it much thought because what they say usually works. If that makes sense?'

'It absolutely does.' Joe pauses. 'I wasn't intending to stay with them. I thought I'd find a more suitable car and take off. I didn't know them from Adam and though they seemed okay, I got the distinct feeling Matt didn't want me around. But something happened. Several hours after we left the motel we stopped at a gas station. They'd been filling me in on the whole 'Hell on earth / end of the world' stuff and despite everything I'd seen, everything I'd heard, I'm still not sure I believed them. I stayed in the car while Luke filled up and Matt went in to the store to pay and collect a few things; snacks mainly, and soda. But when he came out of the store he had a brown carrier bag in one hand and a hand belonging to something that definitely wasn't human wrapped around his throat. He was backing out of the door like the thing was pushing him. I got out of the car but I've no idea what I was intending to do. I couldn't see Matt's face from where I was standing but I thought he must have been scared because I sure would have been. Next thing I knew, Luke was across the forecourt with a knife produced from God only knows where and he sliced the thing's arm clean off, one chop, straight through. He didn't stop there, didn't even pause, plunged the blade into its chest, right between the ribs – assuming it had any – twisted it, pulled it back out and took the thing's head off with one swipe. I could hardly believe what I was seeing; wouldn't have believed it if the thing wasn't still twitching on the ground, its head six feet away!

I remember Luke pulled some paper towel from the dispenser on the side of the pump and wiped the knife with it like it was just dirty and not dripping with blood. Then unbelievably I heard him ask Matt if he remembered the Mountain Dew!'

Gabe laughs, genuine and out loud, and Joe's smiling too.

'That's not the funniest part, because Matt just looked at him, said, 'Fuck! no...' and went back inside! Came out twenty seconds later with a six pack of Mountain Dew and a bottle of Jack Daniels.'

Amused, Gabe lets the silence linger for a couple of seconds. 'I watched Matt take out that demon dog in Williams. One shot in the head, no hesitation, no near miss. Gotta wonder where he leaned to shoot like that, when he stopped being scared.'

Joe sighs. 'Unfortunately I think it was out of necessity. They've led tragic fucking lives those two. I hope it's over, hope they can find some peace, take a break, have a holiday. Although I'm not sure what their idea of a perfect vacation would be.'

'Safari park?'

He's smiling again. 'Maybe, if we could stop them from shooting the animals out of habit.' The timer, which he'd reset, pings again. 'Could you fetch the potatoes? They're just inside the pantry door.'

~..~

Everything's cooked an hour later. Emilie tucks into the food, her wine glass refilled and the log fire keeping her feet warm. If this is the last place on earth she's ever going to see, she thinks she's okay with that. Living on greasy junk food for the last week, and on anything she's been able to get her hands on for weeks before that, has done nothing good for her skin and she's lucky her natural size is skinny because otherwise she would have ballooned out to the size of an elephant. They've avoided meat recently, at least until they arrived at the diner and found it packaged and frozen, cooked it themselves. She might not be squeamish but watching people tearing other people apart is enough to turn even the staunchest carnivore into a vegetarian, and after what they found in Wallace she did lose her appetite for a good few days.

She glances up when Rick takes a seat in the opposite corner of the couch, plate in one hand, fork in the other. He doesn't look cold, doesn't look as if he needs the fire's heat like she does, or even wants it. But there aren't many places to sit. Rick was the last one to join their peculiar little gang after Matt dragged him out of a dumpster behind a strip club in Michigan Bar, saving him from what she would have described as a zombie attack if Joe hadn't banned any of them from using the 'Z' word.

'Why? That's what they are!'

'Why?! Because it's ridiculous, that's why! There are no such things as zombies! It's a Hollywood term, made up by overzealous writers trying to make a quick buck. They're the un-dead and that's what we're going to call them!'

It's the one and only rule (with the exception of the obvious one: don't get yourselves killed) that he's ever tried to impose on them, and even Luke and Matt have attempted to stick to it so she's done her best too. She feels a knot in her stomach when she thinks about the two of them. After Rick came down and told them he was sure they were up in the turret room, she went up to check for herself. Matt has a distinctive, breathy snore that they all got to know well during the week at the diner and she agrees with Rick, it's what she can hear when she presses her ear to the intricately carved door. They can't be one hundred percent certain without breaking the door down, and it looks heavy and solid enough that she doubts they'd be able to. She doesn't think they should try. She just hopes that it is them up there, enjoying a well-deserved rest. She's going upstairs too, after she's eaten, to put her head down on a proper pillow and hopefully sleep for a week. She doesn't hurt as much as she thinks she should but she's exhausted and relieved that the war's apparently over or at least on hold. Whatever's landed them here, wherever here is, she's oddly grateful for it. She isn't sure she has the strength to start fighting again.

'I remember the first time I laid eyes on Luke,' she announces suddenly, more to the fireplace than to Rick. They have talked a little, now and again, in the back of the jeep and keeping watch at the diner. He knows a bit about her, she knows almost nothing about him, but he's never seemed interested in telling her anything. She's usually happy to talk, especially when she's anxious which she has been for weeks now, right up until the battle today, a battle which feels further back in the past with each passing hour.

Rick glances up at her. 'In the hardware store? I am curious how an intern goes from stitching up gunshot wounds to stealing shotguns and ammo.'

He says it with a smile and she smiles back. She's never sure if he's flirting and if he is it's in the same mild way he has been doing since the day they met, something she put down to habit more than any real interest in her on his part. When they did meet he was covered in trash and she was covered in intestines, which didn't make for the best of first impressions.

Not that he's in any way good-looking. His face is thin and his cheeks are hollow. His loose suit hangs off his scrawny body as if he's lost a few pounds since he bought it. His sparse facial hair looks like it hasn't made a clear decision whether or not it wants to grow and the fact that they pulled him out of a dumpster behind a strip joint doesn't help. But in spite of all that he seems genuine enough.

'Short answer, I started to notice that more people than usual were dying in the hospital.' She smiles at Rick's expression. 'I know, people think that patients die all the time but they don't. Believe it or not, the majority at Inter-Community do get better and get to go home. The hospital provides excellent care. But patients started dying when they shouldn't have done: on the operating table due to unexpected complications, waiting for triage in the ER, even just in their sleep. I overheard nurses talking about it, doctors using terms like 'super-bugs' and other interns saying their departments were losing patients after minor procedures. One week the ICU lost every patient due to one complication or another. The cops and reporters started to take an interest. A friend of mine from med school – Katie – said she thought one of the doctors was killing people off like in that book *Coma*, where the surgeons pretend patients are dead then take them to this futuristic lab for use in experiments.'

It still amazes her that the truth is more unbelievable than their theories. One day, if the world survives, someone will make a movie about what's happening. Chances are someone's already writing it, sitting in the trashed ruins of a coffee shop in Hollywood. She hopes Mila Kunis will play her even though they look nothing alike.

'We thought it might be Doctor Franklin. He was this creepy surgeon who always wore latex gloves around the place, even when he wasn't in the OR. We followed him one night but all he did was rent a couple of DVDs, get takeout at the Chinese place around the corner from his apartment block and go home.'

Rick is still watching her, interest and a hint of amusement on his face rather than blank boredom, so she carries on.

'One morning, about a week after it all started, I got to work and two of our nurses had phoned in sick. They didn't show up for work the next day either and neither of them would answer the phone. My supervisor went to their homes to check on them and found them both dead. No symptoms, no signs of violence. Katie had been reading up about deadly viruses that went through hospitals like wildfire, killing off patients;

incurable diseases immune to antibiotics. She and I met up over lunch in the canteen and she'd printed out all these news reports from all over California, stories from other hospitals about patients and nurses dying for no reason. No one knew why. When Katie didn't come in to work the next day, I thought she'd quit. I went over to her place and found her just sitting on the couch, dead, with the TV on. I didn't go back to the hospital. I went home and packed and thought I'd head for my Mom's in Portland. I didn't think it through, not immediately, I just didn't want to stay where people were dying and all the reports Katie had found were from California. Mom always said if anything ever happened I could go home. It wasn't until I stopped to fill up with gas in Bakersfield I realised it was more than people dying for no reason. People were dying for really good reasons too, like other people ripping their heads off. I stole a gun from the gas station and just started to drive, staying off the Interstate, still thinking I should head to Mom's—'

Rick sits forward, fries halfway to his mouth. 'Wait, you stole a gun from a gas station?'

'There was a dead guy on the floor of the store with a shotgun lying next to him. Looked as if he'd been trying to rob the place. The guy behind the counter was dead too. I just grabbed the gun, went through his pockets for spare cartridges and ran. I didn't even pay for the gas. It was the first illegal thing I'd ever done.'

'You went through a dead guy's pockets for spare cartridges?'

'It's a shotgun, only holds two at once, I figured he must have brought more ammo with him in case something went wrong. Don't you ever watch TV?'

He stares at her for a second. 'You didn't call the cops or the paramedics?'

'You don't understand. There were cops everywhere. All I could hear was sirens in every direction. I knew there was something going on. I mean, I've seen all those George Romero films, *Dawn of the Dead*, *Day of the Dead*, *Diary of the Dead*. I wasn't about to hang around to become meal of the dead was I?' Rick shakes his head with an amused smile and she accepts it as a compliment. 'I drove all day and stopped at a diner for something to eat and to take a pee. I was enjoying my vanilla milkshake, waiting for my caramel apple pie, when someone starting screaming, out in the parking lot. When I looked out, there was this guy – looked like any normal guy in a suit – but he was attacking people with an axe! There was a woman lying on the ground bleeding from her head and a kid was holding his arm with blood seeping between his fingers. What kind of man attacks a little boy? So I went out there, got the gun from the back of my car and shouted at the guy to drop the axe. I told him the cops were on the way. But he didn't drop it. He took off this woman's head with a single swing and then came for me. So I shot him.'

It was far from fun at the time but she's pleased with the way Rick's looking at her now, a whole new level of respect even after what he's seen her do over the last couple of weeks, despite what he knows she's capable of.

'He was going to kill me. I wasn't about to stand there and let it happen. I thought I should get out of there quick after that so I had to leave the milkshake which cost me eight dollars, and of course I didn't get the pie so I was still hungry. But I figured the last place I wanted to end up was in a jail cell, it's the first place the zom – the un-dead – would go to look for food and there's no escape. So I took off and no one tried to stop me. I pulled into the parking lot of a half-decent hotel a couple of hours later in Carson City, got some dinner and a good night's sleep. I called Mom the next day. She said there was nothing bad happening in Portland so I decided not to go there in case any of it followed me. She wanted me home but I thought it was too risky. I just kept moving, changing direction every day. Whenever I saw something I thought I could help with, I stopped. I killed people who were no longer people. I stole weapons and ammo whenever I got the chance. That's what I was doing when I first saw Luke, stealing ammo from a store in Red Bluff.' She smiles at the memory. 'Luke was stealing stuff too. Ammo mostly, all different kinds so I knew he must have quite a collection of guns. Course I fancied him from the start. Who wouldn't?' Rick makes a face and Emilie smirks at him.

She thinks Luke's as gorgeous as any of the so-called Hollywood heartthrobs, even with the scar that runs from the top of his right cheek bone through his right eyebrow. It just adds to his rugged masculinity. She hasn't kept her feelings for him a secret when perhaps she should have done.

'Our eyes met across a counter that was covered in blood and broken glass and he gave me this smile.... It was brilliant, one thief to another. I followed him out of the store and we walked straight in to a group of un-dead teachers attacking a bunch of school kids in uniform. Between us we took out all the teachers and after the kids ran off he introduced himself. I hoped for a kiss but he just shook my hand and asked me where I was headed.' In amongst the horror, it's a warm memory. 'I said I wasn't headed anywhere particular. He told me he was travelling with a couple of people and asked if I wanted to tag along.' It isn't quite how the conversation went but it's close enough for storytelling purposes. 'I thought I'd be safer in a group than on my own.' Not necessarily true, and now she knows that just as the others do, but back then it seemed like a safe assumption to make.

In the end, it depends on the group.

'Do you regret it?'

It's a question she's already asked herself. Maybe Gabe does, and Joe, she isn't sure. She thinks Rick does. But she doesn't, she can't, and she shakes her head firmly. She won't regret a single second spent in Luke's company, no matter what the price. It's just a shame she never stood a chance with him and that it took her a whole week to realise it.

'But he never even flirted with you.'

'No.' She allows herself a petulant curl of her bottom lip even though she knows it's childish and pointless. 'But hey, he and Matt, right? No girl's ever going to break into that. They're off in a world of their own most of the time. I tried, the first few days, until I realised he wasn't even seeing me. He's friendly, and he gives nice hugs, but it's like he's blind when it comes to seeing me as a sexual being. I don't take it personally; he's like that with everyone. Remember that waitress in Fort Bragg?'

It was a roadside cafe, the same as all the others they stopped at, some of which were ahead of the apocalyptic tide. They ate in those that were, looking for a brief spell of normality amongst the chaos. Burgers and shakes, fries with everything, ice cream and pie. This one had good coffee, bad food and a waitress who tried to hit on Luke the moment they walked in to the place. She was great looking and she knew it: blond hair, huge tits and legs up to her ears. Luke was pleasant enough with her but she was after a phone number and like every other interested man and woman on the planet she was out of luck. Emilie had already reached this conclusion and it didn't take the fake-breasted girl a week. After four refills and the same number of quiet knockbacks, she 'accidently' spilt hot coffee over Matt's shirt. Emilie did think at the time that Luke's reaction was something of an overreaction, slapping her as hard as he did. But watching Matt kick Luke in the ass on their way across the parking lot, for getting them thrown out before he'd had pie, made it worth missing out on dessert.

So no, she doesn't regret joining their little band of fugitives and if it is over then at least she got to see the finale first hand, up close and personal. All she does regret is falling for a guy who was spoken for a long, long time ago.

~..~

Rick's suddenly seeing Emilie in a whole new light. He knows her well enough to understand she's a plucky chick, nothing much unnerves her and from the start he's thought she's unnaturally un-squeamish, although he supposes that's what comes of working in a hospital. Some of the stories she's shared over the time he's been with them have put him off his food on more than one occasion. That, on top of the things they've seen and done as a vigilante-slash-help group making their way around the South West, means he hasn't eaten properly in a while and he's glad that nothing's transpired to put him off his meal tonight because it's the best he's had in weeks. Joe's a great cook – who knew? Rick's got a clean plate and an empty glass and although he was exhausted earlier and desperate to put his head down and sleep, now he's eaten he doesn't feel so tired. There is, however, a creeping anxiety in his gut that he hopes will be put to rest by another beer, and thanking Joe is a great excuse to go to the kitchen.

Joe and Gabe are just finishing their meals, sitting at the kitchen table, as Rick puts his plate on the worktop next to the sink and offers to do the dishes in return for another beer.

'You're on,' Joe accepts, and Gabe hands him his own plate and cutlery before going into the hall, probably heading outside for a cigarette despite the continuing rain. Joe pours Rick another cold one and sets it down on the side close to where he's running the water, waiting to see if it will run hot, surprised when it does.

'What are the chances of us having Dawn?' He expects the answer to be either a straightforward snort or a sarcastic comment, but instead Joe replies,

'Better than you might think.'

They check the cupboards around them before looking under the sink and, hey presto, there's a new, unopened bottle of dishwashing liquid.

'Would you look at that?' Rick's stunned.

Joe nods. 'I was just saying to Gabe, either someone did actually live here until very, very recently, or someone stocked it thinking the apocalypse is the same as war.'

'Or someone stocked it for us.' It's a faintly chilling thought.

Joe nods slowly. 'The idea did cross our minds but God alone knows what that means. We decided we're not going to question it too hard tonight and investigate tomorrow.' He plucks a drying towel from a drawer to the left of the sink. 'You wash, I'll dry.'

There seems to be plenty of hot water but Rick doesn't use too much because now he's thinking about how wonderful a piping hot shower might feel. Or even a bath. He uses just enough to get the plates in and when Emilie comes through to deliver hers, and to thank the chef for the delicious meal, the water just about covers all four of them at the bottom of the deep sink.

'Emilie was telling me how she got caught up in all of this,' he comments when she returns to her fire, just to have something to say. He reaches in through the bubbles to wash the forks.

'Must be confessional,' Joe comments, and Rick casts a glance over his shoulder. 'I coughed up to Gabe when I was cooking. He asked, mind. Still, it's not something I thought I'd ever talk about to anyone.'

Rick looks around them, at the unbroken windows and the clean kitchen. 'Could be something in the house?'

'Wouldn't surprise me. So, continuing this new tradition, how'd you end up in a dumpster in Michigan Bar?'

It's not something he's planned to talk about either, not ever, because he's not proud of his old life given the good he's done in his new one, even if he has only been living this new one for a couple of weeks. He doesn't feel as close to Joe as Gabe and Emilie obviously do, but sharing as many life or death situations as they have makes Joe a comrade-in-arms. He deserves the truth. Besides, Rick has the distinct feeling that a confessional would be good for him right about now.

So he admits, 'I was a conman.' All Joe does is raise his eyebrows. 'I sold fake insurance door to door, forged paintings at auction houses, counterfeit coins at collectors' fairs. I conned people out of money. Good people too. Then, about a month ago, I was selling pet insurance to everyone with a flea-ridden mutt in this small retirement community called Friendly Hills when I came across something worse than me.' His hands go still in the warm water, the prongs of a fork sticking into his palm. 'Something was conning people out of more than money. Something was conning people out of their lives.'

Joe is silent for a second. 'Lives? Like... life insurance?'

'No, more like... death insurance. There was some kind of document. The moment anyone signed on the dotted line they died, simply dropped dead where they were standing.'

'You saw it happen?'

'Yeah, and I left town that same day. But before I actually saw it, there were stories. I overheard a woman from the soup kitchen telling an old homeless guy that one of their volunteers had been found dead on her doorstep. And in a bar these two construction guys were talking about their friend getting home to find his wife dead in their doorway, the door wide open but nothing stolen. Then one afternoon this tall, thin guy in an immaculate suit walked right by me on this woman's drive. I'd just sold two hundred dollars of fake vet insurance to her for her miniature poodle. The guy was strange and I know we've seen some strange shit lately but there was just something wrong with him. On the surface he looked like any other guy in a suit, like me only better dressed. Black suit, black shirt, red tie. Then he smiled at me as we came level with one another.... He had too many teeth in his mouth, like a clown from some low-budget horror movie, and there was something wrong with his eyes. They were too dark, like there was no white in them. Gave me the creeps so much that I hung around, up the road, until he left. Then I went back to the house to make sure the old lady was okay. I mean, me growing a conscience like that after practically stealing from her minutes before? Out of character, I'm telling you. I found her lying dead in her hall, flat on her back on the carpet with her eyes wide open, staring at the ceiling. No sign of violence, just this piece of paper in her hand; a single, blank sheet with her signature in red at the base of it.' He shudders and returns to washing up. 'It was like someone was taking contract killing literally. I'd been in the house, I knew what the cops would think if they found me. So I left town, just drove, stayed on the road for days, realised something bigger was going on than just one guy. I dodged disaster all the way to Michigan Bar where you guys saved me from those bastard zombies.'

'Which leads me to ask,' Joe starts, not passing judgment on Rick's previous incarnation – for which he's grateful – or giving him a bollocking for the use of the 'z' word. 'What were you doing in that dumpster?'

'Hiding! What did you think I was doing?'

'Looking for lunch?'

Rick glances at Joe in time to see him wink. 'I have never been so scared in all my life as I was that afternoon. I thought I'd had a lucky escape at a bar the day before when I watched a pack of rabid dogs tear apart a waitress who came out for a smoke. I honestly thought my number was up until you guys showed.'

'Emilie rescued you. She did most of the work that afternoon, letting off steam I think. All we did was dust you off once Matt hoisted you out.'

Not a highlight of Rick's life, he's the first to admit, even in a life with very few highlights. He's made up for a few of his sins over the last couple of weeks, just possibly not enough of them. He doesn't want to think about that, so he forces a smile and acknowledges, 'She's an unusual girl.'

Joe laughs. 'Yes, she is. A great shot, an ace with a baseball bat, and utterly unshakable. She's a great asset in a fight.'

'The only thing I've known get to her is Luke,' Rick throws in pointlessly and Joe nods.

'Shame the only thing to ever get to Luke is Matt.' There's something dark underlying his words and Rick is very, very good at hearing the nuances in people's voices.

'I never pegged you as a homophobe.'

Joe throws his hands up, dying towel hanging from the fingers of his right hand. 'Oh, I'm not, believe me. I've got nothing against gay guys and absolutely nothing against Matt and Luke. I am absolutely certain that we wouldn't be here were it not for what's between those two so I'm not criticising them in any way. I'm just saying, for Emilie's sake, it's a shame. Shame she couldn't fall for a boy who can love her back.'

That tone's there again and Rick realises he did misinterpret it. 'You don't think there's time for her to meet someone else?'

Joe looks at him, right at him, and the look in his eyes sends shivers down Rick's spine. 'Do you?'

No, he doesn't. But that means admitting there's no time for him either and that's something he's not quite ready to do because he is most definitely here, right now, and that in itself feels somehow unexpected. 'I don't know,' he lies smoothly enough. He's good at lying; it used to be his chosen profession. 'Maybe.'

'So where do you think we are?'

He moves his head slowly in silent denial of what Joe's implying. 'We've seen some crazy shit recently. This house is far from the craziest thing to happen to us.'

'I don't know. Everything we've seen, everything we've fought, it all made sense in an apocalyptic way. Being transported from a park in California to wherever this is? That ranks very highly in my list of crazy shit.'

'We could be anywhere. Could still be in California. Could be in Kansas.'

Joe snorts. 'Worrying thought.'

Rick sets the last plate on the draining board, thinking about what Joe said. He's never actually blamed himself for anything so he hasn't atoned for any of it, not from the heart. Whenever he stopped to think about why he was doing what he was doing, he always blamed his parents, his upbringing, even television. He managed to fool himself into believing it was the chances he never had that led him into a life of crime. But like it or not, Matt and Luke have shown them all what they can do with excuses like his. Despite both of them losing their parents at a young age, they didn't just become lost in a system that really doesn't give a shit, didn't end up on the street turning others into victims in order to boost their own self-esteem. No, they're the ultimate example of good triumphing over bad. They let their grief lead them into a life of saving folk, educating the few people who would listen, harbouring unworthy idiots like him, saving their asses and keeping them safe. He owes his continued existence to the two of them: he, the others here, hundreds more out there. It must be too late to repent now. He should have done it properly when he had the chance, at the Church of the Fallen Saints when the offer was made for atonement and forgiveness by the priest they liberated from the thing living in the rafters.

'I've done a lot of bad things in my life,' he confesses without really meaning to. 'You kid yourself that conning people out of money is okay because you're not actually hurting them. A couple of hundred dollars here, a thousand there. But I know I was lying to myself. They were vulnerable people who needed that money. God knows how many have lost their spouses because of what I did, or even took their own lives.' He feels a hand on his shoulder and his head snaps back.

'I'm not a priest,' Joe tells him gently. 'No need to confess your sins to me. No point, either. As far as I'm concerned you're even. You've helped a lot of people these last couple of weeks.'

'But you're not the one who dispenses divine justice.'

Joe chuckles. 'No, I'm not. And if you'd said that to me two months ago I really would have laughed in your face. To tell you the truth, I'm still not sure what I do believe because despite everything, I can't bring myself to admit we actually faced down Satan.' It's surprising, because Rick can't see that there's any way of denying what happened in Five Points, but each to their own.

'I do believe and I am going to Hell for deceiving good people out of their hard-earned wages.'

'You're too hard on yourself. Besides, if there is such a thing as divine justice, there's also divine forgiveness and you've definitely earned that. Those school kids in Redwood? They'd have been barbecued if it wasn't for you. That family in Winters? You and I have fought shoulder to shoulder plenty of times. So if it goes to trial you can call me up as a character witness but if there's any kind of justice in the world you won't need to.'

They're sweet things Joe's saying and they put a smile on Rick's face as he hands over the clean cutlery. He lets himself believe it for a while, that he's going to be okay, that they'll see their homes again and their families. Rick's got a family, albeit an estranged one, living in Florida; Lorna and Melissa, a teenage daughter he doesn't know and an ex-wife who hates him. The others don't know about them because he hasn't mentioned them. When all this started he kept experiencing this irrational fear that somehow he was partly responsible for what was happening and that if he contacted them he would just drag them into it. That was the last thing he wanted to do because in his own, possibly meaningless, way he still loves them. He's thinking now that he was fooling himself, something he's exceptionally good at, with his reasons for not calling them, not warning them. If Melissa had told him to fuck off he might have wished some terrible fate on her and he knows he couldn't live with that. So maybe he didn't call them because he's selfish but he doesn't think it matters, not now. He doesn't know if the chaos spread beyond the West because by the time it became clear that it wasn't just a seasonal increase in weirdness and violent behaviour, there was no television, no Internet, no mobile networks, no communications of any kind, not even radio.

Joe described it as the tactics of war, silencing the other side, making it impossible for them to group and plan. That's what their enemy did by blocking every possible means of getting news out to anywhere. How it was done, no one knew. No one they met had managed to work it out. But it was highly effective. Pack mentality quickly took over when normality and routine broke down. In many of the places they drove through there were long-running drunken brawls, destruction and looting; typical panic behaviour. In the first few days Rick was with the group he fought as many humans as he did other things before they started to stumble upon fewer people and more bodies. The closer to the end they got, the quieter things became. Of course at the time they had no idea they were getting closer to the end. Or maybe Matt and Luke did. Matt recorded everything they found and where they found it, building up a map, the map that finally landed them in Five Points.

The greatest strength of human beings, Rick has realised, is the determination to survive. In every town they found pockets of resistance, people fighting something so huge they had no chance of stopping it, something so vicious that they couldn't ever hope to win. But that wasn't preventing them from trying. Wherever they went, Matt and Luke were like modern-day prophets, drawing people to them, quickly dispensing practical advice on how to keep the evil things at bay and what to do if that failed. Rick can't help but wonder how many of the people they met and fought alongside, even just for a couple of hours, have made it, how many are still alive. He can only hope that Mel and Lorna are okay.

He fishes around in the bottom of the sink and hands Joe a stray fork before pulling the plug and watching the water drain away.

'Are you okay?'

Rick nods. 'Gonna finish my beer then go upstairs, try to get some sleep. If that's okay with everyone.'

'I'm sure it's fine.' Joe pats him on the shoulder and leaves him alone in the kitchen to dwell on whether he's said too much.

There's nothing to do now but wait out whatever's happening here and see what comes next. He leans against the sink and drinks his beer slowly, washing out the glass before heading upstairs with a murmured, 'G'night', to the others and a last look at the locked door he's been unable to open.

Upstairs in the luxurious bathroom he stands over the ornate porcelain toilet and stares at his own yellowish stream of piss, trying to remember the last clean urinal he used. Definitely not the one in Hooters in Fresno where he'd been approached by two – two! – guys in the time it took him to relieve himself. In Hooters, for fuck's sake! The world has never failed to surprise him, which probably isn't the best claim for a conman to be making but it's true. He just wishes he could have taken more pleasure in those surprises, seen the funny side more often, found more reasons to laugh. Matt and Luke are constantly laughing, fooling around together. Even under the worst of circumstances they've managed to hang on to their sense of humour and he envies them that. That's how they've managed to survive, he suspects. He hasn't laughed in a long time, not a real belly roar as his father used to call it, one that starts in his lungs, rolls up his windpipe like a wave, into his throat and out of his mouth in a tide of mirth. He wants that now, wants to feel that release of the heavy pressure inside him.

He finishes, flushes, sidesteps until he's standing in front of the sink and looks at his own face in the bronze-framed mirror above it. He half-expects a ghoulish stranger to be looking back at him, or a mutilated face just beyond his shoulder, but it's only him, his reflection staring gauntly out from the glass. He's disappointed that his own imagination still seems to be running riot even after everything he's been through, as if that wasn't enough.

He examines his own image. His face is thinner than it once was, cheekbones showing through not in a ruggedly handsome way but in a starving, skeletal way. His hair is thinner too; red-blond wisps he's insisted all his life aren't ginger. Neither of his parents were ginger but he wouldn't have bet against his Mom having had an affair. His eyes look sunken, dark shadows around them. The others don't look this haggard from their recent experiences. Matt and Luke, the bastards, are in great shape. Then again they were practically born into weirdness.

He turns on the cold water, puts his hands under the stream and splashes his face, lowering his head to do so and looking back up, almost daring the mirror to show him something blood-curdling and horrible like all the things he's seen in recent weeks. But it's still just him, with water dripping from his eye lashes and droplets following the sharp curves of his hollow cheeks. With a small sigh he reaches for the towel on the rail and pats his face dry. It's a luxury not to be using paper towels from gas station restrooms or ratty cloths in motel bathrooms that countless others have wiped who knows what parts of themselves on. Not that he knows any better about this place. It just feels clean and that goes a long way.

He glances in the mirror one last time and bites his tongue to silence the scream his own reflection raises in him. The flesh from his face has been wiped away, leaving strings of muscle and bright white bone. His teeth are locked in a macabre grin and his eyes are deep in their sockets, round and bare. The towel drops from his hands and he looks down, expecting to see the inside of his face looking back at him, smudged and distorted. But the towel's clean, and when he looks into the mirror he's whole again, as if the glass is mocking him, taunting him because he dared it to. He wishes he could be sure that the sights he's glancing momentarily are hallucinations and what he's looking at now is real. But he can't be, because he doesn't quite believe it. He can't help but worry that the house is creating this facade of normal and that the horrors he keeps glimpsing are what's actually real.

~..~

Something's up with Rick, even Joe can see it and he's never been one for bothering to read people. Their conversation in the kitchen is the most the guy's said to him since they rescued him from behind the strip joint, and that means something's wrong above and beyond the usual and the obvious.

But if whatever's looking out for them now can keep on doing so for another couple of days it'll give him time to find out what's up and possibly to help. Before his wife died he was one of those people others looked to for advice, and he was happy to give it. Then Babs passed away and he didn't want to know about other people's problems because they seemed so small and insignificant compared to his own, compared to the gaping hole her death left in his life. This recent insanity has affected them all differently, each in their own way, and it's allowed him to care again about other people. Matt and Luke for starters. If he and Babs had had kids they'd be Matt and Luke's age and however weak that connection might seem it's opened him up to actually giving a shit about them, especially considering the circumstances they've found themselves in. They help so many and they're not alone in doing so. There are unsung heroes in every town, people who made it, people who didn't, people who saved lots of lives, people who saved just one. It all makes a difference. Their little band, stuck here in this odd house, can't be the exception. Out of everyone who's been fighting back, they just happened to be at ground zero at the right time. Although he doubts very much it was by chance because too much has happened for it to be coincidence. There's the map Matt drew up, the map that somehow directed them to Five Points, and if that was where Matt and Luke were always headed it makes the rest of them either privileged or very unlucky.

When the door opens, he and Emilie glance up from where they've been sitting staring into the fire, both lost in their own thoughts. It's only Gabe finally coming back in after sucking on however many cigarettes.

'You can smoke inside,' Joe tells him, watching as he runs his fingers through his hair to comb out the rain before hanging up his coat.

Gabe shakes his head, determined. 'I'm not about to take the rest of you down with me.'

Joe gets to his feet. 'Coffee? Sorry, we've only got instant.'

Emilie declines, but despite his grimace at the idea of freeze-dried granules, Gabe nods. 'That would be great. Thanks.'

Joe switches the light on again in the kitchen, as thankful that they've got power as he is bemused by it. They were lucky the diner in Five Points had its own generator. If it was luck, because whenever he stops to think about everything that's happened he can't help but reckon things might be turning out exactly the way they're meant to.

He runs the cold water, fills the kettle and makes two mugs of coffee. The unexpected discovery of beer and wine in the fridge overshadowed the discovery of the jar earlier, but right now it's just what he needs. Caffeine has always had an unusual calming effect on him.

He doesn't think they need a look-out, but the group works well as a team so he's willing to ask the question and listen to the opinions of Emilie and Gabe. But Emilie's gone by the time he hands Gabe his coffee and sits down opposite him on the couch, facing the locked door Rick didn't manage to open. Despite Joe's usual curiosity, he's not particularly interested in finding out what's behind it tonight. They've found lots of scary and horrible things behind lots of doors. A closed one that stays closed isn't as worrying as it possibly should be. If there is something sleeping behind it, he's content right now not to know. Whatever it is clearly isn't about to spring out and try to eat them or it would have done so already. None of the monsters they've come across have been of the patient variety.

'Em's gone up,' Gabe tells him. 'I told her it was okay. She was exhausted. Do you think we need a look-out?'

'No. But I'm happy to keep you company if you want to wait up?'

He counts Gabe as a friend whereas that term doesn't seem to fit right with Rick or even Emilie. He's known Gabe longer, sure, but not by much and he doesn't have any more in common with the salesman than he does with the other two. Still, Gabe is someone he might like to share a couple of beers with at a quiet bar in a quiet town once this is all over. He's under no illusions that life can ever go back to anything he'd term 'normal' but even if he can't go back to Alpine for whatever reason, he is hopeful of spending the rest of his years in a small town, fixing cars during the day and throwing back beers and shots in the dark hours. That's if they can find a way to leave here and if there's anywhere to go.

They throw a couple more logs on the fire and sit side by side, drinking their coffee while they listen to Rick and Emilie moving around upstairs. Footsteps cross the landing, a toilet flushes and the pipes start to creak and groan in accompaniment to the sound of fast flowing water. A shower suddenly feels like a heavenly idea and Joe would be lying if he said he wasn't looking forward to a good night's sleep, if he can get one. The four of them haven't slept well since this began, especially Rick who looks like he really needs a rest. Matt and Luke sleep like babies every night with an uncanny and, no doubt, self-taught ability to drop off anywhere, under any circumstances, and to wake alert, focussed and ready for action in the blink of an eye. It's the one thing they haven't been able to teach and comes of spending half their lives in places that aren't safe, often under imminent threat. A lack of sleep makes people sloppy, they said, but sleeping doesn't have to mean you let your defences down.

They met others like Matt and Luke on the road, few and far between, people who knew about the battle before the chaos hit. Those people slept with weapons under their pillows, with one eye open – figuratively rather than literally – so as never to be caught off-guard. Matt and Luke are unusual, but in some ways Joe considers them lucky. They travel together, they protect each other, they have one another's backs. And while he's certain there's more to it, he hasn't seen any explicit evidence.

Sure, he's seen them touch to check for wounds, to patch one another up. They aren't physically shy around each other, there are no physical barriers between them. They comfort and hug, they sit too close together. They share a room, double or twin, whatever's available. They might be fucking and Joe wouldn't care if they are but he's never seen anything to prove it, nothing beyond an intense relationship, definitely more than a friendship, forged in battle. They love one another, that's clear, but beyond that he has no clue what they are.

The shower stops, the floorboards creak, a door closes and then silence. The house falls quiet save for the odd small noises in the rafters; beams and joists heating up, stretching and bending and settling again. That, and the crackling of the fire.

When they've both finished their coffee, Gabe nudges Joe in the ribs. 'Go to bed. I'll watch the door. I'm sure it's just a locked door and I'm equally sure there's nothing outside but rain, but if anything comes in from anywhere I'll scream like a girl and attack it with a poker.'

Joe grins, making his muscles ache. 'Okay. If you're sure.'

'I've faced worse than a locked door.' He waves his hand in the air. 'Be gone.'

With a nod, Joe does as he's told, rinsing their mugs out in the kitchen and leaving them on the side to dry before bidding Gabe a good night and climbing the stairs. He heads for the nearest open door and empty bed, kicking his shoes off and lying down on his side on the mattress, above the sheets, finally allowing exhaustion to claim him as he closes his eyes, asleep in seconds.

~..~

Gabe sits in the silence on the couch, poker across his lap, staring into the flames and enjoying the heat on his face. It's nice but he isn't worried about sleep tempting him. He's spent too many anxious hours as a look-out, too many dark nights on watch, to close his eyes unintentionally. Besides, however safe the others might feel, there are odd noises now and again that make his ears prick up. It's probably just the house warming up but it's keeping him on enough of an edge to stay awake. Outside the storm is still raging. He can hear the thunder rolling across the sky and if he glances over his shoulder, through the windows either side of the door, he can see the lightning ripping apart the night and the rain beating uneven time against the miraculously fixed glass. Now there's a phenomenal trick.

He, like the others, has no idea where they are or how they've ended up here. No one seems too bothered tonight but he's certain that will change come daylight. If daylight comes, of course. He thinks he should be concerned about their inexplicable situation but he just can't find it in himself. It's not that he doesn't care because he does. More than anything he would love to return to his old life but he's not naive enough to believe that's going to happen. He is sure of one thing; his life can't possibly get any stranger. And if he's sure of that, there's nothing for him to worry about. They're quite possibly dead but he doubts it because he isn't religious, he's never believed in anything other than good living, and he's never imagined there would be anything after death. He's never felt the need to. So if he's going to stick to those beliefs then this place has to be something else. Maybe a 'thank you', a reward for a job well done. Although if he isn't going to believe in a higher power there's nothing for the reward to come from. And if that's true, it can't possibly have been the devil he saw the morning he left Los Angeles. But he's certain it was and it's this sort of circular thinking that's behind why he's determined not to worry. Because if he's going to worry he'll need to rethink his whole life philosophy and quite frankly he's too tired to do that. It's been difficult enough being an atheist during what he has to admit has really looked and felt like the apocalypse.

Another lightning flash strobes white across the room. There was a storm last night too, their final night in the diner, but that was different. The thunderclaps were loud and hard enough to rattle the glass and the polka-dot blinds in the windows, bright violet bolts threw foreboding shadows across the parking lot and hail stones the size of golf balls cracked the windshield of the jeep the four of them used, following daily in the Mustang's slipstream. This storm feels more controlled, less like a natural event and more like a show. The others might have been right earlier. It could be a celebration because if that was the battle to end it all, they must have won and they were fighting on the side of Good. When he closes his eyes he can still see the explosion of light when Matt and Luke joined hands. There was nothing destructive or evil in that. It was beautiful. This whole thing has been one long mind-fuck.

Dropping his head back he looks up at the high vaulted ceiling, at the impressive chandelier hanging directly overhead. He taps the poker against his palm. He's used to being in possession of something more than hearthside equipment, but their arsenal doesn't appear to have arrived with them and ironware seems to be all they have to defend themselves if the need arises. So far the house has provided everything else they need, so for now he's happy to go along with Joe's assumption that they won't need anything sharper or more effective at killing things quickly. At least until he's proven wrong.

The general aches and pains of the house finally die down and that throws into sharp relief other sounds, quieter sounds. Scratching. He lifts his head, listening, trying to pinpoint where it's coming from. Somewhere off to his right, possibly in the walls. He sits up, tightening his grip on the poker. It could be mice or it could be rats. They've come across some evil bastard rats recently; huge ones with diamond-sharp teeth, blood-red eyes and seemingly insatiable appetites. In a trashed 7-Eleven in the small town of Racoon one bit him on the ankle, leaving a wound that bled through his sock and into his shoe. They had to get him a tetanus shot in the next town over. So he doesn't like rats, so sue him. He isn't inclined to give any of them, even the most distant relatives of the rabid things in Racoon, the benefit of the doubt.

As he listens another noise starts to creep into his consciousness, different from the scratching. A slow creaking, as rhythmic and steady as a heartbeat. It's familiar, something he remembers from way back. He can't quite place it but he can tell where it's coming from this time. It's behind the locked door that Rick failed to open. A slightly sickening dread starts to uncurl in his gut, a feeling that they're not as safe as they've been hoping they are. Slowly getting to his feet, poker in hand, he moves cautiously over to the door. Looking closely he thinks he can make out light spilling out from the crack so aware of squeaky floorboards he crosses to the switch and pushes it down with a soft click. The bulbs in the chandelier all go out and he's plunged into darkness for a moment until his eyes adjust. Then he can see fingers of amber light extending out from under the door, reaching a little way into the hall before pulling back, as if feeling for something on the floor.

It's the light from a fire and he knows where he's heard that slow squeaking sound before; his old Ma and her rocking chair, an ancient wooden thing that she had out on the veranda. She would sit on warm evenings, rocking back and forth, back and forth while she watched the neighbours go about their business. It was her favourite hobby, possibly her only hobby, the only thing she had the time to do for herself. That's what the noise is, and whoever is in there must only just have woken up because even with their talking and the oven and the pipes coming to life, the rocking on squeaking floorboards is loud enough to be heard. Of course, with their talking and the oven and the pipes, whoever it is should have been disturbed hours ago and surely should have come out to see who's in the house. They've made enough noise since their arrival to wake the dead and he really, really hopes that isn't the case.

Turning the light back on, Gabe stands in front of the door and takes a deep breath, brandishing the poker in one hand, turning the brass doorknob with the other. It was locked when Rick tried to get in earlier, but he's acting on a hunch and it certainly isn't locked now. The knob moves in his fingers and his heart starts its all too familiar pounding, body shifting gears into fight-or-flight with well-oiled ease. The door opens inwards with the gentle scratch of rusted hinges and Gabe peers inside, eyes adjusting to the warm glow of the fire burning in the grate as he stares at what's in front of it. He's right about the rocking chair; it is just like the one his Ma once had. There's an old woman sitting in it, rocking gently, the clackety-clack of metal knitting needles restless in her hands.

'Hello?' He keeps his voice low because he really doesn't want to scare her if she's just an old woman, and he absolutely doesn't want to startle her if she isn't. 'Ma'am?' He lets go of the doorknob and puts both hands on the narrow trunk of the poker, one above the other, taking a couple of cautious steps inside. There's a ball of light-blue wool in her lap, a single strand winding its way up to two knitting needles off which hangs something square, perhaps the start of a scarf. He can't quite make it out. He takes another two steps forward, 'Ma'am?'

Her head turns.

He's ready for anything, from the macabre to the plain freaky. He's ready for a skeletal face or no face at all. But she's just an old woman with silver hair and wrinkled skin, big blue eyes staring at him from behind thin-framed specs and a friendly smile with the right number of teeth, give or take.

'Hello, dear,' she greets him, her voice friendly and her expression welcoming.

Gabe stares. The last old lady they met had two obviously broken legs and she still chased them half a mile with the speed and determination of a marathon runner.

'It's all right, dear. I'm just knitting this toy for the orphans. Are you all right? You look a little peaky. Do you and your friends have everything you need?'

Slightly belatedly, Gabe lowers the poker. He keeps staring at her but she doesn't change into anything else, doesn't shift her shape to become something bizarre with bulging eyes, doesn't try to stab him with a knitting needle. She just smiles her crinkled smile and starts knitting again, the sound of needle against needle one of those things that's just familiar and comfortable enough even if he can't recall ever knowing anyone who knitted. Perhaps an aunt, although he doesn't remember ever owning a bright red sweater with Rudolph on the front, even as a child.

'Excuse me, ma'am, but... who are you?'

'I'm Nancy, dear.'

Honestly not knowing what else to do short of yelling for the others, which seems extreme for what doesn't feel like a life threatening situation, he holds out his hand. She makes a show of placing her needles into her left hand and shaking his with her right. It's a strong handshake but nothing out of the ordinary.

'Is this your house?'

'Mine, dear? No. I'm just a guest here, like you. Oh, but don't mind me. I'm happy sitting here with my fire and my knitting. All I ask is that whenever you have the kettle on, you think about making me a cup of tea. Sencha Green if you have it.'

Gabe's the first to admit that bizarre has been the order of the day for quite some time but he can't stop staring at her. Close up he can see the little toy she's making, small and square and blue with stumpy legs and little arms sticking straight out from its sides.

'Are you all right, dear?'

'Yes.' He tries to find a few more words and finally settles on, 'Have you just arrived?'

'I'm not sure. I think so. But my memory is so bad these days.' She doesn't seem remotely disturbed by any of this. 'Come to think of it, I might have been here a while because I usually have a cup of tea when I arrive somewhere, and I don't seem to have had one recently. Or a sherry.' She pauses in her knitting and looks up at him, intelligent, clear eyes sparkling in the light from the fire. 'Oh, do you think you could find me a sherry, dear? I'm quite parched.'

Gabe looks around. There's no sign of a drinks cabinet, but so far the kitchen seems to be well stocked. 'Let me go and see what we have.'

He backs out of the room, still nervous about turning his back on her, and closes the door as he leaves. For a moment he stands outside it, contemplating the doorknob and considering that he might finally have gone insane. He should wake the others but she hasn't tried anything nasty and they deserve to sleep while they can so he keeps hold of the poker and goes into the kitchen, switching on the light and checking the cupboards before the pantry. Sure enough there's an unopened bottle of La Gitana Manzanilla Sherry on a shelf just inside the door, and a set of four small glasses in the cupboard beside the window, next to the stemmed wine glasses, champagne flutes, shot glasses, tumblers and beer tankards. Someone or something has planned for all eventualities. He pours a healthy measure and takes it back through, hesitating for a second before opening the door again, half-convinced she won't be there. But she is, rocking and knitting and humming a tune so softly to herself he can barely hear it. It isn't one he recognises.

'Here you go.' He holds out the glass and she lets her knitting fall carefully into her lap as she takes it with both hands.

'Oh thank you, dear, you're a gem. Now you go off and get some sleep! It's late and you look exhausted.'

'I'm keeping watch,' he explains, feeling foolish. She doesn't look like she could knock down a cobweb with a feather duster, as his Ma used to say. She reminds him of her a bit. And when she frowns she strengthens his feeling of trust.

'What for? Nothing's going to hurt you here, dear. You're all perfectly safe now, I assure you. We won, you know. So you just get yourself up to bed and when you wake up all this storm nonsense will be over and it'll be a bright and beautiful day.'

There's no reason to believe her, then again there's no reason not to except for well-tuned paranoia telling him she could easily be something put in the house to set them up, take them off guard to make way for an attack. But that in itself is ludicrous. Anything could have attacked them at any time, they don't have any defences. They don't have Matt and Luke's frankly astounding collection of weapons, or their hand-to-hand fighting skills. If there's an armoury hidden in the house they haven't found it and a small collection of hearthside equipment – two iron pokers and a pair of sturdy tongs – will only get them so far. Besides, it would probably be better to die in his sleep, unknowing and blissfully ignorant of whatever horror befalls him, although he's not sure that the others would feel the same way.

'Will you be all right alone?'

She pulls a face just like his Ma used to pull. 'I'm an old woman, dear, not a toddler. I can look after myself if the need should arise but I assure you that it won't. Now off to bed with you. In the morning you can make me a nice cup of tea. No milk, no sugar. Thank you.'

Gabe nods. 'Okay. Good night.' He pulls the door closed behind him and stands in front of it, not knowing what to do next. It's one thing for all of them to arrive in this place together. It's another for an old woman to just appear out of nowhere, to know them, to know what's happened. Yes, she's made him feel better for some inexplicable reason, but after months of being rudely awoken by things trying to eat him for breakfast, he's uncertain about leaving them without a first line of defence even if it is just him and a fire poker. Still, he switches the lights off before returning to the couch, hugging the poker to him as he lies down and stretches out, feet over the arm, head on a cushion. He closes his eyes and within minutes he's fallen asleep to the comforting sound of the rocking chair and the crackle and pop of the fire in the grate.

~..~

Emilie wakes slowly, warmth on her face and heat in her body, feeling rested after her first real good night's sleep in ages. Stretching her limbs out under the sheets she opens her eyes and in the daylight surveys the room she's stayed in all night. It's beautiful. The decor is in keeping with the rest of the house, done out in purples, from the violet throw to the amethyst and byzantium in the wallpaper. The large rug covering the bare floorboards is eggplant. The curtains, hanging in the small windows that are at right angles to one another in the corner of the room, are lavender. (Yes, she was a bridesmaid when her best friend from school got married, and their dresses, the bride's dress and the flowers were all in purple hues.) There's a heavy wooden door in the opposite corner of the room, maybe an en-suite, probably just a closet. The bed is the best thing she's known in so long that it's going to be a while before she's getting up to find out. She spreads out, reaching for all four corners with her hands and feet.

After snoozing for what might have been a minute or might have been an hour she eventually admits to herself that she really needs to discover if there's a bathroom behind that door. She wonders if anyone else is awake. She left the bedroom door ajar last night, so that the slightest noise outside the room would wake her, and it's still open. There's no one around on the landing but she can definitely hear movement downstairs so she eventually and regretfully drags herself out of bed and tries the other door, which turns out to be a closet with clothes hanging in it. She crosses the landing to the bathroom.

She showered before she went to bed. It was truly heavenly. And feeling indulgent she takes another just to feel piping hot water raining down hard on her from the huge showerhead. She returns to her room half an hour later the colour of a lobster and wrapped in one of the big, fluffy white towels she found in the cupboard in the bathroom.

Opening the closet again she brushes her fingertips over the line of hanging blouses and sweaters, opens the drawers and lifts out the folded jeans and T-shirts. It all looks slightly too big for her but she finds a pair of jeans which don't fall off every time she stands up and a mohair jumper with a V-neck high enough to cover her breasts. The clean underwear she finds in the chest opposite the bed is a relief. It's not something she would ever have considered a luxury before leaving Malibu but it's been the one thing she's really missed.

There's makeup on a small dresser next to the bed but she doesn't bother with that. She hasn't done since leaving home, except for the day after meeting Luke when she found a woman's makeup bag in a motel room and made an attempt at covering up the worst of the junk food spots to make a half-decent impression. Not that it made the slightest difference. She could have been Paris Hilton; he wouldn't have looked at her twice. She hopes he and Matt are okay.

Dressed and towel-drying her hair she crosses to the windows and opens the curtains. She's in the left-hand corner of the house, looking out over the front yard where they materialised last night. It's a bright morning, if it is still morning and she hasn't slept all day, but it's too hazy for her to pinpoint the sun. It looks as if the sky is wall-to-wall high level cloud so she can't work out north from south, east or west. The grounds appear to run out to a ragged hedgerow some twenty or thirty feet away from the house. Beyond that, through the bare branches of dead trees, she can see a road, if 'road' isn't too grand a description for the strip of broken asphalt that runs straight in both directions as far as she can see. Across the road the light is reflecting off what might be sand, stone or even water. It's impossible to tell without going out there because the horizon itself is blindingly bright and it's an unsettling thought that there might not be anything out there at all. To the side of the house, there's a path running the length of the place, another hedgerow then scrub following the road all the way out to the horizon. There aren't any other houses. There's nothing else.

She has no idea how they got here or where 'here' even is, but nothing's tried to kill her yet and that's a definite, one hundred percent improvement on the last few weeks.

She hears someone out on the landing but by the time she opens the door there's no one there. She does however become aware of sounds and smells from downstairs, a kettle being brewed and frying bacon if she isn't mistaken. She can only hope there are pancakes too. During the week at the diner Matt made pancakes with maple syrup every morning for breakfast. She loves maple syrup. She wishes she wasn't as jealous of Matt as she is.

She pulls the sheets straight on the bed and folds her towel, hanging it up in the bathroom before she heads downstairs. Someone's showering in one of the two en-suite rooms on the other side of the landing. The domesticity of the sound as well as the smell of breakfast is starting to make her feel at home.

Joe's back in the kitchen, Gabe's nowhere to be seen. Hopefully he's the one in the shower because Rick's on the couch with a mug of coffee cradled in his hands. He's dressed in blue jeans with a light-blue shirt and looks as if he's showered too, thin hair pointing in all directions. It makes her wonder just how much hot water there can physically be unless Gabe's taking his cold for some reason.

'Morning.' Rick smiles up at her and gives her a small wave as she steps off the bottom stair. She smiles back.

'Good morning. Sleep well?'

She notices his hesitation before his nod but the aromas coming from the kitchen are very distracting so she doesn't press him, instead following her nose. As soon as he sees her Joe's got the kettle on to boil again and is apologising again about the fact that there's only instant coffee, nothing fresh.

'Whoever stocked this place forgot the really important things,' he jokes.

She's not bothered but it's been a bugbear with Gabe and Matt, the distinct lack of decent coffee since the end of the world began. Once Starbucks closed all its California branches – quite late in the game to be fair – on the grounds of customer safety and there being very few staff willing to risk their lives to bring lattes to the hysterical masses, most mornings have started with the two men complaining about the drop in living standards, as if a lack of frothy coffee marks the downfall of society. There are still diners open, particularly to the north of the state, and they've managed to find more than enough pre-ground coffee on some days to drown internal organs and to maintain, at least in Gabe's case, a resting heart rate of over one hundred. Both he and Matt are three-a-day men. Gabe hankers after a latte for breakfast, macchiato for lunch and an iced vanilla latte late in the afternoon, whereas Matt's happy with anything that's made with freshly ground and, if possible, freshly roasted beans. A jar of instant definitely won't cut it. There's going to be another tirade as soon as Matt puts in an appearance. If he puts in an appearance. For her part she doesn't care what it is as long as there's a hefty shot of caffeine in her first drink of the day. She's never cared much about the actual taste. It's what comes of being an intern, dropping into bed three hours before needing to drag herself out of it again.

'Breakfast will be ready in a few minutes,' Joe tells her. She nods and squeezes his arm in thanks before wrapping her hands around the mug he gives her. 'You found clean clothes too?'

'In my room.' It strikes her now how much of coincidence that is.

'Me too. Just about my size, my shape. Rick was the same. We were trying to work out what the odds are of that happening.'

'About the same as the odds of there being a warm, well stocked house on the edge of a battlefield that we didn't see until the fight was over?'

'I don't think any of us think we're still in California.'

She gazes out of the window over the sink at the dead yard and the bright, clear sky. 'Any sign of Luke and Matt?'

Joe shakes his head. 'Sorry.'

She doesn't know what to do with her disappointment. She can only hope they're still sleeping up in the turret room. 'So what do you think is out there?'

He moves to stand next to her. 'No idea. Desert, probably. It would explain the light you can see, the sand reflecting the sunlight. Not that I can see the sun.... We'll take a look later, go for a walk. Gabe's up for a bit of exploring and I don't want to spend another night here without knowing more about where here is, not if I can help it.'

She can understand the sentiment, but every night for the last couple of months she's known exactly where she is and it hasn't stopped her from being afraid, often uncomfortable, usually cold and, on one occasion, actually wet. Last night was comfortable, warm and dry. She isn't certain that knowing where they are is a necessity as long as nothing tries to kill them.

The water pipes fall silent overhead; Gabe finishing his shower.

'Apparently Gabe has something he wants to show us after breakfast,' Joe tells her.

'Very mysterious.'

'That's what I said. He said he wanted to show us all together and he wanted a shower first.'

'Can't be all that interesting then.'

Joe starts cracking open fresh eggs into a second frying pan. He's obviously not too concerned. Breakfast smells good, she's had a great night's sleep and she has hot, strong coffee in her hands. She's strangely happy right now in a way she hasn't been since leaving Malibu and despite the fragile and mysterious nature of it she's damned if she's going to let anything short of a full-scale attack by a keen enemy change that. So whatever Gabe is going to reveal, she's not going to let it worry her unless someone tells her it should.

Rick's following in Gabe's wake when he strolls into the kitchen a short time later. Gabe's short blond hair is still damp and sticking out at points where he hasn't quite managed to get it to stay plastered to his head. Emilie didn't find a comb either. He's shaved, and he's wearing a fresh white shirt and clean black jeans. She can't help but stare for a second or two because while he's a good looking guy, she hasn't seen him in anything other than that blue Italian tailored suit since she joined their little Scooby gang and he looks better without it. 'You changed your clothes....'

Gabe smiles at her with more than a hint of sarcasm. 'It has been known.'

'Not for the last six weeks,' Joe drops in.

'I was attached to that suit.'

'Surgically.' It earns Joe a swift slap to the upper arm.

'The last vestiges of civilised society,' Gabe points out. 'But it was time to let them go or to at least change out of them until I can find a washing machine. I don't suppose anyone noticed if we passed a Laundromat on the way here?'

There isn't a washer in the kitchen, which seems a little odd, and there doesn't appear to be any sort of utility room. Back at the diner they took advantage of the industrial washer, although after it tore holes in Emilie's grey cardigan, Gabe had refused to put his suit anywhere near it.

'You look good,' she compliments him honestly and he smiles, pleased. She's pleased he's pleased.

'Thank you. I smell coffee....'

Joe dishes up the bacon, eggs and toast and they pull out stools from under the table, the kitchen descending into silence for a few minutes except for quiet slurping and chewing. It's some of the best food Emilie's had in a long time, helped by the lack of threat and fear they've been living with for so long, and she eats it all, mopping up the last of the egg yolk with her toast before pushing her plate away and retrieving her coffee.

'Joe mentioned there's something you want to show us?'

Gabe nods, cleaning his own plate in much the same way she did. 'We are not alone,' he asserts with a final mouthful of toast.

'What?' It's a question spoken in unison.

He gets up, refills the kettle and puts it on to boil, fetching a mug from the cupboard along with a box of Sencha Green teabags, dropping one in.

'You drink tea?' She's surprised after all the fuss he's made about coffee.

He shakes his head slowly. 'It's not for me.'

She looks around the table, they all have drinks.

Joe half-stands. 'Gabe, who's it for? Who else is here?'

'You'll see.'

'Don't you think this is something you should have told us like, immediately?'

'No.'

It's obviously piques the interest of Rick too, because Joe's right, if there's someone else in the house with them, Gabe should have told them already. But he holds up a hand to stave off any more questions or accusations, finishes making the tea while Rick finishes his breakfast, then he lifts the mug and beckons them all to follow him. They pick up quickly on where he's heading – there aren't that many places for someone to hide – and Rick's excited simply because Gabe has apparently managed to find the key that opens the locked door.

'Who's in there?'

Gabe wiggles a finger back at them. 'Patience.'

He reaches for the knob and Emilie realises that she's holding her breath, not in the bad, frightened way she's used to doing but because she's excited. Gabe isn't carrying a poker so whoever it is, it isn't someone to be wary of. For a second she thinks it could be Matt and Luke, even though neither of them drink tea, and her heart starts to hammer. But as Gabe opens the door and lets it swing inwards, she sees that it isn't. It's an old woman in a rocking chair, knitting in front of a dying fire. It's such an unexpected sight that it takes a couple of seconds for her brain to process it.

'What the Hell....?'

It's not a great introduction and Gabe ignores her anyway, bidding the old woman good morning, addressing her as 'Nancy' and placing the mug of tea on the small round table next to her chair. The woman puts down her knitting and smiles up at him.

'You remembered! Thank you, dear, that's so kind. And you've brought your friends in to say hello. That's nice.'

She looks and sounds like any normal old woman; nothing like that witch who chased them through Selma with two broken legs.

Gabe waves them forward. Emilie's the first in line, stepping forward and holding out her hand, staring at the wrinkled visage.

'Nancy, this is Emilie.'

Nancy takes her hand in a strong shake. Given the mysterious nature of their current predicament, an old woman in a rocking chair has an air of normality to it that just shouldn't feel so right.

'Hello, dear. It's a pleasure to meet you. Did you sleep well?' Emilie nods, dumbstruck. 'I'm glad to hear it. You deserve a rest, don't you think?'

Nancy lets go of her hand and finally Emilie manages to form words into a coherent question. 'You know who we are?' There's something open and friendly about the old woman's face, something that invites trust, and that alone is something she's wary of based on past experience.

'Yes, dear. I know who you are. I know what you've done and I know you're safe here. As I said to the lovely Gabe last night, all I ask is that you bring me a cup of tea whenever you have the kettle on and a small sherry in the evening and I'll be fine. You don't need to worry about me.'

'This is Joe,' Gabe introduces him as Joe steps forward. Emilie's not entirely sure that Nancy answered her question.

'Tea and sherry?' she parrots over Joe's shoulder. 'Is that all? Don't you want anything to eat?'

'Oh, no thank you, dear. I'm not hungry. I don't think I need to eat. I've eaten enough over the years. Don't you worry, I'm not going to starve. Just Sencha tea and a nice sherry and I'll be a happy girl.'

Emilie doesn't want to think too hard about why Nancy doesn't need to eat. Instead her eyes fall on the knitting in her lap; a red semi-circle with stubby legs and two knitting needles sticking out at the top like long eyebrows. Nancy's talking to Joe, complimenting him on something or other, quite possibly his youthful looks. Unlike Gabe, Joe hasn't shaved but then again his stubble doesn't actually seem to ever grow out into a beard. The last time she knows he picked up a razor was in Stevinson to slice the throat of a woman trying to bash Luke's head in with a meat mallet. He did the same in Harbor City with a pizza cutter.

'What is she knitting?'

Gabe murmurs, 'Toys, for orphaned kids.'

'Which orphaned kids?'

He shrugs, clueless. 'I have no idea. Last night she was knitting a blue square one. She must have finished it.'

'Really?' Emilie looks around. 'Where is it?'

'Don't ask me.' Considering they probably have more important things to think about than vanishing toys, she follows him out of the room, leaving Joe and Rick in the disarmingly charming clutches of their new housemate.

'Why doesn't she eat?'

Gabe scratches the back of his neck. 'Because she's... dead?'

'But clearly she isn't. And not a single other un-dead person we've crossed paths with has shown the slightest interest in knitting or tea!'

'Honestly, I'm as bewildered as you. But like I said, I don't know. She doesn't seem to mean us any harm. I think she just appeared in that room last night, the same way we appeared in the yard.'

Taking cigarettes and a lighter from his coat he opens the front door, casting a glance back over his shoulder in invitation. Fresh air might be nice, assuming it is fresh, but she leaves the front door slightly ajar just in case in turns out Nancy isn't the only surprise still awaiting them.

Outside the light is unusual, eerie; like the daylight during an eclipse of the sun. There are no shadows, presumably because there's no sun, no single light source that they can see. There's just an odd tinge to the sky, a slightly pinkish hue. And the air is wrong, stilted, dry and stale as if it's been left out too long, unused, with no breeze to stir it. Turning to look at the outside of the house she sees that the windows aren't broken and it is conceivable that it just looked as if they were last night, a trick of the lightning perhaps, yet the whole place looks in a much better state than it did when they first saw it. It's anyone's guess where they've ended up. She wouldn't be at all surprised to see a yellow brick road winding its way into the distance.

The house might look different but the yard remains in the same decaying state it was last night. There's nothing living out here: dead trees, leaves turning to sludge, twigs and sticks that were once plants. They walk around to the back following a path of lifted and broken flagstones to find a similar story. There are skeletal branches of trees tangled over what might once have been a lawn. There's the faint smell of decaying vegetation and a rotting fence that marks the perimeter. Beyond that there's scrubland all the way out to the same bright horizon. Close to the back of the house there's the rusting wreck of an old Chevy, tyres long gone, seats no more than metal and brown springs. It looks as if it's been there for decades. Towards the back fence, facing the building, there's a faded garden bench with its light-green paint peeling and a wooden slat missing from the back but otherwise looking intact. Emilie sits first, hesitant and cautious in case it's been eaten through. When it doesn't collapse under her Gabe sits down too, pulling a cigarette from its packet with his lips and lighting it.

She's lost count of the number of places they've looted for cigarettes for Gabe and it's always a risk. Being inside supermarkets and stores, anywhere with shelves, tends to be more dangerous than open plan diners and bars. There are too many opportunities for being surprised, for being cornered. But Gabe's insisted that until there are no more cigarettes, he isn't about to quit. What his brand was when all this kicked off she has no idea. But in the short time she's known him he's smoked anything he can get his hands on as long as it contains nicotine. He isn't all that particular about whatever else is in it.

She watches him for a few seconds. She actually likes a guy who smokes. It's old-fashioned and she used to have a thing for old-fashioned men. She isn't sure why she's only now noticing how attractive he is. Maybe it's because in the short time she's known him this is the first chance she's had to really look at him. Before now they've been mostly running towards or away from something with barely time to catch their breath. When they were on the road, Gabe would usually ride shotgun with Joe or drive himself. She noticed Luke because he's difficult to miss, he's exactly her type. Gabe isn't. But he's easy on the eyes now he's out of that damned suit. She shifts on the bench, tensing when it creaks and moves under them but it doesn't give way.

'Do you think we're dead?'

Instead of laughing, instead of denying it outright, he tips his head back and takes a long drag on his cigarette, holding the smoke in his lungs for what feels like a painfully long time before blowing it out slowly. It hangs in the air for a second or two like it has nowhere else to go before dissipating slowly. He looks at her and smiles. 'If I was dead, I don't think that would be so good.'

He has a point, because Joe's breakfast this morning was the best she's tasted in ages, and that includes Matt's pancakes. If she's dead, she doubts that sensations would be so vivid. The bed and the shower, the wine and the food, have been awesome relative to how they've been living since leaving their respective homes. But something odd is definitely going on, they're somewhere out of the ordinary.

'If we're alive, where are we?'

He shrugs. He must practise them in front of a mirror because he has a large repertoire of shrugs and each one means something slightly different. This one means he doesn't know and nor does he care. It surprises her.

'Some kind of refuge?' He suggests. 'Clothes, food, warmth. The essentials we need to stay alive.'

'I'd say we have more than the essentials, wouldn't you?'

'Yes. I'll give you that.' Leaning forward, elbows on his knees, he takes another lungful of smoke and lets it out in small rings. 'But you know what? I think we should just concentrate on being here for now. Because it beats everywhere else we've found in the last few weeks. Like you say, we have everything we need and nothing's tried to attack us yet. Ask too many questions and we might start getting answers we'd rather not have.'

That goes against her nature. She's always been one for asking questions. It's what got her into this mess in the first place. Last night she was happy to accept a roof over her head, hot water and a comfy bed. Last night she was happy not to question their apparent luck, the same when she woke up this morning and at breakfast with hot food and strong coffee. But since Nancy's appearance she's becoming increasingly nervous, she's starting to worry about what comes next, if anything comes next. Gabe's right in that for now they're comfortable and seemingly safe, she just can't help thinking about what happens when that changes.

'How did you wind up here?' she asks him in a bid to change the subject. 'I mean, with us. The rest of us have told our stories. It's your turn.'

He doesn't answer immediately and she doesn't push. She waits it out until he's finished his cigarette, dropping it to the gravel and mashing it into the rotting leaves with the heel of his once shiny Italian shoe. Then he starts to talk.

'I,' he announces as if this is going to be something big. Then he lets his voice drop off. 'I was a car salesman.'

She instantly imagines him standing in an out-of-town lot, surrounded by red and white striped bunting and placards announcing amazing deals and offers for the rust buckets parked all around him. But he quickly dismisses that image.

'I worked at a Ferrari dealership in Hollywood. I sold to actors, directors, rock stars; the whole celebrity range. And I was damn good at it. I loved my job, I loved my life. I had it all worked out, had everything going for me. New Ferrari to tool around in every day, men and women falling at my feet – well, my wheels – expensive apartment in an exclusive area with an excellent bar within stumbling distance. My little slice of Heaven. Before the Powers That Be decided to have their domestic right on the doorstep and spoiled everything.'

He taps out another cigarette from the packet in his hands, shielding the flame of the plastic lighter through habit rather than necessity out here where there's no movement of the air.

'There was a man. He came in one Wednesday morning and asked about the cars. He was tall, slim, immaculately dressed in a three thousand dollar suit, black shirt and red tie. Very smart, very rich. He had this smile and I'll never forget it. He had too many teeth and they were a brilliant white like in the toothpaste ads; that white you can't get without spending thousands on dental bills. His eyes were odd too. Really dark. Huge black pupils and small irises. He might have been on drugs and he wouldn't have been the first client I had who was high. I thought he might be an actor, although I didn't recognise him and I tried to keep up to date with the latest who's who so I was able greet anyone who came in by name. The rich and famous like to be recognised.' He laughs with a slightly bitter note that doesn't suit him. 'I guess I should be grateful all this happened to reset my life priorities.' He lets out a deep breath on a long, nicotine-tinged sigh.

'So this guy looked at a couple of the cars and when I approached him he said he wanted something red and fast. As if Ferrari makes anything for the sedate driver. They were his only stipulations, which was a little odd in itself because people tended to have a very clear idea of what they wanted when they came in. They're spending that much money, they've thought about it, even if the money's no object. A Ferrari is a status symbol, it's going to say something about you when you drive it and it needs to say the right things. Most of my clients thought about it, visualised it. Not so much people who are adding to a collection, but the newly rich: lottery winners, actors cashing in their first major movie check. This guy, he was different. It was as if he didn't care which model he bought. He just wanted a fast car.' He shrugs and she can see the regret in the slump of his shoulders. 'He took a Modena out for a test drive. It was already out on the forecourt, I think that's the only reason he chose it. Sales consultants didn't usually go out with the clients because they usually weren't alone. Businessmen tended to have a woman on their arm, celebrities had whole entourages trailing after them. Most models of Ferraris are two-seaters and more often than not the client had a friend to take out with them, to show off. But this guy wanted me to go with him, he had no one else and I wasn't sure I trusted him so I went. He scared the shit out of me, drove like a lunatic. Like the fucking devil. He almost hit a kid on a crossing and narrowly missed ploughing into a van at a red light. I didn't like him, I thought he was crazy. His smile didn't slip once.' He pauses.

'When we got back to the showroom he said he loved the car and wanted to buy it and that was fine by me. I might not have liked him but his money was the same as everyone else's and I could book an exotic holiday for every two sales I made. I took him through to the office and started to gather all the paperwork. I asked him how he wanted to pay. Everyone else I ever sold to produced a credit card at that crucial moment; most were gold or platinum, some corporate, didn't matter. But when I turned around, there was two hundred and forty thousand dollars in cash in a briefcase on the desk.'

Her mouth falls open. 'What does two hundred and forty grand look like?'

He thinks about it. 'It was the most beautiful thing I'd ever seen. It couldn't have been more beautiful if it had been gold bullion. I just stared at it because I had no idea how it got there. He couldn't have had it with him when we went out, there was nowhere in the car to put it! But there it was, larger than life. He asked me if the cash covered it and I told him I'd have to count it. So he waited, and I did. It took me the better part of an hour but it was all there in hundred dollar bills. I called in my supervisor. He put some of the notes under our counterfeit currency scanner. It was real. We shouldn't have accepted it, but we did. I handed the guy the keys to his new car and off he went.

'I told everyone in the bar about it that night but I had a phenomenal week, made another two sales, one to an A-list actor and one to a movie producer I recognised from watching the Oscars on TV, so the significance faded and I didn't think much more about it. Odd things happen, the fabric of life and all that. The bank accepted the cash, it wasn't fake, wasn't laundered as far as I know, there wasn't anything to worry about. Until the following Monday. I was driving to work which usually took an hour. There is – was, I guess – a school on the edge of town. Every weekday morning I would battle my way through lines of parents dropping their kids off in their urban tanks and streams of school buses. I was used to it. But that morning everything was at a standstill. After going nowhere for a half-hour, I got out and walked the quarter mile to the school gates. There'd been an accident, or that's what people were calling it. A family – mom and three kids – crossing the road had been mown down by a speeding car that just ploughed straight into them. There were medics on the scene and about a hundred cops but there wasn't anything anyone could do. They were all dead. Kids were crying, people were screaming. The bodies, what was left of them, were all over the road. The cops weren't able to contain it all. One woman who saw it happen said the car had swerved after it hit them, went careening into the metal railings at the front of the school. I went to have a look and when I saw it I thought I was going to be sick. It was a bright red, brand new Ferrari Modena and I knew it hadn't been an accident. I knew the car and I knew who'd been driving it. The cops were saying he fled the scene but I overheard a couple of hysterical witnesses say he'd just vanished from the driver's seat before the car crashed. I doubt the driver's side door would have opened given the state of it and I knew they were right. Just like I knew the cops would never believe them and would waste their time searching for a driver they would never find. I felt like I was caught in a Poe story.' She doesn't get the reference but doesn't ask about it either.

'I didn't go to work. I turned round and went home again. I didn't get changed, I didn't even pack a case. I left the car I was driving because I didn't want the cops looking for me. I took my old Volvo out of the garage behind the house and left town.'

'Jesus.' At least that explains the suit.

'I couldn't get the guy's smile out of my head. I guess you know, don't you, when something big is happening? You know, right down in your subconscious, before you see anything. That feeling that something's not right.'

She knows that feeling. She left Malibu, her home, her job, her life, based on the same intuition. They all did. He's reached the end of the cigarette and is staring at the ground.

'I had this image of myself,' he confesses, holding onto the glowing butt. 'Built up around what I did, what I drove, what I wore. I saw myself as this suave, sophisticated guy. I told myself that I was a businessman; better, more intelligent than some of the brainless idiots I sold cars to. Society holds actors in such high regard when all they do is muck about all day pretending to be people they're not. You do that on the streets you're a lunatic, a fraud. But because these people do it in front of cameras they're hailed as heroes and treated like royalty. They're not.

Believe me, I've sold cars to enough of them. Most can't even work out how to get into one, never mind how to drive it. Singers, rock stars, they're just as bad. They can't go five feet without seven other people following literally in their footsteps agreeing with everything they say like they need constant validation. I used to tell myself I was better than them. Turns out I was just as bad because when it came to the crunch, I just ran away.'

'You had no idea what you were running from.'

'But I knew something was going on. That's why, when I ran across Matt, Luke and Joe at the centre of a standoff in Boulder City, I actually did something about it. Not a lot, I'll admit. I yelled a lot, ran about and waved my hands in the air, provided that moment of distraction, gave them time to act. But I was proud of myself. Matt and Luke... those guys have been doing this half their lives. They didn't run away from it, they ran towards it.'

She gives him the moment as he finally drops his second cigarette to the dry ground and stamps on it, staring at the flat stub.

'That's why you wore the suit, isn't it? To hold on to just a small bit of that old image of you?' He turns his head to look at her and she can see by his expression that he hasn't given it much conscious thought. He's simply hung onto something out of habit, out of necessity. 'It's the only part of you you can still recognise.'

He smiles. 'When did you take psychology?'

'Final year of medical school.' She grins and nods. 'It's the same reason I need to wear a jacket, because it feels like a layer of protection between me and the horror. It isn't, I know. Bullets, blades, even teeth go through leather as easily as they go through skin. Doesn't matter. It's the thought, the need to hold on to something of who we were. I don't know about you, but I've no idea who I am now, who I've been since meeting Luke and Matt.'

He looks at her for a little while longer before dropping his head back and popping his shoulders. 'I'm grateful to them for what they've done for me, everything they've done for me. They've not only kept me safe, just running into them gave me a chance to actually do something worthwhile. But as meaningless and pointless as my life was before all this, I was enjoying it. I could have happily lived and died not knowing any of the shit I know now.'

They all have their stories and each one of them is amazing and sad and terrifying in its own way. They've been through a hellish time together and wherever they are now, whatever happens next, she's confident that they can deal with that too, simply because they don't have much of a choice.

She and Gabe sit for a couple of minutes listening to nothing. All around them is silence, complete and flawless. No birds, no cars, no noise of any kind. It isn't right. She's never been anywhere before without noise. There's life even out in the desert. But here there's nothing.

'Where do you think we are?' she asks him again, more to break the silence than in hope of getting an answer.

'At the end of the world,' he breathes, tapping out the last cigarette, emptying another packet. He stares into it. 'Almost time to quit.'

~..~

Joe's finishing washing the breakfast dishes, enjoying the simple domesticity of it, when Rick comes in from the hall. Whatever was wrong last night, he seems worse this morning: jumpy and nervous as a virgin on his wedding night. In the short time he's known the man Rick's been something of a drama queen, the first to wash the blood off his hands after a fight, the first to change soiled clothes into stolen clean ones the moment the chance has arisen. But that's not to say he hasn't pulled his weight and killed things that needed killing. He looks worried but then he always looks worried.

'Is everything all right?'

Rick's eyes are wide, lips pale. 'Can you hear something?'

Joe pauses with his hands in the warm soapy water and listens. 'No.'

'Neither can I.'

It's a peculiar exchange even in these circumstances and the look Joe gives Rick tells him so. But Rick shakes his head.

'I mean, I can't hear it in here. But I can hear it in the hall. Come through.' He seems enough on edge that Joe decides to indulge him, wipes his wet hands on the drying towel and follows him out into the hall where they both stand silently, Rick with his finger at his lips in a 'hush' gesture. It takes a second or two, but Joe can hear something; scratching, maybe mice or rats.

'I think it's coming from inside the wall.'

Crouching down, they both listen with an ear each pressed to the wall dividing the hall from the room Nancy's in.

'What do you think it is?' Rick looks at him, fear in his expression. Joe resists the urge to roll his eyes.

'It's just mice.'

But in the next moment Joe hears something that changes his mind, another sound over the scratching, a sort of incessant chattering like teeth in the cold, but at differing pitches.

'Gremlins? Elves?' Given recent events neither suggestion seems too farfetched. Rick looks at him and Joe can see him edging towards panic. 'Remember those critter things in Hollister?'

Joe isn't likely to ever forget but he doesn't think these are critters. They were more the gnashing of teeth type, angry little buggers, biting anything that came within their jump radius which was pretty damn wide. These sounds are more like things communicating with each other, not that he's about to say that out loud in case it's the final push that sends Rick hurtling over the edge of reason into full-blown hysteria.

'Then, what?'

'I don't know.' Experimentally, and with some misgivings, he taps on the wall with his knuckles and immediately the noises stop.

'Are you sure that's such a good idea?'

'No....' Joe hesitates. 'But there's no reason to immediately assume whatever it is means us any harm.'

'Oh, you mean unlike every other thing we've run into?'

He has a point but Joe still thinks he's overreacting. Nothing in the house has tried to hurt them so far and whatever these things are, they sound small, although that in itself doesn't mean they're harmless. The critters were short enough to tread on if you could get one underfoot but they were still vicious little bastards. Gradually the noises start up again, and now he's certain there's more than one of them.

'Sounds like they're trying to figure something out.' He didn't mean to say that out loud.

'Like, how to get out of the wall?'

'If they're in the wall, how did they get there in the first place?'

Suddenly the din moves away from them towards the back of the house, becoming muffled when whatever they are reach the bookcase. Rick and Joe follow, still crouched, edging sideways like aged crabs, listening and watching the wall in case something does start to break through.

'What do we do if they get out?'

Joe opens his mouth to say something sarcastic then shuts it again. It's a very good question and he rises and turns to grab a poker that's been left next to the sooty fireplace.

'Your answer to everything,' Rick quips, but there's no real commitment to it and he grabs the other one.

The noises stop, and it's as if they're being listened to in return. He shushes Rick and leans closer to the wall just as the front door opens. The sudden noise surprises the already tightly-strung Rick, who loses his balance and drops back, his ass hitting the floorboards.

'It's just Emilie and Gabe,' Joe sighs. 'What's going on with you?'

Rick just glares at him and if something is wrong he isn't going to talk about it.

Emilie's understandably staring at them. 'What are you doing?'

Joe glances up. 'We think there's something in the walls.'

Gabe comes over to crouch at his side. 'I thought I heard something last night.'

'Why didn't you say anything?'

'Because it was before I found Nancy and after that I didn't hear them again.'

'It sounds like... creatures.' Rick whispers.

Gabe frowns at him. 'Last night my first thought was mice. Or rats.'

Joe nods. 'Mine too. But I think they're communicating with one another.'

Straightening, Gabe looks thoughtful. 'We could break into the wall.'

'I don't think we need to. I mean, they're not exactly threatening us right now.'

'You're sure? Remember the critters?'

Not bothering to reply, Joe stands up. 'I say we leave them alone unless they decide to make something of the fact we're sharing their place.'

There seems to be a general agreement so Joe starts back towards the kitchen, determined to finish off the dishes, to keep the place clean and tidy. After Babs passed away he kept their house tidy, just as she would have liked it. Thanks to the apocalypse his life's been a mess for months, so while he has the option of order he's going to take it.

He's stopped by the very last thing he expects to hear; a knock on the front door. They all freeze except Gabe who makes a hasty grab for the poker Joe's left propped against the arm of the couch. They exchange glances and Gabe murmurs,

'Expecting someone?'

Given the white-knuckle grip Rick has on his poker, Joe decides Gabe is his best backup. He knows the others will wait for him to make a move before following his lead; it's the mode of operation they fell into whenever Matt and Luke weren't around to bark out commands. And a few weeks' worth of habit formed under threat will take a lot longer than twelve hours of assumed safety to break.

Another knock.

He has to make a decision, but his options aren't exactly in double figures: answer it, don't answer it, hope whoever it is will go away. The last option seems stupid because it's hardly going to be a door-to-door salesman asking if they're likely to change their windows in the next twelve months.

The handle on the front door dips and slowly the door opens. Rick steps forward, poker raised, and Joe holds up a hand purely on instinct, the same way Matt and Luke do when they're all armed and primed and waiting for the perfect moment to start shooting.

'Relax,' he murmurs quietly. 'It could be anyone. Could be the boys.'

He sees Emilie move out of the corner of his eye and he's about to tell her to keep back when the door swings inwards.

He isn't sure what to make of the man – he supposes it's a man – standing on the top step. Curly dark hair, a round face, high cheekbones, curved nose. His brown eyes are huge, like he's stoned. So far so normal. But he must be getting on for seven feet tall. He's wearing a long, ruler-straight blue coat buttoned up from chin to ankles, black boots just visible underneath. His arms are rigid at his sides, fingers looking as if they're locked together like a doll's.

'Hi.' Joe thinks he would be able to see the line of any weapon secreted under that coat, it's so tight on the pencil-thin body. So he takes a step forward and holds out his hand. 'I'm Joe.'

There's a pause, everything holding steady, no one making a move. It's a moment that's been all too familiar recently, when a situation can go either way. Then the stranger is inside the house, standing in front of the mysteriously closed door. He's upright as a pillar, unblinking eyes falling on each of them for a time before settling on Joe. He doesn't accept the handshake but then Joe can't be sure his arms even move. He does, however, speak.

'I am here to check on you.
To ensure you have all
Items you need.'

It's an odd voice; flat, toneless, devoid of any emotion. But what's more disturbing is that the words seem to come from his throat without his lips moving. It's kind of macabre, but no worse than the other stuff they've witnessed and this does come just as Joe's starting to think that nothing will ever surprise him again so it's almost welcome, because a life without surprises would be very dull. 'Excuse me?'

'I am here to check on you.
To ensure you have all
Items you need.'

No one else has moved and Rick's still holding that poker as if at any moment he's going to do something violent with the spiky end.

'Who are you?'

The stranger's arm does move, left elbow bending to a right angle like an old toy soldier, his hand rotating twice at his wrist in a way that definitely isn't human before he points one long bony finger down towards the floor. Joe thinks can he can hear sounds behind the movement, like grinding metal.

'I am the landlord
Responsible for this house for
Your comfort here.'

Joe glances at Gabe who shrugs, obviously with no more idea of what he means than Joe does.

'Landlord?'

'Landlord of this house.
Responsible for providing the
Things you need.'

He's about to say 'we need answers' but Emilie beats him to it. She steps forward, pushes down on the end of the poker in Rick's hand until he lowers it, and demands to know, 'Where are we?' in a voice that's a little too high, a little fearful, but still rock steady.

The stranger turns his head without moving his neck and his face cracks open into the most ghastly smile Joe's ever seen, thin lips literally curling back like the tops of sardine tins to reveal two straight lines of skeletal teeth that don't move when he talks.

'You are in the house.
This is a well deserved chance
For you to get rest.'

Joe can't argue with that but then it's strangely hard to argue with anything spoken in Haiku by a guy who looks as if he's been put together by, at best, an apprentice. It's clear he's not telling them everything, he's not really telling them anything, but it might be that he can't say what he doesn't know. Or that he can only say what he's been told, instructed or programmed to.

'And what did we do to deserve this rest?'

'You saved the world.
Were triumphant in the fight
Between good and evil.'

Okay, that's great news. 'I don't suppose you could leave off the poetry?'

'This is what I am.
I can't be anything but
The thing that I am.'

Joe has a million questions, he's sure they all do, but it's difficult to hold a conversation with a stick man talking in riddles and he has a suspicion that this is as specific as the guy's going to get. He doesn't think there's much point in whacking him with a poker and trying to get the information out of him by force. In fact, something tells him that it would be a very bad idea.

'You are not prisoners.
This place is safe to explore
Where they want.'

'Who wants?'

'The designers of the house.
Everything comes from them is
Built from them.'

Joe doesn't understand a word of that one. 'Designers?' he parrots, and the landlord nods, his head tipping so far forward Joe's scared for a moment that it'll fall off. He's reminded of those nodding dog toys he's seen in the backs of cars and the thought of the bolt in the neck that holds the dog's head in place makes him feel a little nauseous. Then, without warning, the front door is open again and their visitor is standing on the top step without apparently having moved. He's disconcerting but he's hardly threatening. How quickly everything becomes relative.

'Wait.' Gabe raises his hand like a school kid in class. 'Are we supposed to look after Nancy?'

The landlord's eyebrows lift as if they're being pulled up by strings, big eyes grow impossibly larger and Joe realises he doesn't have a clue who Gabe's talking about.

'Nancy,' Joe points to the closed door. 'The old lady in the rocking chair?'

There's a definite hesitation before the response.

'I will check.
Let me get back to you...
On that.'

Then the stranger's gone. Vanished. Nowhere to be seen. They go outside but they're alone. They can see for miles in all directions, there's nothing but the house and the yard they're standing in.

'What the Hell is going on here?' Joe mutters under his breath and just to himself. He doesn't have a clue so it's doubtful the others do either. That their self-proclaimed landlord didn't know about Nancy is an important detail, because if he didn't bring her here it means that he isn't in control. So the important question has to be, who is? He seemed to be suggesting that they were but Joe certainly doesn't feel like he's running the show.

They really need Matt and Luke. The two of them have been fighting longer than Joe, Gabe, Emilie and Rick put together, they might know how and where to find answers. But if they are up in the turret room, they'll come down in their own time. For now the questions will have to wait. There is at least something they can do.

He moves to Gabe's side.

'I think we should stick to what we agreed last night,' he suggests. 'I think we should explore.'

BOOK TWO ~ MATT AND LUKE

thirty-one years ago

This is the night Luke won't remember. He's six months old, riding in his baby seat in the back of the car. It's Christmas Eve. There's snow in the trees and ice on the ground. Catherine is telling Carl that he's driving too fast, telling him to slow down. He's arguing with her. He isn't driving too fast but they're late for dinner with her parents who've never liked him and being late tonight won't make a great impression.

Bright lights cut in through the windshield. The car swerves. Catherine screams. The sound of twisting, tearing metal is followed by a silence that's broken only by Luke's cries until calloused but gentle hands reach in to pull him out of the wreckage.

~..~

nineteen years ago

This is the night Luke won't ever forget. A beautiful summer's evening, the light just starting to fade, the air holding on to the balmy heat of the day. A car moves along Route 395; two adults in the front, two kids in the back. Dad's driving. Mom's twisting around in the passenger seat to ask her young sons,

'Did you enjoy the play?'

Luke doesn't like the theatre, it's boring, but it's better than the opera or the ballet which are stupid and boring.

'I didn't understand it,' little Matt declares before Luke can answer.

Luke didn't understand it either. There were loads of people in the cast but apparently three of them were invisible, although he could see them just fine, and at the end one of them said that the man in the long coat was made of clockwork. That was a crock of shit. He didn't look clockwork and he bowed like everyone else.

'The clockwork man was lame,' Luke complains, tone flat.

'Didn't you think he had a very poetic way of speaking?'

'No! It was annoying.'

Mom smiles and promises, 'I'll read you the story one night.' She turns around again, and to two boys that sounds more like a threat. Luke glances at Matt and rolls his eyes up into his head, which makes Matt laugh like it always does.

Ages later they're still not home. Mom's humming softly to the music on the radio, some classical stuff that makes Luke think of Sunday mornings. Matt's been shifting in his seat for a few minutes, and Luke knows what's coming when he starts to whine.

'Mom...'

'Mom, Matt has to pee.' He talks in a sing-song over his little brother, pulling a face when Matt sticks his tongue out at him.

Dad looks at them in the rear-view. 'Can you hold on, Matthew?'

Matt shakes his head firmly.

'Are you sure, honey?'

Matt's sure, so Dad pulls over. There're on a sheltered section of the road, quiet at this time.

'Go on, but don't be long.'

Luke opens his door at the same time Matt gets out. 'I'm going too.' Their parents don't try to stop him. Mom sighs like she always does when one of them follows the other somewhere but it's useless trying to stop them.

There's a steep bank at the verge, Matt scrambles up it and Luke follows. On the other side there's a gentle slope down to scrubland and in the distance a collection of low buildings. Matt turns his back on Luke and a couple of seconds later he hears the splash of urine on the dusty ground. He groans. This is gross. But he was the one who wanted to come too and if he says anything Matt will tell him so in that smug voice he puts on whenever he wins one over on his brother. So he says nothing, looks pointedly in the opposite direction, at the farm or ranch or whatever it is way over on the other side of the field, and waits for Matt to stop peeing.

He hears his mother scream. He wants to run back up the slope but for a second he's frozen to the spot, feet like boulders, refusing to move. There's the ear-piercing sound of tearing metal and terror sets heavily into his stomach making him want to retch. Suddenly Matt's running by him, almost pushing him over. Luke grabs one leg of his jeans to stop him and he falls, face first, into the dirt. Luke throws himself down next to him, one arm across his back to hold him in place.

'Lu—'

'Shut up!' he whispers as loud as he dares. 'Stay here.' He stresses it in a way he hopes will make Matt stay put and crawls on his front up the bank until he can see their car. Matt does as he's told for once, staying where he is, watching Luke with wide, scared eyes.

'What can you see?' he whispers, but Luke can't tell him because what he's seeing must be a dream. There's a wolf, huge with grey hair, tapered teeth and sharp claws. It's standing on its hind legs in the car, in the space opened up by the ragged tear in the roof where the metal's folded back on itself like paper. Mom isn't screaming anymore because her head is in its claws, held up like a trophy, her body still in the passenger seat. He can't see Dad. There's blood on the windshield, too much to see through.

Luke holds his breath, stares at the wolf. And slowly it turns its head and bright yellow eyes look back at him, mouth open, dripping with red.

Luke scrambles to his feet, pulls Matt up and hisses, 'Run!'

Matt doesn't question that and they run as fast as they can across the scrub, Matt clinging to Luke's hand, dry roots grabbing at their jeans, clumsy feet tripping over rocks. Luke looks behind him just the once but the only thing following them is an unearthly howl. They make it to the sprawl of buildings in minutes and crawl through a space in the old wooden fence. Luke leads the way as they pass silent stables and open outhouses until they reach the front of the main house. With a swift kick to the locked door, the way he's seen people do on television, he gets them inside. The air's still but it isn't stale. It's quiet. There's no one here but it doesn't feel abandoned.

They stand together inside the dark hall, the light fading quickly, panting for breath, neither of them saying anything.

In the end it's Matt who breaks the silence. He doesn't cry like Luke expects him to, he just says, 'They're dead, aren't they?' and Luke nods. 'What did you see?'

Luke replies, 'A werewolf.'

~..~

here and now

Lazy rays of dusty light reach through the ratty curtains, falling across the polished floorboards of the turret room. The decoration is perfectly in keeping with the rest of the house; dark wood and red wallpaper with gold detail. In the centre of the room there's a large, hand-sewn rug, threads of colour matching the walls, faded and dusty, coming unravelled around the edges but still grand, and standing on the rug is a four poster bed of solid oak. Carved into the footboard there's a scene depicting angels and demons locked in battle, while God and the Devil watch over the fight from the headboard. Serpents twist around the thick bedposts, mouths open, hungry for the birds in flight on the inside of the bed's high canopy.

The sheets are silk, the quilt is hand-stitched, a tapestry telling a violent story. There are wolves with red eyes standing on their hind legs, their long claws extended towards hordes of fleeing people, the threat sending them hurtling into other kinds of danger; the awkward, crooked forms of the un-dead and the tall, thin figures of blood sucking vampires. In the centre of the horror, there are six humans armed to the teeth, fighting and helping those trying to run away.

Matt and Luke are asleep in the centre of it all, tucked under the messy sheets and the woven representation of their story.

Luke is dreaming.

In his hand he's holding a silver knife with a sharp, wicked blade pressed up against the vulnerable skin of Matt's throat. The curved edge hugs the line of his jaw with deadly intention. Matt is looking right at him with love shining in his eyes, standing close enough that they're breathing the same air. Luke can feel something sharp at his own throat and doesn't need to look to see the second knife in Matt's hand. He's calm. He trusts his brother unconditionally. They wouldn't hurt one another. He knows this and believes it even as he feels a sharp tug at the skin just below his jaw, sees a blood drop slide over the silver blade to collect in the curve between his index finger and thumb—

Luke's eyes snap open. Matt's still asleep, a foot away from him, lying on his side with his arms folded across his chest, breathing out into Luke's face. He turns onto his back to get away from it but twists his neck to keep looking. There's no sound except for Matt's soft snores and that's unusual because there's always something: old movies, raised voices, breaking glass, gun shots.... Maybe the world ended and everyone died. Maybe they're in Heaven. He wouldn't actually mind that much because Matt's with him and that's all he's ever really cared about, all that's ever mattered. He feels a thousand times better than he has done in a while and that has to be a good thing. They've been living on junk food, coffee and adrenaline for months. Uninterrupted sleep has been as rare as cold beer. He feels less like he's been trampled by something huge with claws, even if his mouth still tastes like the inside of a trash can. It's daytime, judging by the light coming through the curtains, although he's no idea what the actual time is. His body clock feels screwed up, like how he imagines jet lag to feel although he's never been on a plane.

Pushing up to his elbows, he looks around. This isn't their usual run-of-the-mill dingy motel on a dusty road between Craptown and Shitsville. This place looks and feels more like a five-star hotel, albeit one in desperate need of modernisation. It's nicer for sure than what they're used to even if the curtains look like they've seen better days, days before they were food for moths and whatever else has been chewing holes in the thin fabric. He and Matt have lived out of motels for half their lives. They can sleep through domestic rows, heavy sex, heavy metal, even gangland shootings. But they'll wake instantly at anything that signals their kind of trouble: screams, wanton destruction, unusual silence. Trouble they need to shoot at or, in very rare cases, get well away from. There's silence now, but it feels safe. And don't those sound like the ramblings of a guy who's finally lost it?

Matt stirs next to him, strands of his hair falling across his face. It's lighter than Luke's and he wears it longer, long enough to touch his shoulders. When they were kids they used to cut each other's hair. They still do, but Luke likes to keep his short because, and this isn't something he'll ever say out loud, he likes Matt cutting it, likes the feel of fingers combing through it, nails scraping across his scalp. Matt tends to hand over the scissors only when his own is long enough to be pulled up into pigtails while he's sleeping. Luke's teased him about it mercilessly for years, particularly over the last couple of months when they've had to jerk each other's chains just to stay sane. It's only when he reaches out to push the errant strands back behind Matt's ear to stop them tickling his face that he realises his hands are filthy; stained brown with dried blood, dirt under his fingernails. He stares at them in the dusty light. He doesn't want to think too hard about the battle on the hill, that last fight which was more a test of wills and in some ways more painful than the physical attacks they're used to. The sickening sensation of being ripped into, of being opened up and laid bare, is still a sour taste at the back of his throat, a curl of nausea in his stomach. But he remembers looking over at the end, looking into Matt's eyes, straight into his soul and letting him see his own. He'll never forget what he saw; a truth he's always known but never acknowledged, a truth that he knows, without a doubt, lies at the centre of him too.

He needs a shower but he's loathe to leave Matt to wake up alone, so he waits. Even if his face resembles something from a teenage slasher flick he knows it's better to wake up to the sight of a battered face than no face at all. Besides, they're used to it. If he could ever have called himself good looking, the scar across his right eye – courtesy of an overzealous blood sucker – ended that fantasy years ago. He has, on occasion, been told that it gives his face a certain character. Matt agrees, insists he looks like 'a crazy, cat-stroking *James Bond* villain' and laughs, then kisses the ugly mark just below Luke's eye line before Luke can punch him. He does things like that, throws out an insult then follows it up with something so achingly sentimental Luke can't retaliate. It's a defence mechanism from their childhood, one he's never grown out of.

He closes his eyes again, the ends of Matt's stupid hair twisted loosely around his bloodied fingers, listening for any warning signs, any sounds of impending trouble. There's nothing for a long time and he starts to doze off but something jerks him back to consciousness and instinctively he slides his hand under the pillow where it would usually meet the cold metal of a fully loaded Colt 1911 A1, .45 calibre semi-automatic. But while it's always been there in the past, solid and reassuring, now there's nothing.

'Where are we?'

Matt's voice, rough with its morning gravel, startles him and his head snaps round. Brown eyes look at him expectantly; Matt's fully awake and tensed, reacting to the tension in Luke's body. This is how they've survived, by reading one another, following each other's lead without questions, using their ability to communicate without a word. Just a glance between them can telegraph a warning or a command. Luke relaxes a little and Matt responds in kind.

'Morning sleeping beauty.' He shrugs as casually as he can manage. 'I don't know where we are. But nothing's tried to get in so I don't think we're in any immediate danger.'

Matt stretches his arms above the sheets and leans up on one elbow. 'Last thing I remember is standing at the top of the hill with that guy.'

'Are you hurt?'

Luke watches as his brother mentally checks his torso and extremities for pain or numbness. Eventually he shakes his head. 'No. But I was hurt. I'm sure I was.'

'I thought I broke at least two ribs but they feel fine.'

'We could be dead.'

'So this is Heaven?' Luke looks around. 'Not what I'd imagined.'

Matt laughs and flops onto his back, reaching out to press fingertips against Luke's hip, keeping the physical contact. 'Do you think we won?'

'I have no idea. But I gotta pee.'

'Thanks for sharing.'

Waking up in a strange place isn't anything new to them. They're long over letting it worry them. Establishing where they are usually comes in as a lower priority to other important points, such as 'is anyone threatening to kill us?' or 'have we killed anyone we shouldn't have?' If the answer to preferably both those questions is no, next up is 'are we still fully clothed?' followed by a quick calculation of the amount of alcohol, and the type, consumed prior to them passing out. But top of the list of questions to ask upon waking in a strange place is, 'where's the nearest john?'

Luke smirks as he climbs out from under the sheets, noting the silk and glancing down at himself to see what he's wearing. Torn and filthy black T-shirt, jeans stained with blood. Some of it's probably his. Most of it hopefully belongs to the hordes of things they were fighting. He casts a glance over to where he threw back the sheets. He can see Matt's white, bloodstained T-shirt.

'Might wanna double-check for wounds,' he suggests as he makes for the door that's ajar, assuming it's the en-suite. He's right, and he pulls the cord to turn on the light, but he doesn't really see the detail of the room until he's midstream and the pressure is off his bladder. Only then does he look around and his eyes widen at the dark, gleaming marble surfaces and floor tiles, the walk-in shower tiled in shining gold, the porcelain bowl on the marble cabinet with tall gold faucets, and the bidet that just for a moment makes him think he's pissing in the wrong bowl.

'What the fuck is this place?' He mutters to himself, and gives a quick shake before he zips and flushes. He runs the cold water into the sink for a second before splashing it over his face, washing his arms and hands before cupping them and taking a drink. He thinks about sticking his face under the flow, but he isn't sure it'll fit and there was that embarrassing incident in Sugarloaf when he got his nose stuck in the end of the cold faucet and Matt had to use liquid soap to free him, once he'd picked himself up off the floor and managed to take a breath before he laughed his fucking face off. Dumbass. Still Luke grins at the memory, scoops several handfuls of water into his mouth then goes back into the room, climbs on to the bed and puts his wet, cold hands on Matt's face.

Matt screeches like a girl, grabs Luke's wrists and pulls his hands away, wrestling him onto his back and using his long legs to clamber over him, trying to force Luke's hands down onto his own skin where the play fight is causing his T-shirt to ride up his stomach. Luke's suddenly very aware that Matt is definitely not a girl, sitting heavy across his thighs, looking at him steadily, neither of them backing down as quickly as they have done in the past.

All Luke says is, 'Matt,' and he's off him, rolling his eyes and clambering off the bed, heading for the bathroom. Just as Luke didn't, he doesn't close the door, but he wolf-whistles at the opulence.

'What is this place?' Matt calls back. Like Luke knows. 'Hey, why are there two toilets?'

The genuine confusion in Matt's voice puts an evil smile on Luke's face. 'For number ones and number twos, bro! Why'd you think?'

There's a pause, then, 'Huh. Which is which?' Luke can't help the laughter that bubbles up. 'Bastard!'

'You could try the one with the flush.'

Another pause. 'Oh. Yeah. So what's the other one?'

Sitting up, Luke glances across at the open door and hears Matt start to pee. This easy intimacy between them is something that's just happened over the years but sometimes, as far as Luke's concerned, it can be a little too easy, a little too tempting to take advantage. He turns his head and stares at the window.

'It's called a bidet,' he explains, voice raised. 'It's to wash your ass.' There's silence, except for the sound of Matt urinating and Luke knows he's thinking about it, working out the logistics in his head. 'Please don't ask me.'

Matt doesn't, thankfully.

Getting off the bed, Luke pads over to the window and pushes aside the curtains. When he first woke and looked over he thought they were moth-eaten shreds of material hanging on determinedly to the iron pole. But they're not; they're just made of thin, light-coloured material. Not a single hole. He does have to rub some of the grime from the glass to look out but that's okay, he's got worse stuff under his fingernails. He can't see much. It appears that they're in a room at the top of an old house. There's a gravel yard below, enclosed by the winter skeletons of trees. There's a hedge some way off, then a road which looks like it has seen better days, the asphalt cracked, pot holes gaping. Not a road he'd like to drive the Mustang down, if the Mustang made it. He doesn't want to think about that either. It's just a car but it's been good to them by not breaking down at critical moments over the years. He isn't sure what's on the other side of the road. The uniform brightness looks hot and cold at the same time, like a beautiful northern winter's morning.

He hears the toilet flush and Matt's footfall muffled by the rug as he crosses the room and stops close behind him. Big hands drop to his shoulders, skate down his back and settle at his waist. 'This can't be Heaven.'

Luke's hyperaware of the touch, Matt's fingertips hot on his skin below the seam of his T-shirt.

'Why not?'

'Dirty windows for one. Plus nothing's growing out there, it's all dead.'

'Kinda looks like Kansas.'

Matt's chin settles on his shoulder and it's too irresistible not to tilt his head, stubble against stubble, to get closer. 'I guess the question is how did we get here and what are we doing here?'

'That's two questions. And I have absolutely no idea. But it's not the weirdest thing that's ever happened to us and so far it's okay.'

'Unless there are things waiting to eat us on the other side of that door.'

'Oh, you're cheery.' He feels Matt take a deep breath. 'I think we won, though. That last fight... that was something special.' The memory makes him feel sick but he adds, 'We kicked ass.'

'We kicked the biggest ass there is.' Matt moves around him, perches on the low sill and looks out across at the bright horizon.

'What do you remember?' Luke asks him, tracing the wooden window frame with one hand, putting his other onto Matt's shoulder.

'About the battle?' Matt leans into Luke's touch. 'I remember wiping out the first wave of un-dead and thinking maybe we were the only ones still left alive. I remember hacking through that pack of Hellhounds, one of the bastard things getting its teeth into my wrist before I smashed it's skull against a tree trunk.' His voice is calm, almost devoid of emotion as he lifts his wrist for Luke to see that there's no injury, not even a bite mark. Luke understands his detachment. If he relaxes, even just a little bit, cracks might finally begin to appear in the walls they've both constructed over the years. 'I remember reaching the top of that hill with you next to me, and coming face to face with the guy in the suit.' Luke remembers him too; the guy in black with a red tie and a smile that looked too big for his mouth. 'Then... all the terrible things we've done, flashing through my head, being forced to watch it all back like the worst movie ever made; Catherine Chambers in Cambridge, that family in Oregon, those kids – Alan and Joanne – in Maine. Terry Banks, Adam in New Orleans, Lawrence, Bodie, Arrowhead... all of it coming back, wave after wave, until you took my hand.'

Then everything changed.

Matt looks up at him.

Luke saw the movie too, a replay of his whole life, even stuff he didn't know; the inhuman thing that appeared in the middle of the road the night his parents died, the tracker who came from nowhere to kill it and keep him safe until the cops arrived, the unpleasant way that guy died only two months later.

But when he took Matt's hand something happened. The horrors of their lives stopped instantly to be replaced by a different montage.

Matt continues quietly. 'Every victory, every time we made it out alive. Every private joke and shared smile....'

Luke felt it too, like the best acid trip ever, his heart singing, the giddy feeling of happiness spreading through him, expanding his lungs, settling his stomach, seeping into his muscles until he felt invincible, that with Matt at his side he could triumph in every battle, win every fight.

'I felt like we could rule the world,' Matt tells him, shaking his head. 'No fear, no pain.'

And then, from nowhere, a blinding light like the blast from a nuclear explosion, rushing outwards, cutting through the man in the suit, and the trees, rushing out to the horizon until there was only light. After that, nothing.

But Luke remembers something before that moment. He remembers looking around and seeing the devastation. The scorched earth, the shards sticking out from the bellies of felled trees, the body parts of the faithful to the wrong side all around them and their little band of desperadoes still standing amongst the carnage; Joe and Gabe, Emilie. Rick.

'Wonder where the others are.' It speaks volumes that it's the first time either of them have mentioned the four. They've only had company for the last two months. Joe joining them first, Gabe two weeks later. They picked Emilie up four weeks or so ago, somewhere north of Reno – he can't remember where – and Rick was last, south of Sacramento. After a while all the towns, even the states start to merge into one. They've crossed the country more times than Luke can count, but recently all the action's been centred around the South West: Nevada and California particularly. Time's started to blur too and sometimes the only way they've known what day it is has been the clocks on their cell phones or glancing up at CNN in bars. Of course, neither has been possible lately, what with there being no television, mobile coverage or Internet.

Then again, there have been a couple of years when the only way they've known it's Thanksgiving or Christmas is by the change in weather, the crap that fills the shops and the lights and decorations that spring up almost overnight in every town from coast to coast, crisscrossing the streets, building to building, adorning everything from dental surgeries to funeral parlours. Every year, Luke insists that they celebrate Christmas. So they hang stolen baubles on half-dead firs, secretly buy and wrap ridiculous gifts in gaudy paper; a new razor and a silver lighter one year, chocolate body paint and strawberry flavoured lube the next. They suck back eggnogs and watch *James Bond* movies on cheap motel televisions. On one day of every year they pretend they live normal lives. But they're glad they don't.

For as long as it's counted, it's just been the two of them, so Gabe, Joe, Rick and Emilie joining them over the last eight weeks hasn't meant all that much, not really. They didn't need the company and when it became clear that Joe was with them for the long haul they picked up a second car so he didn't have to ride with them, something that wasn't too difficult by then. Vehicles were being abandoned all over the place and they're adept at stealing cars. Joe wasn't too happy about the arrangement, that was obvious, but they're used to it just being the two of them and that's the way they like it. They know they're completely wrapped up in one another and they're aware it's unhealthy but it's kept them alive. Luke just isn't sure it hasn't become an obsession on both sides.

They're both hoping that the other four are okay, and Luke thinks they were still standing at the end even if he can't remember seeing Rick, but Matt is Luke's entire world and has been forever, a lifetime. He's going to be upset if anything has happened to any of their posse, but he will kill himself if he ever loses Matt. It's the one thing he knows for certain in a life that's been nothing but shocks, side swipes and underhanded blows by Fate herself.

Luke feels Matt's warm fingers wrap around his wrist. He tries to pull his hand back but Matt doesn't let go. He slides their palms together and presses his fingers through Luke's.

'I know what I felt at the end. I know what I saw when you looked at me.'

'Yeah.'

Luke knows it too, he can't deny it now and he won't. But they've avoided talking about it since Matt hit puberty. They've been a constant source of strength and comfort for one another. They've patched each other up countless times. They've been medic and nurse, the Easter bunny and Santa Claus. They've been everything to each other except for this. This has been the great big elephant in the room for the last few years.

Matt's childhood ended at the same time as Luke's and he had to grow up too quickly, equal to his older brother from the beginning. From the start they fought side by side, together killing the werewolf that killed Mom and Dad, and so many more monsters since. Matt never cried, never whinged, never complained. He never asked to live a normal life, to stop the madness, to let someone find them a new family, a real home, even to go to school. Luke managed to connect up illegal cable so they could pick up whatever the Discovery Channel had to teach. He tried to give him space, didn't follow him to bars when he started going out, didn't give him a hard time when he came back to the Airstream in the early hours even though he wanted to, because Matt gave him the same freedoms.

Eventually functional touches started to linger too long and meaning started to creep into the careful searches for hidden wounds, broken bones and internal injuries. They both stopped trying to hide it when they jerked off in the dark, awareness of one another slowly growing. It should have been impossible to deny something so obvious when they were together twenty-four-seven, but they succeeded, both of them denying the attraction neither of them wanted. Life was already difficult, unpredictable and fucked up enough, the idea of adding something so morally questionable and fraught with danger wasn't one either was willing to contemplate.

But maybe the state of their lives is the whole point. What's another layer of insanity on top of a stratum of madness?

Sex doesn't seem like it would change anything either way. They're as caught up in one another as it's possible to be. There's no real reason to assume the fight is over, it's just a feeling. Sure, last night – if it was last night – felt like a finale but it could just as easily have been the mother of all battles between two stronger-than-usual sides. Whatever it was, wherever they are now, they're still together, whether they're alive or dead. Why shouldn't they celebrate? Why shouldn't they finally have something for themselves?

Matt rubs his thumb over the small bones in Luke's hand. 'If I'm right, if this isn't Heaven, where do you think it is?'

'Purgatory? Limbo? Nevada?'

Matt huffs in amusement. 'You really think we're dead?'

'We're definitely not in California anymore.'

78

'I thought the end would be louder.' That makes Luke laugh. Matt looks up at him and murmurs, 'Love you,' and Luke repeats it back to him. No big deal, they've said it before, a few times over the last fifteen years, when they've pulled things back from the hairy edge. They know it, it doesn't have to be said but now and again it's good to hear. They live for one another, they would die for one another. They've come close on a couple of occasions. Sometimes Matt needs to say it and Luke needs to hear it because the only thing they have in the whole world is each other.

One particular night, after a humiliating and almost fatal fight with an acheri in the body of a little girl left them broken, bloodied and bruised, they curled up together on one bed in a cheap motel and spent the night clinging to each other, unsure whether or not they could go on. Alone, Luke might have put a gun in his mouth but leaving Matt was unthinkable. When they go, they'll go together.

This though, Matt's fingers stroking his hand, this is different. This isn't comfort and they both know it. This is something that runs much, much deeper. This is them, finally, as open to one another as they're ever going to be.

Matt stands up, keeping hold of Luke's hand as he steps around him, pulling him away from the window, his other hand settling at his waist. They're close and they've been this close a thousand times before but it feels like all the arguments against have turned to dust, all the rationale is suddenly, irrevocably pointless. There's strength and heat in Matt's fingers, determination in his eyes. They're both strong willed but Matt's tired of dancing around this thing and Luke doesn't have the will to fight it any longer either. Their love is unconditional, the only boundary set by a moral code that doesn't belong to them.

The way Matt's looking at him.... There's always been love and affection in his eyes, but now there's something else, something he's seen hints of before but never this bright, like it's burning up from inside his soul. Lust: pure, simple and breathtakingly beautiful.

'You gotta be sure. We both know there's no going back from this.'

Matt doesn't answer, he's always been brave. He just smiles and nods. Then he pulls on Luke's hand.

Not about to play the chick in this, Luke pushes Matt backwards towards the bed, stumbling as he trips over one of his brother's oversized feet. The backs of Matt's knees connect with the mattress and he falls on to his back, pulling Luke down with him.

Luke turns the dial and waits for the water to come through before stepping into the shower. He's used to waiting until the water's hot, but it's instantly there. He's sticky in places he hasn't been sticky in for a long time and he can't decide if it's gross or not, because he's been covered in many more disgusting bodily fluids in the past, of all colours, consistencies and origins. He decides it's not so bad, could definitely be worse.

'You use up all the hot water, I'm gonna shoot you,' Matt calls from the bedroom.

Luke grins. Finally kicking the elephant out of the room isn't going to change the habits of a lifetime. He turns the flow to full and washes every inch of himself twice in the slightly too floral soap that he finds in the dish next to a bottle of apple shampoo. This is the best place they've woken up in by far. It's in their nature to be suspicious but it feels safe to both of them even if it's nothing but a time out, a break in hostilities. Since picking a side, and yeah, only monsters side with monsters, it's been one hunt, one fight after another; everything from Shelob-sized arachnids to flesh eating zombies, bakus to vampires, crocottas to wraiths.

It's a slight concern that he hasn't seen a gun since he woke; they don't appear to have any weapons at all. But then there hasn't been an obvious menace in however long they've been sleeping because they would have known about it. They haven't stayed alive this long without being able to sense danger in their sleep. And at least Matt can't carry out his threat, although it's starting to seem like using up all the hot water will be more of a challenge than usual.

He can still feel layers of dirt being washed from his skin. This is the first proper, honest-to-God shower he's had in a decade. It's like standing under a waterfall in comparison to most motel showers which feel like having a dehydrated man pissing over him. Whatever this place is, it's the kind they've only dreamt about, the sort of comfort they never even bothered to fantasise over because they've never had the means to afford it. No one in their right mind would turn it down but it hasn't exactly come free. The price they've paid over the years is incalculable.

'Hey!' He looks up moments before a stark naked Matt is wrestling him out from under the water. 'My turn!'

Luke laughs, gives up the shower before one of them ends up cracking their skull on the tiles, and towels himself off. 'I think we'll be the equivalent of human prunes before we run out of hot water. Something's definitely not right about this place. I mean, how many motels have we ever stayed in with heated towel rails?'

Matt stares out at him from under the flow. 'One thing I am sure of is that we're not in a motel. And it's not just the towel rail. What about the second toilet just to wash your ass?'

Dropping his towel on the tiled floor, Luke turns on the hot water over the sink just in case, but it makes no difference so he shuts it off again and strolls naked into the bedroom. He starts opening drawers until he finds clean clothes. It's lucky, because their clothes are trashed. No way is he putting on his old blood-stained jeans after he's managed to get this clean, and exploring in the nude is something he's reluctant to do even at the best of times.

In the free-standing set of drawers there's underwear and socks, jeans in both their sizes, T-shirts in black and white, and the narrow wardrobe contains button-down shirts of varying colours hanging next to a couple of hoodies and dark jumpers. He pulls on a black T, jeans and a black top. Matt's still in the bathroom but the shower's stopped running, so Luke bounces on to the bed and teases him mercilessly about plucking his eyebrows and blow-drying his hair until a wet towel hits him in the face and Matt comes out.

'What are the odds?' he speculates out loud as he pulls on a pair of light blue jeans and Luke notes the lack of underwear. It's not a case of odds and they both know it. He suspects they didn't just arrive here by accident, something brought them. It's time they left the bedroom and went investigating, however much they might want to curl back up together under the sheets. Matt pulls on a fresh white T-shirt and a dark red button-down.

'You think everyone made it?' Luke asks him, wanting to know if Matt maybe saw the same thing he did. Or rather, didn't.

'I think so. I think they were all alive at the end of it.' Something in Luke's face gives him away. 'You don't?'

'It's just... at the end, I remembering looking up, seeing Rick, and I thought....' But he doesn't finish, instead he shrugs. 'I could have imagined it. By then I wasn't sure what was real and what wasn't.'

'We'll find out,' Matt promises. 'And if he didn't make it, we'll have a drink for him and raise a toast to his memory.'

'And if we didn't make it?'

'Not a bad way to spend eternity.' He hesitates. 'You know if we both weren't....'

Luke stands close, rests his forehead against Matt's and closes his eyes. 'I know. Me too.' He just lets himself feel the relief for a few long seconds before stepping back. 'Come on.'

Luke spots Emilie at the same time as Emilie sees him. A moment later she's up the stairs, meeting him halfway, flinging her arms around his neck. He huffs in surprise and briefly falls back against Matt, steadying himself. He hugs her back for a second or two before disentangling himself. Her shout brings someone up from a battered leather couch and to his relief he sees Rick getting to his feet with a smile on his face. At the base of the stairs he shakes Rick's hand firmly as Emilie gives Matt a slightly less enthusiastic, but nevertheless just as heartfelt, hug.

'Good to see you,' Rick tells him, and Luke nods.

'You too.'

As much of a relief as it is to see them there's a pang of regret not quite overshadowed by the tinge of guilt that immediately follows it. Picking up strays wasn't their best decision ever, the last thing he wants is to be burdened with them if the fight is over, no matter which side won. Letting Joe tag along was his decision, something Matt hasn't let him forget even though they've never had reason to be sorry he made it. But there have been times in the last couple of months when they've wished they were alone the way they're used to being. The two of them against the world is something that's ingrained in them now. They're grateful for the assistance but if they're at the end of the battle or the end of the world, they both want to go back to the way things were, even if it's just for the chance to explore the new way things are.

'I thought you two were up there,' Rick tells them, and it seems he's been more convinced about their survival than they've been about his. 'We didn't think we should disturb you, thought you should be able to get some rest finally.'

Luke glances back at Matt and smiles. 'Yeah, thanks. We got some sleep. Are Joe and Gabe here?'

'They went for a walk,' Emilie explains, leading them into the kitchen.

'Do you know where we are?'

She shakes her head. 'No idea.'

Luke is about to ask her if there's really any place to walk to given that he didn't see anywhere from the window upstairs when his attention's arrested by the lingering aroma of bacon and eggs.

'Oh my God... you've had a fry up, seriously? There's food in this place?'

'There's apparently anything you want,' Rick clarifies and Luke doubts it's true but he's willing to put it to the test.

Emilie pipes up that she'll cook but Matt's already way ahead of her. He's found the frying pan and he's got his head stuck inside the fridge. 'Sausage and eggs?' he calls back, and Luke thinks he's going to start salivating.

'Yes. God, yes.' He hears his own tone and grins.

Matt glances up at him, over his shoulder. 'I was actually offering food, bro.'

'Laugh riot.' But embarrassingly he might be blushing. 'Anything I can eat would be great. And I am talking about food.'

There's no way Rick and Emilie aren't going to pick up on the change in the banter between them. Before today they've stayed well away from that untapped potential in their relationship. Not anymore.

'I want coffee,' Matt announces predictably as he pulls the sausages, eggs and milk out of the fridge and dumps them on the counter, heading for a door Luke's hoping is a pantry and doesn't contain anything that isn't food.

'I'm shocked,' he grouches in response. Luke's had fifteen years of faking loyalty cards from Starbucks, Caribou and Tim Horton's. They learnt of Gabe's addiction only hours after picking him up, when he practically begged them to stop at a Starbucks just a hundred miles from the carnage they'd left in Boulder City. Matt actually paid for the coffee for once. Gabe loves his lattes and frappes, for Matt it's just the caffeine, no frothy milk watering it down or some too-sweet flavoured syrup making it taste like something it isn't. Straight up, the stronger the better.

'There's only instant,' Rick apologies, and Luke's about to say something sympathetic when Matt points to the far corner of the kitchen.

'Except for that.' They all look, and what do you know? There's a De'Longhi Espresso machine sitting resplendent on the work surface under two wall-mounted cupboards, all plumbed in, green light indicating its readiness for use. 'Just need the beans and a grinder.'

'That wasn't there before,' Rick states with conviction but Matt isn't listening. He's too busy digging a bag of roasted coffee beans out from one of the cupboards on the wall and fetching what Luke knows, from years of lectures he's only half-listened to in the front of the Mustang, is a burr grinder from behind the door by his knees. Going by the looks on Rick and Emilie's faces these are all things they didn't know were there, and that's a surprise with Gabe in the house. He, like Matt, can smell coffee a mile away. Luke pulls a stool out from under the table and the other two also take up residence there while Matt grinds beans and cooks breakfast.

He's not bad in a kitchen. He picks things up quickly, did so even when he was a little kid. He was at home in the diner, but then he worked a temporary job in a burger van for five weeks one winter when he was sixteen and they needed the cash. He knows his way around an industrial griddle. He looks happy in this kitchen, especially once he has a strong black Americano in his hands. He puts one in Luke's hands too, and smiles happily. Luke wants to tell him he loves him but instead he just lifts the mug to his lips and savours the taste. It's strong enough to make his throat burn.

'Jeez, bro!' He gets a slap on the shoulder and Matt goes back to his frying pan. 'So what have we missed?'

Before anyone can fill them in, they hear the front door opening and the unmistakable sounds of Gabe and Joe returning from their exploratory walk. They see Matt first through the kitchen door and Joe's over in a couple of strides to hug him tight. He lets him for a second or two before pulling back. Luke's next, a little awkwardly because he doesn't get up, and happily Gabe just settles for handshakes.

'Damn good to see you boys,' Joe tells them as Gabe pulls a couple more stools out from under the table. It amuses Luke the way he calls them boys, mostly because Matt hates it. Neither of them have been 'boys' for a long, long time but Luke can see the funny side whereas Matt doesn't exactly have a sense of humour about this stuff.

'Good to see you too,' Luke tells them and means it on the surface. Glad you're alive, glad you made it. When are you leaving?

Predictably for a man who can find a Starbucks without a map, Gabe's smelling the air and his eyes come to rest on Luke's mug.

'Is that real coffee?'

'Yes. And it's mine.'

'But there's only inst—' He catches sight of the espresso machine before Luke has to point it out. 'Where did that come from?'

Luke grins. 'Don't blame us if you're all blind.'

'I'm not blind. I need some of that. Right now. More than I need air.' Gabe's never been one to worry about where his caffeine comes from as long as nothing gross is floating in it, but Joe looks dumbfounded.

'I swear that wasn't there before we left.'

'Well, it's clearly there now.' Matt's already making him a latte between buttering bread and making sure the sausages don't burn. He would make someone a great husband, even a great dad, if Luke could ever conceive of letting someone else have him. If Matt could ever consider being with someone else.

Luke wraps his hands possessively around his mug just in case Gabe gets any bright ideas. It's taking Matt way too long to make Gabe a mug of his own and by 'too long' he means anything over a minute, two tops.

'Any idea as to where we are or how we got here?'

'No.' Joe shakes his head. 'One minute we were in that park. There was a blinding light, like an explosion, from the top of the hill you two went up and the next thing we know we're standing in the yard out there. That was last night. There was a storm and this place and nothing much else.'

'Just the four of you?'

'Yeah. We had no idea if you two made it, although Rick was sure you were up in the turret room, he thought he could hear Matt snoring.' Matt gives Rick a stony look which he pointedly ignores. 'We did get an interesting visitor this morning.'

'Who?'

'This... guy, I suppose, turned up out of nowhere. I say 'guy'.... About seven foot tall with mad eyes and a coat the same height as he was, more or less. Said he's the landlord, that he's responsible for the house. We asked him where here is, but he didn't tell us, just said we were here for a rest. In Haiku.'

'Haiku? The little Japanese poems?'

Rick looks up. 'Is that what that was?'

Joe ignores him. 'He did say we saved the world.'

Luke shares a smile with Matt as he stands up. 'Guess we did win.' Reaching for him, he pulls his brother into a hug. This is what they've been fighting for all their lives. Matt squeezes him tight. 'We did good,' Luke murmurs in his little brother's ear before releasing him.

'Yeah, we did.'

They don't say anything else, there doesn't seem to be anything more to say, and Matt goes back to making breakfast as if nothing's changed. Maybe it hasn't, not really.

He hands Gabe a mug and there's a moment when Luke's sure Gabe's going to plant a sloppy wet kiss on Matt's cheek. They haven't had real coffee since they left so-called civilisation to hole up in the diner for a week, reduced to Mountain Blend granules and long-life milk.

Gabe settles for, 'You're an angel,' and Matt laughs.

'I promise you, I'm not.'

'So the landlord?' Luke addresses Joe. 'Not entirely human?'

'Definitely not. More like a... a robot. A badly designed one.'

He isn't sure what he can say to that. Without actually meeting him, it's tough to know what to make of what Joe's telling him. 'Emilie said you've been exploring. Find anything?'

Joe spreads his hands and glances at Gabe. 'Nothing.' Gabe confirms it.

'Nothing?'

'Nothing. We walked for half an hour in one direction, turned around, came back and walked for half an hour in the other. There's nothing. Just the road and the horizon. Have you looked out?' Luke nods. 'On the other side of the road, it's not sand, it's stone. Smooth, hard and the colour of sand but not sand. Real peculiar. But what's even more peculiar is that despite us walking for what felt like thirty minutes out, it took us more like five to walk back. I don't think we were ever more than five minutes away from the house. Walking in the other direction, we kept looking back and the house was never as far behind us as it should have been.'

'Okay, that is weird.' But weird isn't unusual and they've come up against many things just as bizarre, possibly more so. Possibly. The sound and smell of frying sausages is seriously distracting him from worrying about their less immediate problems.

'Anything else we've missed?'

Rick lifts his head with a smile that looks slightly forced. 'Apart from us being better off food and drink-wise than we've been since this whole thing started?' Luke doesn't bother to remind him that it all started long, long before they got involved. 'There's a mad old woman in a rocking chair in the lounge, and we think there might be creatures in the walls.'

'An old woman, and creatures in the walls?'

Joe confirms, 'Possibly. Well, not the old lady, she's definitely there although she hasn't come out of the lounge. She claims she's happy knitting and would welcome a cup of green tea whenever we're making one. She's also apparently partial to a sherry in the evening.'

'Sencha Tea?'

Joe nods and Luke meets Matt's glance across the kitchen. 'Sounds like Grandma.' Matt gives him the hint of a smile. 'And the creatures in the walls? They attacked you?'

'No. But I'm sure when we heard them they were talking.'

He looks up at Joe. 'Talking?'

'Communicating.'

'But you haven't actually seen one?'

'No. We've just heard the scratching and these sounds... like teeth chattering.'

'Sounds like Grandpa,' Matt murmurs with a smirk, and Luke grins.

'There is something I would like to know,' Emilie starts and Luke recognises that tone. She's great in a fight and he does like her but now and again her crush on him gets annoying. 'And that is what you two have been up to.' She's looking straight at him, expression bordering on crude, and he knows there's no point in denying anything but it's definitely not her business.

'Nothing that concerns any of you,' Matt assures them in a tone that translates directly to 'end of conversation'. He's never been bothered by her attachment to Luke, he's always been confident that one day they'd end up doing something about what's been simmering between them for years. Luke hopes they're all paying attention because he doesn't want to have this conversation more than once. They are, apparently. Joe's sizing them up from where he's sitting and at the other end of the table Gabe's smiling, drinking his coffee like a guy who knows where the next one's coming from and isn't about to do anything to endanger that.

Rick though, Rick just has to open his mouth. 'I thought you'd been up to *nothing that concerns us* all along.'

Luke honestly doesn't care what they think but they have to be a broadminded group after what they've been through.

'We weren't,' he clarifies. 'Now we are and it still doesn't concern you.'

'Okay.' Rick's nodding. 'Fine. Great. Glad we sorted that out.'

Gabe leans over, mug clutched in his hands. 'What he's trying to say is that we're all very happy for you.'

Matt's obviously ignoring them as he puts breakfast in front of Luke: three sausages, eggs over easy and two doorstop slices of fresh white bread.

'Thank you.' It's heartfelt as Luke picks up the sausages with his fingers and dumps them on a slice of bread, covering them with ketchup and making a sandwich fit for a king. The ketchup leaks from the sides over his fingers and he licks it off before taking a bite of his breakfast. Matt pulls a stool out and brings it around, elbowing Luke until he shifts over and gives him space for himself and his own plate. Then they tuck in and for a few long minutes there's nothing but the sound of hungry men eating.

When he stops for breath, Luke inquires, 'Who wants to tell us about the old lady?'

'Probably best you see for yourselves,' Joe suggests. 'When you've finished, obviously.'

Luke nods. It's important to get priorities right at times like this. All too often they don't know when their next meal is coming or if they'll still be alive to eat it. So when they have food, good food, everything else can usually wait.

~..~

Rick watches them eat, abruptly distracted by the ketchup dripping from bread to plate. It's putting him in mind of blood drops falling from white skin into silver dishes, ruby lips and a forked tongue licking at bleeding wounds in glee. He gets up from the table and goes out into the hall.

'You okay, Rick?' Joe calls out and he chokes back,

'Yeah, I'm fine.'

There's something about the smell of cooked meat that's turning his stomach and he's not sure why. They lived in the diner for a week and by the end of it they all stank of cheap beef and fried onions and he didn't mind at all. He rubs his chest to alleviate the stinging sensation that feels like heartburn and opens the front door to step outside into air that tastes just beyond its 'use by' date. Nothing's changed out here, the yard's still a mess and he feels a sudden urge to find a rake and clear up a bit.

Staring out at the bright horizon he tries again to remember exactly what happened at the end of the last fight because the details keep scattering like the remnants of a dream. As he stands on the top step and closes his eyes it starts to come back to him, slowly at first, then all in a rush so it takes his breath away.

They knew where to go, when to go, somehow. Matt was constantly going on about signs and they were following a kind of map he'd been constructing since long before Rick joined them, a map that eventually led to Five Points. They stopped at the diner because there was nowhere else; the last town they drove through had been looted and pillaged until all that was left were streets filled with shattered glass. The small shops had been gutted, homes ransacked. There was a cafe in the main street but the stench was too bad to even approach it. They never found out what happened to the 254 residents catalogued on the 'Welcome to Three Rocks' billboard. They were just gone. There was no sign of anyone anywhere and they didn't want to stay in a ghost town so they moved on and came across the diner. There was electricity from a still-functioning generator and the cold store was well stocked. It was relatively comfortable and with a couple of modifications they made it easy to defend. Not that they needed to and that was the final sign, Matt said, that they were at the centre of the storm. He knew where they needed to be and when. He didn't make it clear up front whether he was talking about all of them or just himself and Luke, but for a week they all lay low. They rested, caught up on some much needed sleep, even if it was squashed into booths with various limbs hanging off the bright red PVC seats. They didn't talk much but it didn't matter. It was nice.

At the end of the week, Matt told them time was up and that if they wanted to follow it had to be voluntarily, of their own free will. It was important for some reason he didn't explain. Of course they all went. Matt and Luke were their saviours, they owed it to them and what choice did they really have? They didn't know what would come next. So they walked in silence to the battleground, a park, a mile or so up the road from their temporary shelter, where families once walked their dogs and children played. Their little band armed to the teeth and led by two young men they'd known for a matter of weeks.

There, they fought.

At first it wasn't unlike the kind of fights they'd been involved in before. The first wave came at them from the perimeter; the un-dead, the possessed, the disease-ravaged. They systematically hacked them down, a long hour of carnage that left them bloody and battered but still victorious. As they knew from previous fights, the things most people became when they were bitten or infected weren't intelligent or fast or particularly strong. They were easily to kill in ways that meant they stayed dead.

Rick remembers Joe tipping his head back and yelling up at the sky, 'Is that all you've got?' He remembers thinking at the time that Joe was shouting in the wrong direction, and of course the answer was another wave of Hell's spawn, hounds amongst them. They chopped and slashed their way through, their significant stash of bullets all but used up, sheer determination boosting and bolstering them. They put to use everything Matt and Luke had taught them, staying close, working together as a team. He remembers hearing Emilie shouting Luke's name when the second wave was down to its last few un-dead, some with limbs missing, swaying and staggering, and he looked up to see Matt and Luke break away, heading for a low hill at the north end of the park.

Then something happened to him. He can't remember what but he knows it hurt because he can recall the flash of pain, sharp and sudden but dulling quickly as everything seemed to go red before it went black, cold following heat a moment before his body flared hot. After that there's nothing until the flash-bang of the storm and finding himself standing in the yard with the others. Between the two events there's a void that he doesn't want to dig into too deeply.

He hears voices behind him and turns, stepping back into the house as the rest of them come out of the kitchen.

'Okay, Rick?' Joe asks again and Rick nods, forcing a smile. He may well be, he just isn't sure, but the creatures in the walls and the old lady in the previously locked room are enough to take his mind off the other things for now.

'We heard the scratching again.'

He can hear it too. It's getting louder and it seems to be coming from under the stairs. Matt and Luke crouch down in front of the bottom step, Emilie and Joe leaning in while Gabe's again goes for a poker.

'What if it's critters?' he hears Luke whisper and watches Matt pull a face.

'Urgh. But, no. Critters were about a foot tall. These sound shorter.'

Rick's about to ask but Joe beats him to it. 'How can something sound short?'

'The sounds are coming from close to the floor.'

'Maybe they're trying to burrow out.'

Which is just great, if Luke's right, because if whatever those things are do get out he doubts the sight of a man brandishing a poker is going to look like the friendliest of greetings. He hears a cracking sound, breaking wood and the others are scooting back, Gabe stepping forward with the poker raised.

'What the fuck...?'

Not critters then, judging by their reactions. He peers around Joe and sees that they're staring at a hole in the stair, about five inches across, wooden splinters at its edges and something peering out from inside. As he watches, a short orange arm reaches out of the hole followed by a stubby orange leg and with difficulty something clambers out. It's nothing more than a square body, about the size of Rick's palm, with short arms and legs and a face with black circular eyes, an oblong mouth and triangular white teeth, the tip of a pink tongue poking between them. It looks like it's made of wool. And it's looking up at them.

'Ahhhhh!'

One minute it's alive, or some definition of 'alive', and the next it's dead. Or some definition of 'dead'.

'Jesus, Gabe!'

'Fucking Hell!'

Gabe's brought the poker down hard on the thing and practically chopped it in half.

'Have you just been waiting to use that?' Emilie sounds more irritated than upset, staring at the orange body that now has a wide trench in the centre of its torso where the poker landed. It's no longer animated, its teeth no longer real but made from felt like the rest of its features, torn strands of wool spilling out from where its insides should be.

'I know what it is,' Gabe tells them as Luke picks it up and turns it over in his hands, saying,

'It's just a toy.'

Rick catches sight of Matt nudging Luke's elbow and pointing back at the hole in the step. He looks to see what Matt's pointing to. There's a second creature peering out at them. This one's purple. Amusingly, Luke hides the 'dead' one quickly behind his back.

'Luke,' Matt's whisper has a worrying urgency. 'Grandma Nancy.'

Gabe is still talking, 'I've seen these things before,' and Rick sees recognition on Luke's face just as Gabe concludes, 'Last night. It's what the old woman was knitting.'

~..~

Luke exchanges glances with Matt. Their individual intuitions tend to be well honed, but if they're both thinking the same thing at the same time, ninety-nine times out of a hundred they're right. The second, purple toy is out of the hole and standing on the wooden floor, possibly looking for the first one that he's keeping out of sight in case they were friends.

'You want to introduce us to the old woman?' Matt's voice is heavy with inevitability.

Gabe looks up at them and there's caution in his expression. 'I don't know. Do I? Do you already know who it is?' But he's up and heading for the lounge door with them in tow, opening it with dramatic flair.

Luke knows just by the shape of the old woman's head exactly who it is, and he knows Matt does too. They walk around to stand in front of her and she looks up, a great big toothy smile on her face, false teeth gleaming white thanks to the power of Polident.

'Luke! Matt! It's so good to see you boys again! It's been so long. How are you?'

It's frustrating but totally believable that these things are still happening to them. Neither of them answer her, they just look carefully at what she's knitting – an orange oval toy with long arms and even longer legs – nod once and smile in unison then return to the hall, pulling the door closed behind them with the others watching, waiting for an explanation. Luke hands the 'dead' toy to Joe.

'It's Grandma Nancy,' he states with a slight curl of his lip. 'She was our Mom's Mom. Really weird woman. Used to sit and knit toys for homeless and orphaned kids all day. Whenever we stayed at her house, Matt and I used to make up these stories about the toys coming to life, living behind the bookcase in the hall, moving around the house in the walls and eating all the spiders.'

Joe nods. 'Okay, so we don't need to kill her, right?' Luke's about to respond with an emphatic 'No!' when Joe's expression changes almost comically, his forehead creases, his eyes narrow and he manages two more words. 'Wait.... What?'

'I know. Highly unlikely as it might be, that's who she is. She died like... twenty years ago.'

'No,' Joe's shaking his head and now Luke's getting confused.

'Yes. She did, we can promise you. Mom made us wear black suits to her funeral. And there was this really creepy vicar who kept checking out Matt's ass...'

'No, I mean... what are you saying? Your Mom? Your Mom or Matt's Mom?'

Luke looks at him and there's a bad feeling creeping into his gut like he the times he's had milk that's gone off.

'Our Mom.' Joe looks as if he's been slapped and that bad feeling morphs into the first stirrings of anger. 'You know we're brothers! We fucking told you! When we first met, we told you our parents were killed by a werewolf when we were kids.'

'I thought... I mean, I assumed you were talking about both sets of parents, I assumed they knew each other and they were in the same car. I didn't know you were brothers! You're... I mean... you're....'

'Having sex?' Luke's suddenly furious; everything they've done for these people, everything they've been through and this is what Joe decides to have a problem with?

He feels Matt's hand tighten around his arm, 'Luke—' But he's on a roll and he doesn't want Matt, the voice of reason and calm, to butt in quite yet.

'Why do you care, anyway? What gives you the right to judge us? You can't imagine the life we've had. We lost our parents, brought ourselves up. Two kids on our own with nothing and no one but each other. Matt's the only person I've ever loved. We're both consenting adults and it isn't anyone's business but our own.'

'Luke!'

He takes a deep breath and lets it out. He's not finished but Matt isn't going to let him go on. So he rolls his eyes and backs down, letting Matt explain.

'Luke's parents were killed in a car crash when he was six months old.' He reveals it quietly with reverence. They've never talked about it, there's nothing to say. But after Mom and Dad told Luke on his tenth birthday about what happened to his real Mom and Dad, and promised that they would always love him as their own, Matt had wrapped his skinny arms around his big brother and told him that he would always love him too. 'My parents adopted him before I was born. We're not related by blood.'

For whatever reason, though, Joe isn't about to let it go. 'Would it make a difference if you were?'

It seems like an odd question to Luke and he's still trying to process it when Matt gives a calm and level answer.

'I don't know. I don't care.'

Even though it shouldn't be, it is good to hear that, and to hear the honest admission in his voice. Luke's asked himself on occasion whether things would be any different between them if they had both been born to the same parents. He can only hope so.

'It doesn't matter does it? We're not. And it's still none of your damn business.'

Luckily Gabe, the other voice of reason, steps in, still grasping his favourite poker in a not entirely non-threatening way.

'He's right. What they are to one another isn't anything to do with us. But *they* are.' He points with the end of the poker at the purple creature still staring at them from next to the hole in the stair. 'You said you used to make up stories where your Grandma's toys came to life and if that's your Grandma in that room then it makes sense that those are her toys coming to life. So—'

'So you're suggesting we're doing this?' Luke turns to face him. It's crazy. 'You don't think if we had three wishes we'd have gone for something less...'

'Less like the crap we've put up with our whole lives?'

He can always trust Matt to finish his sentences when he can't.

'Maybe it's not wishes. Maybe it's just... happening. I mean, that espresso machine wasn't there until you got down here.'

'But you said Nancy was.'

'True. So... it could be all of us.'

'One of you wished our mad Grandma back to life?'

'Clearly not.' Gabe steps away, hunches his shoulders and scratches his back carefully with the poker's small iron hook. He isn't giving them grief about the other thing, he doesn't look like he cares one way or the other, so Luke's happy to give him the benefit of the doubt while half-listening to Matt talking quietly to Joe.

'Try not to think of it in terms of a normal, everyday, run-of-the-mill relationship.' His brother's rationalising. 'Try to think about it more in terms of our lives being so completely twisted around that a little bit of sex on the side really isn't anything we're going to lose sleep over. How's that for you?'

'I don't know, quite honestly.'

'Okay. Fine. But after everything that's happened we deserve to be happy, we deserve something good and whatever you think of us now, legally, morally or whatever, we are happy and we are good. We've been everything to one another since we were kids and this is just hands, dicks and bodily fluids. So get over it.'

Sometimes Luke loves Matt so strongly it takes his breath away. He resists the urge to grab him and rub Joe's face in it by sucking on Matt's neck.

Rick's got the coal tongs from the fireplace and is jabbing them at the purple toy, which is alternating between aborted attempts to run off across the hall and experimentally biting at the tongs as if it's trying to work out whether or not they're edible. As Luke watches, Rick makes a swift and sudden grab for it and catches it, holding it out and away from him as it struggles. It doesn't have a great deal of body strength and its arms and legs aren't very long so it can't get purchase on the metal plates it's clamped between. It makes a fast, chattering sound, panicked, possibly warning others to the danger. But its struggle is futile and eventually it stops trying to escape and just hangs there.

Luke stares at him. 'Now what?'

'Can't we just stop her from making them?'

'Oh sure!' He doesn't want to imagine how that would go. 'You want to piss off an old, un-dead woman with knitting needles, be my guest.'

'We don't know how many she's already made, how many are in the walls.'

'We don't know if they're even a threat to us, Rick.' He snatches the tongs and lowers the toy to the floor. It tips back to look up, growls at them, then runs on its squat little legs across the wooden floor to the bookcase where it crawls through a second hole in the skirting board, one that's been hidden from view.

'See!' Rick points out, actions apparently justified. 'They've made more holes! What if they gang together?'

Luke rolls his eyes. 'If they are from our stories, there were never dangerous. They ate spiders and once we made up this one story where they went after Grandma's cat and tried to ride it like a camel. So quit your worrying.' He hands back the tongs and turns, catches his brother's gaze. 'Walk?'

'Definitely. Where to?'

~..~

BOOK THREE ~ TILL DEATH DO US PART

nineteen years ago

'What do you think our next parents will be like?' Matt asks as Luke makes him peanut butter and jelly sandwiches.

Whoever lives here at the ranch, they haven't been gone long. There's milk in the fridge that hasn't spoilt and the bread's dry but not mouldy. He's worried about Matt. His question sounds cold coming from the mouth of an eleven year old. Mom and Dad haven't been dead a day, they were attacked by something that shouldn't even exist, and he's been waiting for the tears and the histrionics that just haven't come. They slept in a single bed in an upstairs room at the back of the house with a door that locked from the inside and a lean-to under the window in case they needed to make a run for it. But no one came in the night. Matt didn't cry in the dark. He turned his back on Luke until the light was out then he turned over and buried his face in his brother's coat. Luke wrapped his arms around him and they slept like that until the sun rose. There were no tears and no bad dreams to wake them.

He pushes the sandwich under Matt's nose where he's sitting at the huge kitchen table. Matt stares at it then lifts his head and looks at Luke with big eyes. Here come the tears, he thinks. But still Matt doesn't weep.

'They won't split us up will they?'

Relieved, Luke shakes his head. 'I won't let them, I promise.' But even as he speaks he knows there's only one way he can make sure they stay together. If the cops haven't already found the car they will soon. They'll put the deaths of Mom and Dad down to an animal attack. He can bet that he and Matt left clues to their direction as they ran across the scrub and in the day-light those will be found and the authorities will come looking. They'll come here. 'We need to leave, to run away. If they don't find us they can't split us up, can they?'

'No.' Matt takes a bite of his sandwich, looking happier.

'Are you sure you're okay with this?'

He doesn't speak, he just nods.

While Matt's in the bathroom Luke takes a look around. He knows stealing is wrong but he isn't stupid, if they're going to survive they're going to need more than luck. He finds clothes that will fit him and bundles them into an old sports bag he pulls from a closet in the master bedroom. They'll be too big for Matt but it can't be helped. He'll grow into them. Then Matt comes out of the bathroom holding a clear plastic bag full of dog-eared hundred dollar bills bundled up with elastic bands. Maybe luck is all they'll need after all.

They leave very soon after, heading in the opposite direction to the road with no idea where they're going or what they're going to do but with the means now to live for a while without the intervention of adults.

They run at first then walk. They don't stop except to buy chocolate and soda from a lonely store on the corner of two dirt tracks. By the end of the day they're hungry and tired. Just as it starts to get dark they fall into a dusty road. Matt hasn't cried once but he looks like he's wanted to sometimes when Luke's glanced at him. Luke feels a little like crying himself when he catches the toe of one shoe in a rusted can and falls flat on his face into dry sand and dirt. He swears instead, a word Mom would definitely have grounded him for using, but when he lifts his head he's staring at a collection of old rusted trailers that he recognises from when Mom and Dad were looking for a tourer: four abused Airstreams, a couple of Keystones and a Spartan right at the back. There's a splintered sign on a rotting wooden stick, faded red paint still visible: 'Morgan's Trailer Park'. The plots are overgrown and the entire park looks as if it was abandoned years ago, the trailers left to disintegrate. A quick scout over the ground turns up a tyre iron and a pair of rusted bolt cutters. He hands the iron to Matt and tells him to break in to the Keystones and the Spartan to see what kind of a state they're in while he opens up the Airstreams. He warns him to be careful and asks if he's all right. Matt nods although his eyes are too wide and a little bit watery.

'We'll be okay,' Luke promises with more conviction than he feels. As he watches his little brother go off on his own, he's both relieved and terrified that Matt seems to believe him. He waits, keeping an eye on him as he approaches the nearest trailer and hoists up the bolt cutters that look huge in his young hands. Luke turns away, pride surging through him, pushing back some of the raw grief.

He pries open the door of the first Airstream like a can opener. The inside is trashed. Whoever lived here left in a hurry; all the drawers and cupboards are open, there's a sick-inducing stench and the bed sheets are gross, stained dark. Luke would rather sleep outside than sleep in that bed.

The second trailer's full of old electronics. There's a rank smell of acid so sharp he can feel his eyes start to water and his nose close up. When he gets back outside he calls to Matt.

'Found anything?'

Matt calls back from top step of one of the Keystones. 'A dead cat and a possible crime scene.'

Luke can't tell whether he's being serious, but he hears metal snapping under pressure so whatever he's seen hasn't put him off looking. He's suddenly overwhelmed by a sense of relief that his brother's not a cry-baby like some of the kids in his class at school. They might not share the same parents but Luke's glad Matt's his kid brother.

'Be careful, bro,' he shouts back and goes on to the third Airstream, one of the big ones: a Starship or an Overlander if he remembers right. Levering open the door he sniffs the air before going inside. It's slightly stale but nowhere near as bad as the other two. There's no sign that rats have got in, the place looks tidy and clean except for a layer of dust that would give Carol-Anne, Mom's maid, a mild stroke. But otherwise it's not bad, definitely salvageable. The big bed at the far end has no sheets but the mattress looks okay. There are cobwebs in the bathroom and a huge spider right in the middle of the shower stall, but that's not going to put him off. Matt can get rid of it.

Standing in the middle of the kitchenette, he knows they could stay here. He's no idea why he ran instead of waiting for the cops last night, but he knows why they ran today and something inside him is telling him this is the right thing to do. They don't need the authorities to turn them into paperwork and burdens. He won't risk them being split up even though he has no idea how likely that is. They can look after themselves, he's sure of it.

Leaning out of the door he calls across, 'Matt! Come here, I found one.'

There's the sound of footsteps running on hard ground before Matt appears in front of him, excitement on his face when he looks inside. 'Are we going to live here?'

'For now. Is it okay?' Matt nods. 'The cash from the house will buy food. I'll think of something before it runs out, I'll get a job or something. I'll take care of us, I promise.'

Matt looks at him with absolute trust. 'I know you will. Are you sure no one's coming back?'

'Yeah.' He's sure. He doesn't know how or why but it's that same feeling of *right*. 'Stay here. I'll go find us something to eat. There must be a store close by.'

'I'll come with you.'

'Matt—'

'I don't want to be here alone.'

It's his first sign of weakness. He's eleven years old. His parents were killed last night. Luke feels a wave of protectiveness so strong he can't speak for a minute so he nods, pushes Matt out of the trailer and pulls the door to, catching it on the latch. The lock is screwed since he destroyed it.

There's a 7-Eleven a mile down the road. It's got bars over the windows and they have to wade through trash to reach it, but they get microwave Burritos, Doritos, Hershey Bars and giant sodas. They can't live on shit like this but he'll come back tomorrow, once they've checked if there's a generator on the park he can get working. If not they'll find another way to cook. He asks the clerk if anyone lives in the Morgan's Park trailers and the spotty kid laughs.

'All the drug dealers and white trash left town years back.'

Luke wants to disagree but he keeps his mouth shut and just thanks the guy.

Back at the Airstream they find a couple of working flashlights under the bench in the living area and sit up talking until it's later than Mom and Dad let them stay up.

'I wanna find what killed them,' Matt declares when they've finished all the food. 'And kill it.'

'You want to find a werewolf?'

'I know how to kill them. Silver bullets.'

'I don't know if that really works....'

'It must do. If werewolves are real, silver bullets must be too.'

He has a point and Luke doesn't feel like arguing. 'Okay. We'll do that. We'll find out where it lives and kill it. Just as soon as we're sorted here. All right?'

Matt nods.

Eventually, when Matt's fallen asleep with his head on Luke's leg, Luke turns the flashlights off and they stay on the bench all night.

~..~

What a rush!

Luke yelps in excitement, adrenaline coursing through him as he runs through the undergrowth, blade held high, half-listening for his brother's heavy footfalls. When he reaches the edge of the forest he stops, plants his feet in the soil, his hands on his thighs and takes in deep gulping breaths of air. Matt isn't far behind, breaking cover from the thick foliage with a whoop and slapping him on the back.

'That was crazy!'

Luke laughs and looks up, the mirth draining fast. 'Hey, are you hurt?'

Matt looks down at himself, 'No, it's not mine.' He's practically covered head to toe in whatever it was they've just tracked and killed.

Relief washes in, Luke's smile returning. His heart feels like it's trying to break out from his ribcage. They've tracked things down before, evil things that should never have been given life, but this is the first time it's gone to plan, the first time they've worked together in perfect sync, the kill executed without a single mistake. For the first time, Luke believes they can actually do this.

'I really need a shower,' Matt points out and Luke straightens up, looks at him and grins. He's so proud right now. Matt is thirteen years old. Most kids his age are causing havoc in the playground, bullying or being bullied, kicking around a soccer ball and trying to work out what girls are for. Matt has just sliced the throat of something significantly older than he is and more than twice his size. Luke's still not sure he did the right thing by running the night their parents were killed, but at least now he knows it wasn't the worst thing he could have done. His brother's an intelligent kid, chances are he could have been a straight-A student, attended an Ivy League school and become a lawyer or a doctor, even a chef. He's equally sure his own future lay inside a coffee shop or at best a garage. It's all irrelevant now. They can't go back. He doesn't want to. It's selfish but he hopes Matt feels the same. He looks like he does, grinning ear to ear as he stands there covered in something else's insides.

Luke nods. 'Shower. Right.' Together they turn and start walking the five miles back to the trailer park.

~..~

fifteen years ago

'How old are you, boy?'

'Nineteen, sir.' It's a lie that comes smoothly now. Luke looks it, easy. Matt's tall for his age too, he's passing for eighteen, older when they're lucky. The motel's overweight owner doesn't really care, none of them ever do. He takes the cash and hands over a room key.

Over the years they've become serial criminals and damn good trackers. They've made the trailer into a home of sorts with a working generator and illegal cable. They've leant how to live with barely any money and no one to look after them.

The first time they went after the werewolf they ran into two women, Donna Clay and Samantha Weston, who stopped them from making the fatal mistake of thinking they knew what they were doing. They stayed with Matt and Luke for a few weeks at the park, camping out in one of the Keystones that Luke had cleared out in case he or Matt needed some space away from each other. Both women were in their forties and called themselves 'trackers', the first time Matt and Luke heard the term. They said they'd been killing inhuman things for ten years, since something ate their husbands while they were on a men-only fishing trip in Wyoming. 'Everyone has a story,' Donna told them after listening to theirs.

They taught Matt and Luke how to shoot the semi-automatics they found in one of the other trailers, showed them how to do research – which books were of real use and which were fiction – and how to ask questions which might otherwise have people calling the cops. They taught them other stuff too: how to get credit cards without a fixed address, how to hotwire a car, how to patch up a bullet hole or a knife wound. Not once did they mention going to school or finding a foster family. Not once did they treat them as anything but equals.

Four years on, Matt and Luke are moving around a bit. They're still based at Morgan's Park but now they're spending a few days a month on the road, sleeping in shitty motels and eating the healthiest food they can get their hands on. When they're back at the Airstream, Matt cooks; he's developed a flair for it after watching too much of the Cookery Channel. They stole a 1994 Ford Mustang three months before, three states over, from the parking lot of a strip bar. No one's shown the slightest interest in it and Luke thinks the owner probably hasn't reported it as nicked. He has a fake driving licence and he's planning on getting Matt one for his sixteenth birthday.

They've amassed a small arsenal of weapons including the pistol which shot the silver bullet that killed *the* werewolf, the one that murdered their parents. Going on a tip from a guy they ran into at a motel outside Las Vegas, they brought it down one full moon, six months ago. They're expert trackers now, professionals, schooled in the arts of credit card fraud, identity forging and grand theft auto.

Matt, as it turns out, is an ace with a pool cue. He can look so innocent and naive when he wants to that no one ever works out they've been hustled even when they're handing over the cash. They've been eking out a meagre living that way while tracking down and killing things that have no right walking on the surface of the Earth and sending them back to Hell.

They both know that someday soon having a base just won't be practical. These things are everywhere and they need to be on the move not only to do what they've made it their goal to do, but to carry on living the way they are. Staying in one town too long will eventually draw attention to them. It's okay while they're still just kids, no one suspects them of anything serious, but when they're older they're going to need to stay under the radar, as Donna and Sam told them. A couple of months back they picked up word that the two women had been killed tracking a trio of witches in South Dakota. They still consider them their mentors, their graves may be unmarked but Matt and Luke will never forget them.

Luke opens the most recent motel room door and they both stare at the incredible decor that greets them.

'You have got to be shitting me,' Matt moans.

Luke slaps him the top of his arm, hard muscle absorbing the blow. He's tougher than any kid his age should need to be.

'Watch your language!'

'Ow! Jesus, Luke!' A genius hustler and a crack shot he might be, and he's not exactly a typical fifteen year old either, but he still whines on occasion. Not about the important stuff, just when the motels have the wrong kind of shampoo, or they get back to the Airstream to find his garlic's gone off. He has the right to complain now and again, Luke reckons. He's been educated by cable television and they're lucky that Matt's parents were rich and interested in giving their children the best start possible because it meant they already had the capability to pick truth from embellishment. Dropping out of school at thirteen and eleven obviously cut their chances of going to college or getting a job on Wall Street but they can read, they can write, they have solid groundings in mathematics, Latin, history, American geography. They just know more about living in the real world than a lot of school kids.

The motel room's done out in bright pink, with black lace everywhere. 'Explains why it was so fucking cheap,' Matt points out and Luke kicks him in the shin. 'Do we seriously have to stay here?'

'What's the matter, bro'? Not confident in your sexuality?' Luke drops the holdall he's carrying and bounces on the bed nearest the door. He always takes that bed, that way anything that comes in has to get through him before it reaches his brother.

'How am I supposed to be confident in something I know nothing about?'

It's a response that Luke thinks he might be pondering for months to come.

'Would you and the porn channel like to be alone tonight?'

'Really?'

He takes pity on Matt and leaves him alone for a couple of hours, walks to a bar a quarter mile down the road and buys a beer. He gets talking to an older woman who buys him another beer then takes him back to her apartment where he loses his virginity on red sheets and never learns her name.

It's gone midnight when he walks back into the motel parking lot, triumphant and high until he sees Matt come running out of their room wearing nothing but his black boxers, holdall in one hand, shotgun in the other. He spots Luke, yells at him to get in the car and they peel out of there like roadrunner, with a squeal of rubber on asphalt.

'What the fuck...?' Luke demands once they've put enough miles between themselves and the motel for Matt to start breathing normally again.

'I have no idea, some mad bitch came barging into the room and tried to eat me! I blew her brains out all over the bed!' He twists in the seat and looks back one last time, checking they're not being followed. He's actually laughing. 'But fuck, Luke, before she attacked me... I think I might like guys.'

Luke doesn't bother to pick him up on the swearing. Not then, not ever again.

~..~

twelve years ago

The attack is so sudden neither of them actually remembers waking. All they know is that one moment they're sleeping soundly in the Airstream and the next they're struggling with something eight feet tall with lots of hair and very, very sharp teeth. Luke hears Matt's whistled intake of breath, a sign of pain that years ago would have brought forth a scream but not now.

They're not prepared for this. The guns are in the living room on the table instead of stowed under the bed, but they might as well be in the car because they can't reach them. They were cleaning them before they climbed exhausted into bed at just after two. It's only an hour later, still dark, and something is trying its damnedest to sink its teeth into Matt's throat.

The closest thing to a weapon at hand is the beer glass Luke knows is on the floor about a foot away because he's tripped over it twice in two days and still, thankfully, hasn't moved it to the sink. Getting to it is a problem. He has to climb over a pair of gross hairy legs as well as those belonging to the creature. (Funny joke, he'll share it with Matt as soon as he's sliced through the spinal cord of whatever it is that's attacking them.) He manages to snag the tankard between two fingers, drops it on the floor where it shatters helpfully and he snatches up a long piece of glass sharp enough to cut into the palm of his hand. He stabs it down fast and brutal into the back of the thing's neck. It grunts and collapses, Matt shoving it off him immediately, uttering a string of profanities Luke can't blame him for. It lands hard on the floor and Luke checks that it isn't going to get up again before he checks that Matt isn't about to bleed to death from the wound in his throat.

With an off-white patch of gauze covering the cleaned and treated bite, and fervidly hoping that whatever it was they've just buried behind the Spartan doesn't pass on its mutation in the same way as werewolves, they sit side by side on the metal grated steps of the Airstream, squashed together, half-empty beer bottles hanging from blood-stained, dirt-encrusted fingers.

'It's escalating.' Luke hates pointing out the obvious but they need to acknowledge it. He's surprised that Matt doesn't fight him on it, that he just nods and presses cautious touches into the area around his neck, checking for heat. 'Okay?'

'Yeah. Hoping I won't get hairy and start to howl during a full moon.'

Luke doesn't mention the joke he thought up earlier. 'It wasn't a werewolf, bro'.'

'You think it's time to hit the road, permanently?'

He really hates to admit it, but yes, that is what he's thinking. 'At least until whatever this is building up to is over. If it's ever over. Sorry. I really wanted this to be home for longer.'

Matt shakes his head. 'No. You did great. It's been home, been everything we need. But now we need to get out there, figure out what's going on, find others, people like us who might know something.' He drops his head to Luke's shoulder, an old, familiar thing and Luke turns his face into the long hair, dry-kisses his scalp like he's been doing since Matt was eleven.

'We'll come back. One day.' He can hear his own lie and he's immediately sorry.

Matt laughs softly. 'No we won't. But it's okay. As long as it's you and me. We'll be okay.'

~..~

here and now

They have no idea what time it is. The clock in the hall has stopped and there are no other clocks that they've found. There isn't the sun to go by either, the light is uniform outside. The road surface is broken up from underneath, as if there's been a bad earthquake sometime in the recent past. It's not that Matt doesn't believe Joe but he crosses the road with Luke following and crouches down to touch the ground on the other side. It's just like he said, smooth and hard like marble with a pinkish hue the colour of human skin. He looks at the road cutting a path through the nothingness and the house with its yard full of dead trees.

'Tickets to a Bon Jovi gig would have been enough,' he murmurs and his voice sounds strangely flat in the bleak terrain.

Luke closes up to him. 'What?'

'If the Powers That Be wanted to say thank you.'

His brother's eyes bulge at him. It's just a random band he picked, the first one that came to mind, but it is fun to let his brother believe otherwise.

'Bon Jovi? Seriously? Could you be more gay?'

'You tell me.' He gets a punch to his arm in reply.

They walk into the centre of the road, stepping carefully over potholes and torn up fragments of asphalt. It's not hot, it's not cold. It's like standing in a room without air con on a warm day. Everything's still, slightly stagnant, not a hint of a breeze.

'Which way?'

They head left away from the house, walking close together, arms bumping now and again. They've done a lot of walking over the years. They don't exactly have Green Flag cover so when the Mustang's died on them they've had to walk to the nearest garage for parts or a tow-truck and a mechanic. They are lucky that Joe's a skilled mechanic, as well as being good in a fight, and he's filled in the blanks in Luke's knowledge when it comes to the intricacies of the internal combustion engine.

'What I wouldn't give for a cold beer and a game of pool in a good, old fashioned roadhouse,' Luke declares and it sounds good to Matt too. But he knows there's something else on his brother's mind and it's only a matter of time before the explosion comes. 'I can't believe him!' There it is. 'All we've done for him, taking his sorry ass in.'

Usually the best thing to do when Luke gets like this is to let him rant without with any input. He doesn't want another opinion at times like this, he just wants to vent his own frustration and wants everyone else – Matt – to shut the fuck up. But following the best course of action isn't something Matt's ever been very good at.

'What's going through his mind is exactly what's stopped us for the last fifteen years,' he points out. 'He probably made the assumption that we were sleeping together. And if he hadn't before this morning he knows for certain now. He's not going to immediately make the connection that we're brothers as well, is he?'

'That's my point!' But Matt really doesn't think it is. 'Joe's spent two months on the road with us, fighting every sick, demented thing we've come across, hacking the heads off zombies and cutting the hearts out of wendigos with a fucking axe! Which part of that suggests we give a shit about what's normal?'

'We've been out of the world for twenty years. Joe's been out of it for two months. He had a wife. We're about the right ages to be his kids. He doesn't think like us. You should be glad it's just him and not the others too.'

Luke rolls his eyes. 'Gabe's probably tried everything once. Emilie presumably thinks this is 'hot' and Rick... I never know what Rick's thinking. We barely know the guy and I'm actually quite glad about that.'

'You know what? I don't care what they think and neither should you.'

'We cared enough not to do anything about it for fifteen years.'

'That's my point! And it was our choice.' Actually, more Luke's choice but Matt hasn't pushed the issue.

'I still can't believe it. We saved his life. We told him what was happening, kept him as safe as we could. Hundreds, possibly thousands, of people died and he hasn't because of us. And now he's got the nerve to give us grief about actually finding something good in all this?' He's back in full rant mode, hands flying.

It's all Matt can do not to laugh, because that would definitely earn him another slap. 'To be fair, he hasn't. Not really.'

'Didn't you see the way he was looking at us?'

'He's in his fifties, he accepted the idea we're sleeping together even though we weren't, then he finds out we're brothers—'

Luke interrupts. 'Adopted! Different parents. Different blood.'

'But that's never made a difference to us, why should it to him?'

'Hey, if we were related by blood, no way I'd have done what we did this morning!'

'Really? So why did we wait until now?'

That shuts him up, even if it's just to send him into a sulk. 'Why is their first assumption that we're lovers?'

Matt does laugh at that, incredulous. 'People have assumed that for years! We're all tangled up in one another. When was the last time you picked someone up in a bar? You know what we're like. We exclude people. We got a second car for Joe within two days of him joining us because we didn't want anyone else in our space.'

'That's not the point.'

But Matt knows he's getting through to him. 'It's exactly the point. Last time I was with a guy before this morning was two years ago in Rockridge. John. Black hair and blue eyes.'

'I remember him.' Luke matches the fond smile on Matt's face. Rockridge was good to them. 'I remember his sister, Zoe, too. Long hair, huge tits.' He taps Matt's arm. 'Hey, you know it's just you and me now, right? I haven't slept with anyone for a long time because I haven't wanted anyone else. Even Paula was just to remind myself how to do it!'

Matt nudges his shoulder in another 'love you too' moment. Then he frowns. 'Who the fuck was Paula?' But Luke's stopped dead in his tracks, staring straight ahead and when Matt sees what he's staring at, he doesn't care about Paula anymore either. 'Oh my God.'

A huge smile is splitting Luke's face almost in half. A hundred yards in front of them there's a wooden shack at the side of the road with two neon signs in the windows at the front, one flashing 'BAR' in red and the other offering 'POOL' in green.

'Sweet.' Luke sets off towards the place at a determined pace but Matt doesn't follow immediately.

'Is that a mirage?' he calls.

Luke stops. 'A what?'

'A mirage. You know... hallucination.'

'Oh.'

He joins Luke a couple of steps ahead and watches curiously as he rolls something in his hand and down through his fingers before lifting his arm and lobbing a stone hard and fast towards the shack, narrowly missing the neon. There's the sharp sound of breaking glass as a window breaks and Luke grins. 'Definitely not a mirage.'

'Where did you get that stone?'

'I picked it up.'

'No you didn't.'

'Sure?'

'Positive.'

'So where did I get it?'

'That's what I asked you.' Sometimes it occurs to him that a lifetime of conversations like this one should have sent them both insane long ago.

'It was in my hand.'

'Because you needed it to be, to throw it at the window.'

'Your point being...?'

'My point being, that bar is exactly what you wanted, what you wished for. The espresso machine back at the house that Joe swears wasn't there yesterday? That's the same make as they had in that coffee bar in Bangor.'

'The one you made us stop at eight times in one week, despite it being a ten mile round trip just to get there?'

Matt doesn't grace him with an answer. 'What if Gabe's right? What if wherever we are, we get... wishes? What if we're wishing for this stuff and it's appearing?'

Luke closes his eyes, takes two breaths and opens them again. 'Nope, doesn't work.'

'Hey! You've got to be careful with this stuff! What did you wish for?'

'A Ferrari.'

'What? Why? You hate sports cars!'

'Do not.'

'Yes, you do! That poor guy in Boston, the lottery winner haunted by his dead wife? You told him his brand new Aston Martin would break down every twenty miles, bankrupt him for fuel and made him look like a selfish prick with a tiny dick and low self-esteem.'

'I don't want it to drive! I'd sell it on that auction site you bought those crosses from – the ones with the blades in the top – and pocket the proceeds!'

'Why not just wish for the money?' Matt loves his brother, lives for him and would die for him without hesitation. But sometimes, just occasionally, he imagines getting his hands around his throat and squeezing. Just for a minute.

Luke holds out his hands. 'Can we get a drink before I die of thirst?'

'What makes you think you're still alive?'

'Right now, if I can get a cold beer, I don't care if I'm alive or dead.'

'Unbelievable.'

Luke grins and Matt gives in. They're going for a beer in a bar that wasn't there a minute ago and in their world it isn't all that strange.

'Hey, isn't it good to know that we get the good stuff and not just weird relatives from our past?'

It's a point Matt has to concede as they head into to the roadhouse, towards the sounds of laughter, pool and Rascal Flatts on the jukebox.

~..~

Inside it's perfect. It's exactly what Luke wanted and Matt's right, that's curious bordering on highly suspicious. There's a drop in the volume of conversation as they step inside but only for a second then everything's as it was. Luke orders drinks at the bar – two beers, two tequila chasers – and watches Matt watching the two guys at the pool table end their game amicably and walk away. He knows what's coming, sees the silent question in Matt's eyes and he nods and smiles. His brother bounces up the two wooden steps to the raised platform where the table stands, under a window coloured by the neon signs, and racks up the balls. He chooses his cue and chalks the tip while Luke sets the tray of drinks on a low table close by and does the same.

Matt breaks hard.

His brother's skills in this game have helped them survive over the years. In his first shot he drives five balls to the rails, pots two solids and, much to Luke's amusement which he absolutely doesn't keep to himself, the cue ball.

They sink the tequila then Luke takes his shots, potting a stripe with his first, missing everything on his second. He's never been quite as good and they've used that to their advantage in the past, letting punters win against him until Matt steps in with a challenge they can't turn down.

While Matt lines up his next play, Luke looks around. The other customers are all but ignoring them, chatting quietly in small groups, drinking around tall, circular tables beneath the random collection of neon and hammered-out metal signs adorning the walls. The quiet cacophony is made up of conversation, heavy boots and high heeled shoes on the wooden floor, the dull thud of darts hitting the board, and the background music playing on the jukebox. There are a couple of hopefuls trying their luck with the barmaid and Luke tries to remember the last time he did that.

It's all so familiar.

Matt finally takes the shot and misses everything. Luke can't help but laugh. Apparently Matt can't help but flip him the bird and he laughs even harder. They're brothers first and foremost and some things won't ever change.

'You know,' Luke starts. 'This place is very similar to the roadhouse at the Locked Crossroads.'

It's an urban legend, the Locked Crossroads, so-called because the stories claimed people that who travelled to the centre of the cross were never able to leave, that whatever direction they travelled in they would always end up back in the centre. And when eventually they went mad trying to escape, the road would open up and Hell would swallow their souls. Just for a laugh someone built a roadhouse there in the seventies, called it *The Gates of Hell*. It attracted a lot of bikers. The interior and exterior here are more than a little reminiscent of the *Gates*. The stories are bullshit, obviously. He and Matt went, enjoyed a couple of beers and a game or two of pool, uninterrupted mostly, before heading off on their way, driving west. They never saw the place again.

Matt straightens and looks around. 'It's not similar, it's the same place.'

Luke isn't sure he can remember it that well. 'Maybe. I think the layout's wrong.'

He glances out through the glass in the closest window pane. He can see the house some way back in the distance, but there's nothing else just like there wasn't when they walked here. And now he's wondering where all the people have come from, because there are no cars out front and no other residences as far as the eye can see. It gives him an uncomfortable feeling to think that they've just appeared because he wanted a beer and might have to disappear again when he and Matt leave.

Matt leans his ass against the edge of the table, cue still in his hand. 'What if something's taking our memories and using them to create this place?'

'The roadhouse?'

'All of it.'

'Why?'

'As a reward?'

That's a depressing thought. 'This is what you want? A rundown house in the middle of nowhere, four people we barely know and our dead grandma who keeps knitting toys that come to life?'

'You wanted the bar. I wanted coffee.'

'That machine was probably there all along and they just didn't see it. That corner of the kitchen is dark.'

'Gabe the coffee addict failed to spot an espresso machine the size of a mini bar?' Matt turns back to the table and Luke watches him work out his next shot before bending at the waist to line it up, shuffling his feet apart. It gives him ideas he still isn't one hundred percent comfortable with. 'What about this place? Are you saying Gabe and Joe missed this too?'

He shrugs. He will admit it's strange, especially given the other stuff. But there has to be an explanation and he's hopeful it'll be one that makes sense. 'Maybe they didn't walk this far.' Just as Matt pulls back the cue, Luke experimentally slides his hand into the back left pocket of his jeans.

'Hey!' Matt straightens and turns to protest and Luke holds up the neatly folder hundred dollar note he found there.

'What the fuck...?'

'I want another round.'

'So... you're saying you wished that to be there?'

'I'm saying I want another round and I need cash. Also I was trying to put you off.'

Matt indicates the table. 'Can I just...?'

Luke shrugs, leaves him to take the shot and goes to the bar, returning with two more beers, two tequila shots and some girl's phone number which he promptly tears in half the same way he's been tearing phone numbers in half for a number of years. He doesn't want to think about that because as happy as he is to defend them to the others, a reality check brings him to the simple fact that he did spend the morning jerking his brother off. However not related they are he was still there when Matt started school, when he fell off his bike and bled all the way from the driveway to the bathroom without a single tear to get Luke, rather than Mom, to clean the wound. Mom wouldn't have wanted to get blood on her clothes no matter how much she loved her son. Both her sons. There was never any doubt about that. But Matt turned to Luke when he needed something, not to his parents, that's how it was. What they did this morning, it feels like the final extension of what they've been up to now – everything to each other – and the rounding off of this complete co-dependency they've developed over time. He doesn't mind, he's never minded. It isn't right by anyone's definition of 'right', but it sure feels like it was meant to be and it's better than anything he's ever done before.

Matt's hand on his backside startles him back to his beer. 'Thinking about me?'

'What are you doing?'

'Seeing if I can magic a hundred dollars out of your ass the same way you did out of mine.' He comes up empty handed. 'Um. Not fair.'

Luke grins and winks. 'Feel free to keep trying.'

They play a few games, drink a few more beers, get a little drunk. The light starts to fade outside.

'How long do you think we've been here?' There isn't a clock and he's starting to speculate on whether or not time as a working concept even exists here.

Matt glances out through the window. 'A couple of hours?'

'Think we should get back?'

'No.'

They play another game, buy another round. As Matt strides around the table looking for his next shot, he asks, 'What do you think we should want, if we could have anything?'

Luke considers this. There have been rare times over the years when he's wished they didn't know what they know, wished they hadn't found exactly what they went looking for when they started out. There hasn't been a single day when he didn't wish Matt could have had a normal life, endured through high school and cut loose at college, even if that meant their relationship turned out differently. Even if it meant both of them not being the men they are. He knows Matt feels differently, that he wouldn't change anything, possibly not even the werewolf attack and that should be more of a concern than he's ever let it be. Matt was closer to Luke than he ever was to Mom or Dad. They weren't Parents of the Year, but while they were alive they made sure their sons were provided for, kept safe and loved. For whatever reason, Matt has always treasured their relationship over everything else. Not that Luke doesn't, he wouldn't give Matt up for anything in this world or any other. But on occasion, when the situation's been bad, when it's been too damn close with some of the terrible things they've faced and the injuries they've suffered, Luke has seriously considered finding a small quiet town and just stopping, renting a place and living like normal people for a while. Maybe forever.

The problem is he can't unlearn or deny all the things he knows and one of those things is that normality is just a veneer covering the world. People don't see beyond it because they don't want to. No one can know and still go to work in an office every day, sit in front of the television at night. Once they knew, they were cursed with that knowledge and they had no choice but to live the way they lived. Of course, when things really started to kick off, three or four months ago, when more and more people started to see through the cracks, he and Matt were suddenly the lucky ones; self-trained, qualified to survive. They stopped being the lunatics and started becoming the heroes.

So if he only had one wish it definitely wouldn't be for a normal life, whatever one of those is. But to not need to fight, not need to track down and kill Hell's spawn because they're no longer a threat, that would be sweet.

'Luke?'

'Sorry, bro'. What would you wish for?'

'A Hilton.'

It throws Luke because it isn't what he's expecting. 'What?'

'A Hilton hotel. Indoor pool, gym, bar, restaurant.' It's weird. 'Hey, it's a valid request.'

'Not saying it isn't.' And now he knows what he would wish for. 'I want a house.'

Matt gawps at him. 'I think that's what we got.'

'I mean, for you and me. A nice house, with a lawn and a back yard. Even a white picket fence.'

'No picket fence.'

'No?'

'No.'

'Okay.' He shrugs. 'Can I have a garage full of power tools?'

'Why?'

'Why not?'

'How about a garage full of weaponry?'

'I want not to need weapons. That's kind of the point.' But it sounds almost perfect for a pipedream. 'That's what I want,' he finishes, leans over the table and takes his shot. He pots a ball, just not one of his.

He feels Matt's hand brush his waist. 'Think we could settle down?'

No, he doesn't, not really, even if he has considered it now and again, imagined what it would be like to live in a small town with bad winters, to get a job as a mechanic, spend his evenings drinking in a bar and his nights figuring out just how far he and Matt can go before it got weird. If it ever got weird. But even if the war is over he seriously doubts everything that ever escaped from Hell has been sent or pulled back down. Their particular skills will still be needed. There's never any rest for those who know what they're doing.

Matt's hand comes to rest on his shoulder. 'Me neither.' He takes his final shot and pots the 8-ball. 'Yes!' It's a small celebration but it takes their minds off their hypothetical and fundamentally pointless conversation. Except that it's set Luke's mind running about the potential possibilities of this place they've found themselves in. He isn't sure what he would do with those possibilities if they really existed.

Eventually they start back to the house. As he suspects it's a five minute walk, just like Joe and Gabe said.

'I wish we had the car,' Matt muses as they get close. It's dark now but there are no stars out. There's moonlight in the same way there was sunlight, blanket cover across the sky but no actual moon. There's just enough light to see by so that they don't trip over their own feet while they're walking but they have no clue as to where it's coming from.

'We have the car. It's parked behind the house.' It's a long-shot, and Luke doesn't elaborate despite Matt's pointed, curious look. When they arrive they walk around back to find the Mustang parked on a concrete standing close to the fence. It's useless, of course, because Luke's almost certain there isn't anywhere to go. He suspects they would end up five minutes away from the house even if they drove for hours. But that's hardly the point. 'Did I do that?'

Matt's poking the driver's side door like he isn't sure it's real. 'I don't know. It might have been here all along.'

It's comforting in one way, seeing it, but in another it's freaky, the start of an astonishing power rush. 'And the roadhouse?'

Matt looks at him over the car. 'You didn't get the Ferrari.'

That's a good point. 'I didn't... need the Ferrari. I don't need it. But we needed the roadhouse to relax, chill out, play a couple of games and grab some beers. I needed that stone you said I didn't pick up to throw at the place to prove it was real. You needed real coffee. The car's been an escape route, rescue, shelter, it's been with us years.'

Matt rests his elbows on the Mustang's roof, arms stretched, palms up. 'Okay. So what else do we need?'

Luke leans over the car and reaches out one hand, pushing his fingers into the sleeve of Matt's shirt to stroke the inside of his wrist. He can feel his brother's heartbeat.

'Proof. Something big. Something that can't just be coincidence or chance.' The roadhouse is from their memories, like the espresso machine, Grandma Nancy and her knitted toys. 'The wine cellar.'

Matt curls his fingers around Luke's wrist, warm and just a little bit arousing. 'What wine cellar?'

'The one in the basement at Uncle Harold's place. Remember?'

As kids, Matt and Luke adored their Uncle Harold. He was one of those family members who wasn't related by blood but still referred to as 'Uncle' not only by them but by their parents too. A sworn bachelor at the age of sixty, Harold lived in a tiny coastal town north of Los Angeles, in a Craftsman house that he maintained with an enthusiasm bordering on obsession. He was retired although no one ever said from what. Luke liked to pretend he was once an assassin, a gun for hire. Matt thought he'd worked for the Government in some secret guise. He surfed, he collected fine wines, and he played in a small band every Friday night down at Lenny's Laundromat where he did his washing. When Matt and Luke's parents wanted a week away without them, they were deposited with Uncle Harold and spent days at the beach and nights playing hide and seek in the extensive wine cellar under the house.

'You think just because you say that, there's now a wine cellar in the basement of this house?'

Luke holds up his free hand. 'Just testing a theory. Let's find out.'

~..~

After trying several different foods, they've dropped a steak on the floor next to the hole in the stairs and several little wool creatures are nibbling at it happily. The animated toys haven't tried to attack anyone and Joe's made Gabe promise he won't maim any more of them unless they turn nasty. Rick asked Grandma Nancy as nicely as he knew how to stop knitting but she just replied, 'Oh, I can't do that, dear. They're for the orphaned children, you see.'

No one wants to tell her that they're coming to life as ravenous things with teeth. No one wants to find out what her reaction would be. Heart attack or a smile, they're both bad. No one wants to deal with the possibility that she knows what she's creating.

Joe's looking up recipes for peppercorn sauces in a book he's found in one of the cupboards. He hasn't mentioned Luke and Matt's revelations again – either of them – and Rick's glad no one's brought the subject up. He's got enough on his mind without worrying if two guys who've been fighting horror their whole lives should or shouldn't be making the floorboards creak together no matter what else they are to each other. As far as he's concerned, it's just sex. At least someone's getting some.

He cleans out the grate, sweeps up the ash from the fire the night before and sets another, placing the kindling and the logs and feeding the flames until they catch. He's doing it for Emilie. Ever since they arrived here he's felt hot, too hot. The others don't feel it. Emilie stayed close to the fire last night until she went to bed, Gabe kept his coat on until the place warmed up and Joe's spent most of the time slaving over a hot stove. Presumably it's making him happy. Rick's too hot within thirty seconds of the fire taking hold and gets up, away from the heat. But as he backs away a single impression comes unbidden into his mind like a flash from a camera; there one moment, gone the next. It leaves behind an imprint, a blurred idea, vanishing too quickly for him to get anything more than a suggestion of heat and pain. It's like a dream on the edge of waking and he doesn't know what it means.

~..~

'Where have you two been?' Joe grouches when Matt and Luke arrive back at the house. He's obviously still pissed off at them but Luke doesn't rise to it. They haven't answered to anyone since they were kids and they're as far from starting now as they've ever been.

'To the bar down the road.'

'There isn't a bar down the road. There isn't anything down the road.' But the seed of hope in his voice isn't difficult to miss.

'Something else too. There's a wine cellar in the basement.'

'What?' He looks up from whatever's simmering in the small saucepan on the hob. 'There isn't even a basement.'

They lead the way into the hall and Matt unlatches the new door under the stairs, letting it swing open for dramatic effect. Gabe's first up off the couch, eyes going wide.

'You're serious? How did we miss this?'

'We didn't.' Joe's voice is flat but he's still through the low doorway and heading down the narrow spiral iron stairs before Matt and Luke who follow behind to the stone floored cellar. It has the same dimensions as the ground floor of the house. The air is cool, the perfect temperature possibly. Rows of handmade floor-to-ceiling wooden racks, stacked between weight bearing pillars, hold bottles resting on their sides. The question of whether or not there's a bar down the road is shelved for the time being as Gabe and Joe move between the racks in reverent quiet, speaking in whispers.

Emilie reaches the base of the stairs, stepping around Luke.

'What the fuck...?'

Joe peers out from the end of an aisle with a frown. 'Ssh!'

She rolls her eyes, making Luke smile. 'It's a wine cellar, guys, not a church.'

'This is a place of worship,' Gabe corrects her from somewhere in the far left aisle.

'It wasn't here before,' Emilie shoots back. Luke nods at her. She's right.

Like the roadhouse, this place has been recreated directly from their memories. And whatever's doing it is getting better, because while the roadhouse is incredibly similar to *The Gates of Hell*, this is a perfect replica. An aficionado of wine, Uncle Harold delighted in taking them down to the cellar to show them his new acquisitions and to explain to them why some wines were worth thousands of dollars while others were worthless. They never listened, but they did love playing in the cool dark and they took in some of the names of the grapes, vineyards even the odd wine maker just by way of natural osmosis. So while Luke's certain there will be some duds in the collection, he's equally sure there will be a few bottles to get excited about.

'Oh my God!' Apparently there are. 'A 1959 Mouton Rothschild!' Gabe is holding the bottle like it's a new born, staring at it like a proud new father. 'Beat that.'

Joe's rejoinder comes from the end of another rack of reds, '1971 Mazis Chambertin, Armand Rousseau.'

'Damn!' Gabe moves to the whites. 'Okay – Jesus! Montrachet DRC, 2007.' He's obviously in awe. 'This stuff goes for three grand a bottle.'

Sins forgiven, Luke thinks. 'How about you two find a few bottles to go with the steak?' he calls out, following Matt back upstairs. As real as it is, as flawless a copy, it's still something from their past, their previous life, and it doesn't feel quite right.

'Sure thing.' It sounds like Joe's far away, lost amongst the racks. Whatever, it actually feels good to do something for their little band of loyal followers. The fire is burning away when they get back up into the hall and they drop down into the couch in unison.

'So... we have God-like powers here, huh?' Matt muses.

'Well, the car, a bar and a wine cellar. What have you done?'

He grins. 'Made my dick two inches longer.'

It takes Luke a second, and a glance down at his brother's crotch, to get that Matt's kidding.

'Laugh riot!'

They sit in silence for a time, listening to the squeaks of excitement from the wine cellar and to the fire as it cracks and pops, watching the embers and the smoke rising to the chimney stack. Matt's hand settles on Luke's leg, nails picking at the denim until Luke laces their fingers to stop him.

'We can't stay here forever,' he asserts gently. 'We have to try to work out what's going on.'

Matt nods his head against the back of the couch. His eyes close and for a moment Luke actually thinks he's going to cry. It stuns him because he can't ever remember seeing him cry and he realises now how wrong that is, how weird, since he's known him his whole life. Then suddenly he does remember one time, but the memory is too fleeting, gone too quickly for him to place it.

Matt doesn't cry. Instead he lifts his head, opens his eyes and locks his gaze with Luke's. 'We don't get to play God indefinitely you mean.' A tiny smile quirks his lips and Luke mirrors the expression. 'I get the feeling we're waiting for something, or something's waiting for us.'

'Something like what?'

His smile widens and he moves his head side to side. 'I have no idea. So we may as well enjoy the wine.' The conversation's on hold, that's obvious by the lightening of his tone and the way his eyes slide away. He follows Matt's gaze and sees Joe standing in the doorway, two bottles grasped tightly in his hands.

'A 2000 Montrose. Four, in fact. Perfect. Steak'll be ready in ten.'

Behind him, Gabe's carrying another two bottles. He follows Joe into the kitchen while Emilie heads upstairs and Rick seats himself on the arm of the couch.

'That door wasn't there before you two got back.'

There's no point in denying it. Luke explains, 'This place is shaping itself around us, around our memories and experiences, but we can influence it. The Mustang's parked around back. Now we have a wine cellar in the basement and a roadhouse within walking distance.'

'Why? How?'

Luke doesn't have an answer to either question and while Matt might have got close to something when they were alone, he isn't putting it forward now and Luke has to respect that. They can talk about it later. 'We don't know,' he replies.

'You found a bar when Gabe and Joe didn't find anything.'

Matt sits forward and before Luke can comment, he reassures Rick that it's nothing new. 'Believe me, Luke can find a bar anywhere.'

He can't argue with that. He found *The Gates of Hell* using a barely legible newspaper clipping printed in 1978 and sheer determination.

'Guys!' Gabe calls them into the kitchen and they rise but Rick stays put.

'Not eating?'

He shakes his head. 'Not hungry.'

Luke's starving after those hours spent drinking and playing so he shrugs, whatever, and they leave Rick in the hall.

Emilie joins them and they perch on stools around the kitchen table. Someone's found some pillar candles of various shapes and sizes and they're arranged in a huddle in the centre of the table, flames licking at the semi-darkness, shadows dancing on the walls. Conversation, predictably, revolves around Matt and Luke's ability to change things, their influence on their surroundings. The question of water into wine comes up and Luke dismisses it, refusing to even try, pointing out that the wine cellar is stocked to the rafters and preventing the idea that they're gods in this place from ever taking hold. It's bad enough he's thinking that way, it needs to remain in the privacy of his own head. They speculate on whether the bar down the road will still be there if just the four of them went out to it without Luke or Matt, and Joe decides they should find out once they've eaten.

The steak's good. The wine is incredible. They start to bounce theories between them but each one they come up with falls down when they add Grandma Nancy and her knitting in to the equation. She and the wool creatures just don't fit; a dead relative and old childhood stories made up by two kids trying to scare each other in the dark. Matt and Luke were never that close to Nancy and they both agree that she wouldn't be their first choice of family member to resurrect from the grave. The only thing that makes any sense at all is the idea that it was a first attempt, trial and error by whatever power is interpreting their thoughts. Emilie suggests one of them could have been dreaming about her at the time and they just don't remember. Luke supposes that could be right although he doesn't think it's likely. He hasn't thought about her in twenty years and Matt hasn't mentioned her since the funeral.

But the suggestion reminds Luke of the dream he did have and does remember; he and Matt standing with knives at each other's throats. It makes him feel slightly nauseous and he's glad he's finished eating the rare and bloody rib-eye. He pushes his plate away and takes a gulp of wine, shifting closer to Matt and putting his hand on his leg under the table. He needs to tell him about the dream, will do as soon as they're alone, and no sooner has he made the decision than a wave of calm passes over him so intense that he feels his whole body lighten, the load lifting, as if he's let go of a secret he didn't realise he was keeping.

There are no other working theories so they stick with the one they have and talk around it, trying to extrapolate to a sensible conclusion. But there isn't an obvious one. Why they're here, where they are, how they got here, exactly how much power and control Matt and Luke really do have; it's all speculation, at least for the time being.

True to Joe's word, he, Gabe, Rick and Emilie head out once plates have been scraped clean and glasses and bottles are empty, leaving Matt and Luke to wash the dishes by candlelight. Luke's got his hands in the warm, soapy water, Matt's drying.

A few quiet minutes pass after the front door closes behind them. Then Luke starts, 'There's something I need to tell you.'

'Okay....' Matt's tone is immediately wary.

'Last night, or this morning, I had this dream. You and me, we were in that room upstairs, I think, and I was holding this knife. It had an ornate handle and a wicked sharp blade and I was holding it—'

'—to my throat.' Matt interrupts him, finishing his sentence.

'Yeah, how do you...?'

'I had the same dream. I had a knife to your throat and you had one to mine. In your dream, was I...?' Luke nods. 'And we were looking at each other like we'd agreed to do it, agreed to cut one another?'

'I think I was going to kill you.'

Matt nods. 'Me too.'

Luke drops the plate he's holding back into the water and wipes his hands on his jeans, turning. 'Whatever happens, I'm not about to do anything like that.' He says it like it's obvious, like he shouldn't even need to utter the words.

Matt dumps the cloth onto the worktop and takes a step forward, closing the gap between them, reaching for Luke's damp hands. 'It was just a dream, this place messing with our heads. After everything we've been through, if we were going to commit suicide, we'd have done it years ago. We're stronger than that. Nothing is going to make me hurt you and nothing is going to make you hurt me. We're fine. Whatever it is, we'll deal with it the same way we've dealt with everything else.' He sounds so sure, so confident, that Luke nods his agreement without questioning it. This is the way it's always been; one bolstering the other when they get low. 'Okay?'

'Okay.'

Matt lets go of his hands and they go back to doing the dishes like they promised Joe they would, finishing them off in silence.

They take the candles through to the hall, throw a couple more big logs on the fire and settle again on the couch. Matt casts a glance at the door to the lounge, which they keep closed, and asks Luke if he thinks they should make Grandma Nancy a cup of tea or fetch her a sherry. Luke looks at him like he might have finally gone mad. 'Bro', she's not real. She's just the same as those wool creatures.'

'Joe's been feeding them raw steak!'

'He shouldn't encourage them. Who knows how many she's knitted by now.'

'He's a softy at heart.'

Luke snorts. 'Not too soft that he hasn't wasted a shit load of evil bad things over the last two months. Or given us grief about us.'

'Feeding those things could be his way of atoning.'

'I think it's a little too late for atonement.'

Matt turns to him. 'You think we're going to Hell?'

He's dumbstruck for a minute. 'Yes, I think we're going to Hell!'

'But we saved the world!'

'We've killed things, lots of things. We've killed people.'

'People who deserved it. People who weren't human. Bad people who were threatening others and on many occasions actually eating them. That doesn't make us bad, it makes us good. We struck out, we did something. That has to count in our favour.'

'I'm not sure there's going to be a trial with a jury of our peers who decide if we're sent up or down. I think God plays judge, jury and executioner.'

Matt's expression changes from bewilderment to curiosity. 'You believe in God?'

Luke gapes at him. 'You don't? Given everything we've seen and everything we know? If there's a Satan, how can there not be a God to balance things out?'

'We don't know for sure there's a Satan, and besides he's just a fallen angel. He's not God's opposite, exactly.'

'He's the leader of the opposition. If there's the Devil there has to be God, like Republicans and Democrats. If there's evil there has to be good.'

'What about what that priest told us, the one in White Rock?'

The Church of the Fallen Saints, Luke remembers it well, and the priest they protected from whatever that thing with claws was that they found living in the rafters of the old building. He'd gone on and on about good and evil being the same thing seen from different perspectives. Depending on what corner you were standing in, he claimed, good could be evil and evil could be good. There was no war except the war that man made. Luke had been pretty damn sure at the time that no man had made the bird-like creature they killed in a hail of bullets and a shower of feathers.

'He was nuts,' Luke said firmly. 'It's simple. Murder's bad, saving people is good.'

'But what if the act of murder saves someone else?'

'You can't know for sure that it will, not every time. Okay, if a guy's got his hands around a kid's throat, then shooting him in the head is absolutely the right thing to do. But stabbing a guy outside a bar because he tries to steal your cigarettes? That's wrong. Even if you don't, and he goes on to hold up a convenience store at gunpoint. That priest was delusional.'

'He wasn't making up the part about the monster in the rafters.'

'No, but he also said he'd seen Death, remember, standing at the altar with his scythe, black robe and everything.'

'Maybe he did.' Matt shrugs. 'If you think the Devil and God exist, why shouldn't Death be real too?'

'Gabe said he sold a car to Satan.'

'He's convinced himself it was Satan.'

'Just go with me here. Say he's right, and the guy we saw – the same guy in the black suit on the hill at the end – was the Devil. Satan in a meat suit mixing things up by killing a family with a two hundred thousand dollar sports car is a far cry from the Bergman image of Death in a cloak playing chess for some guy's soul.'

'Why is it?'

Luke ignores him. 'What would Death be doing in a church anyway?'

'I imagine he was there for the priest.'

'You really think he saw Death?'

'Why is that harder to believe than Satan mowing down kids in L.A.?'

He has a point, and it's a circular argument with no end, so Luke lets it go. He drops his head back and closes his eyes, pulling his brother's hand into his lap, parting his knees slightly and pressing Matt's knuckles into his groin. Matt chuckles softly, a surprisingly hot sound, and his fingers trace the denim seam between his legs. It makes Luke wish for an empty movie theatre showing a crappy film, just to be sat on the back row paying zero attention to the screen. He wonders if there's room in the house for a cinema.

By the time the others get back, they're spooned together on the couch, Matt's arm hooked over Luke's hip, his hand down the front of Luke's open jeans. They're awake but they don't bother moving. The four are drunk as skunks. They make some crude comments about how the 'boys' have spent their night before climbing the stairs as quietly as a herd of elephants. Luke overhears an argument about which bedroom is Emilie's, hears toilets flush, doors slam, and after a good twenty minutes, the house falls silent again.

'Guess they found the roadhouse,' Matt comments sleepily.

'Guess they did.'

'Want to go up to bed?'

'No.' He's comfortable and warm. But in the morning they'll want to have more sex and that might be problematic if the others wake first. 'Okay, fine.'

They take the candles with them, the shadows following their progress as they climb to the landing and up the spiral stairs. It's so spooky but it's also starting to feel like a home, something they haven't had since leaving the Airsteam twelve years ago. It's a dangerous thing because it means the longer they stay the less they'll want to leave.

Once inside the room, with the candles on the dresser and the door locked, Matt steps into Luke's space and runs his fingers through his hair, nails scraping across his scalp the way he loves it. For a second Luke closes his eyes and savours the sensation then he reaches for the buttons on Matt's shirt, popping them one by one.

'You know the last time you undressed me I was....'

Luke drops his hands, interrupting him. 'You carry on with that thought and my hard-on's going to wilt faster than spinach.'

Matt nods. 'Right. Sorry.' His expression changes and Luke recognises it, waits for it... 'You know that spinach wilts?'

'Shut up.'

'I thought I was the only one watching the Cookery Channel.'

Luke ignores the tease. Matt's fingers are at the hem of his hoodie, pulling it up slowly, the heels of his hands skimming Luke's ribs as he lifts it and Luke has to raise his arms to get it off over his head, T-shirt going with it.

They don't kiss, they haven't kissed, but Luke sort of wants to just before Matt wrestles him backwards onto the bed. Then he wants to do other things more.

~..~

Rick stays awake as long as he can. He couldn't eat dinner, couldn't face steak. Even if he'd asked for his done as black as charcoal the thought of watching the others eat bloody rare meat still makes him feel queasy. Despite not having had any food, he isn't hungry. He's being plagued by the distinct feeling that something is close by, following him, watching and waiting. He keeps thinking he feels fingers brushing against him, indistinct touches to his back and his shoulders. But when he turns around there's nothing there. This isn't like those wool things downstairs, this is dark and threatening.

He sits on the edge of the bed and stares out of the window at the strange light outside, moonlight without the moon. He wishes he had the guts to leave, to just walk until he drops dead from thirst or smacks his head on the edge of the world. He's had a bad feeling about this place from the start, but that's turned into a heavy sensation of dread, sitting in his stomach like bad Chinese food. It's obvious the others aren't experiencing any of this. Emilie, Joe and Gabe seem happy, taking the opportunity for a break. He keeps asking himself what's singled him out, why he's alone in this.

It was fun at the bar, slamming down tequila shots like they were back in reality, pouring fizzy lager down their throats like he used to before the world started to end. Sitting at a table, taking it in turns to pick someone out of the thin crowd and take bets on which out of the four of them they would prefer to sleep with. In the end they decided everyone would sleep with Gabe and he was more or less happy to sleep with anyone. Joe's still bothered about Matt and Luke, but Gabe doesn't care and, despite her interest in Luke, Emilie thinks it's the hottest thing since Michael Lucas' *Dangerous Liaisons*, whatever the hell that is. Rick couldn't give a shit. It's none of his business. They're not hurting anyone, they're grown men. He doesn't understand Joe's argument that they shouldn't because they're brothers.

'The same blood doesn't run in their veins,' Gabe argued when they were in the bar.

Joe spouted more garbage than Rick's ever heard in his life, although he thinks it might have been the whisky talking. As far as Rick's concerned, even if they were actual brothers, given the amount of blood they've undoubtedly lost over the years he doubts there would be any left that they actually shared. It's not as if they're about to start making mutant babies and frankly he has more important things to worry about. He enjoyed the night out but now he's back here in the house with the scratching in the walls and the vague noises he thinks only he can hear; far away screams and wet sounds of torture.

His only hope lies in the fact that he's all too aware of the sheer volume of alcohol he's imbibed tonight. That should mean he's alive. But whatever it is that he can feel behind him, it's getting closer, gathering strength. Soon enough he's going to know what it is and he doesn't want to, not ever. If they still had their weapons he might have chosen to put a bullet in own brain, but the only choices he has if he wants to kill himself are the steak knives or the gas oven, and neither option is appealing. His liver may well save him the bother and fail all by itself, but it's a long shot. Besides, suicide would probably just land him in more trouble and the question remains, is it better to keep living with the horror he can already feel or to die and face the unknown?

Eventually the drink gets the better of him. He flops back on the mattress, focusing on the ceiling as best he can until he can't keep his eyes open any longer and unwillingly falls asleep.

He dreams the same dream, only tonight it's more vivid, more real. He can feel the heat in the orange flames. The screams so close he can taste the blood. Wet sounds fill his ears. And it's all happening to him. It's his body on fire. His screams. His pain. It's his skin being peeled from his muscle, his muscle ripped from bone, things tearing into his organs while something keeps him alive. It's never over, it'll never end. A demon with red skin and black eyes leans over him, opens its mouth and breathes out with a acrid breath so strong what remains of his stomach clutches and heaves. The demon reaches out a long hand, inhuman fingers with too many knuckles and talon nails that it uses to scrape the skin from his face in fleshy curls. He howls in agony and the thing before him laughs. 'You're mine,' it shrieks in a voice like metal cutting through metal. 'Soon you'll come to stay and I'll never let you go.'

Rick wakes, pulse racing, heart hammering, low wail dying in his throat. It feels like he was gone for hours but it's still dark, it's still night. His throat hurts, raw from screaming except he hasn't been screaming, couldn't have been otherwise the others would have come running. He sits up, looks down at himself and he's surprised to see he's still wearing his clothes, still wearing his skin. But he knows now what's waiting for him in the shadows, in the dark places behind the facade.

Hell is waiting.

He remembers it now, the end of the battle, the crazy man with no eyes running towards him, wailing like a banshee. He didn't see the blade until it was deep in his stomach, pushed in to the hilt, blood covering the gnarled old hand that held it. His blood. No one else saw it. They were busy with their own opponents. He has no idea if they made it but he didn't. He remembers falling to his knees when his legs gave out, smacking his head against the thick tree trunk behind him, the cold wet grass soaking through his pants as the screeching maniac pulled the blade back out. The pain flared, white hot and incredible, searing through the numbing shock, embracing him until it was all he knew. Then it was gone and for one blissful moment he looked up at the stars, watching them wink out until everything went black. He remembers his own death.

And his subconscious mind remembers Hell in macabre detail, even though he can't have been down there very long before he was pulled back. The void in his memory is starting to fill with the vivid, horrific knowledge of the horrors of Hell. It won't be long before he loses his mind. Maybe that won't be a bad thing, because despite being here he doubts he's been saved.

He doesn't deserve to be in Hell! He isn't a killer or a rapist, he's just a petty criminal who tried to make amends after he came face to face with the really bad guy.

He needs to stay here. He can't leave. Because he only has one place to go and it's the last place anyone would ever want to be. Matt and Luke seem to be in control here, to a point. They have to be able to make it so he can remain even if the others leave. He could even ask them to create more. He doesn't need much: a roof over his head, hot running water, ideally the bar down the road for when he wants company. Not a lot, not really. He's not even hungry most of the time. Given the alternative, he'll settle for a lot, lot less as long as he's allowed to stay, as long as Hell can't get him. These are mad thoughts but that was just that one dream, if it was a dream, a moment that lasted a fraction of a lifetime and was still more than he can bear. An eternity of it is unthinkable. The idea alone sends his mind skidding towards insanity.

Back when he was a child in Sunday School, the vicar made it perfectly clear that Hell is for very bad people; murderers and paedophiles. Evil men and women. All he's ever done is con people out of money. He knows it was wrong, he's always known it. But there should be a difference between wrong and evil. He's spent the last two weeks helping people, saving people! He never imagined that he'd already crossed the line between forgivable and damned.

The first time he conned poor, unfortunate Ben Massy out of his lunch money the kid told him he was bound for Hell, he just never believed it. Until now it has been a fictional place, a nightmare used to frighten and brainwash children. Now it's a reality worse than anything any Hollywood writer has ever dreamt up.

He isn't going to sleep tonight. He doesn't think he'll ever sleep again. There's no reason to if he's dead. He gets up, pulls his shirt sleeves down and wriggles his fingers. When he looks at them a flash of memory overlays them with the image of bloody stumps and if he looks down he knows he'll see his crushed, severed fingers on the floor in front of him. Clamping one hand up over his mouth, he makes a dash across the landing to the bathroom and throws up in the toilet bowl. Sliding to his knees he grips the white porcelain and his stomach heaves again, acid vomit spewing from his mouth: burning tequila and flat lager.

It's a while before the retching stops. He's shaking as he flushes and eases up to his feet, turning on the faucet and using his cupped hands to bring cold water to his mouth. A few deep breaths and a couple of cups later he's feeling a little steadier. He dries his hands then heads downstairs, getting a glass of water from the kitchen before hesitating in the hall.

Grandma Nancy is just another creation from Matt and Luke's memories, but she might know something about what brought her back. She didn't give much away before but she also didn't seem confused or surprised to be here. The others haven't stirred despite the noise he must have made upstairs so unless he wants to wake them, the old lady is his only option right now.

He opens the door quietly in case she's asleep but she isn't. He doesn't think she sleeps, doesn't think she has to. He pours her a sherry without a word, from the bottle they've left on the small empty bureau next to the door, and takes it over to where she's rocking slowly back and forth, knitting needles clicking together in the process of creating another toy that's going to come to life and join its friends in the walls.

He sets the petite glass down next to her and she smiles up at him, no surprise, just gratitude. He pulls one of the high backed chairs around until it's close to hers, his back to the fire, and he's about to sit when she suggests,

'You look like you could do with a drink too, my dear.'

She's right. Despite his unsettled stomach he pours himself a glass and sits down, sipping the sweet, strong liquid, getting used to the taste. It has a slight burn to it, like caramelised sugar, and it feels like fire in his throat. He almost throws up again but manages to swallow.

When he can speak, he asks, 'Do you know why you're here?'

She stops knitting and hesitates before lowering the half-finished pink circle into her lap.

'I don't, dear. I don't think I'm supposed to be. I was in another place, somewhere bright and warm and now I'm here. But I'm not worried because I think I'll be going back when it's over. And you boys keep bringing me tea and sherry. You're all so good.'

'How do you know you'll be going back?' He tries not to let fear creep into his voice.

'It's just a feeling. You know what I'm talking about, don't you, dear?'

His eyes rise to her face. She's no longer an old lady, not Matt and Luke's Grandma, she's something else, something scary. Black seeps into the whites of her eyes, her teeth elongate to sharp points while her face melts and her chin drops, making her mouth impossibly wide.

Rick scrapes his chair back across the floorboards, dropping his sherry glass which spills and rolls but doesn't break. He glimpses the reflection of the fire in the cut crystal and when he looks back Nancy's just an old lady again, gazing at him with concern in her kind eyes.

'Sorry.'

'Are you all right? You look as if you've had a shock. Have another drink and you'll soon feel better.'

He doubts that. 'Do you know... where I'll go, afterwards?' He isn't sure he wants to hear the answer but he has to ask the question.

'I presume you'll go home with the rest of them,' she says, like she hasn't just turned into a vision of horror right in front of his eyes. Maybe she knows what's really going on, maybe she doesn't.

He remembers the landlord, and the definite feeling that he did know more than he was letting on. Of course there's no way of contacting him, none that immediately springs to mind. He popped in then he vanished. There has to be a way, though. Perhaps Matt and Luke can summon him.

He leans down to pick up the fallen glass before standing unsteadily and asking if there's anything else Nancy needs. She tells him that she's fine and that he should get some sleep, so he bids her goodnight and closes the lounge door behind him. In a way, he envies Matt and Luke. They have something to do to keep themselves occupied, to pass the time. Not sleeping leaves him a good seven or eight hours alone and he's not the best company for himself right now. The last thing he needs is the opportunity to sit and think but he's stayed in better equipped low-rent motels. There's no television, no wifi. There isn't even a radio. There is the bookshelf behind which the wool creatures are hopefully asleep and when he looks he finds an array of books on a hundred different subjects from aviation to zoology, and fiction by everyone from Isaac Asimov to Timothy Zahn. Opening the glass doors he tilts his head and scans the authors' names, quickly coming across his favourite, Christopher Brookmyre. He slides the book out with reverence as a crazy thought slips into his mind. Perhaps he put it there. They've been presuming only Matt and Luke can change things here but it could just as easily be all of them, couldn't it? Last night he'd been thinking about beer when Joe found bottles in the fridge. And now this; his favourite novel by his favourite author.

It's been a while since he read Brookmyre's *Pandaemonium*, the plot of which revolves around a group of high school students who inadvertently find themselves at a retreat half a mile from a top-secret military base where the US army has just opened a portal through which demons are escaping. It feels oddly like the right thing to be reading given his predicament. He takes the book over to the couch, glancing at the dying fire, the orange sparks from the last spluttering embers. He doesn't want to rekindle it, doesn't ever want to see fire again.

He's opening the book cover, skipping to the first page of narrative, when another idea comes to him. If he and Nancy have been brought back from the dead, there's no reason to think that any of them made it. They could all have been killed. He should feel sorry or sad or guilty but he doesn't. All he can feel is horror and terror at his own plight and misery famously loves company. But if the others are having the same hallucinations they haven't said and they certainly don't look as shell-shocked as he feels. He can't think of any way of confirming his theories tonight so he settles down to read, all the time wishing for the landlord to pay them another visit, hoping he can make it happen.

~..~

They lie on the bed in a tangle of bare limbs, forehead to forehead, palm to palm.

'You know we could do anything, right?' Luke murmurs and Matt nods against him. Luke squeezes the sweaty fingers pressed between his own. 'What do you want to do? What would you create?'

'Nothing. I've got everything I want. I've got you. I've never wanted to change anything. I know you think I should have had a different life but I've never wanted anything other than what we have. Except for this.' He tightens one leg around Luke's knee. 'Now I have this. I'm happy.' A small quirk of his lips and he adds, 'Although pumpkin pie would be great. Remember that diner in Queens, years ago? Best pumpkin pie ever.'

Luke chuckles. 'That's probably what you're getting for breakfast now.'

'Fine with me.' He presses his foot into the back of Luke's shin. 'Actually, you know what else I want?'

'What?'

'I want it to snow like it did in Whistler. I want to build snowmen and win another snowball fight.'

'I won that snowball fight!'

Matt ignores him. 'It was so beautiful. If we ever settle I want to be somewhere that gets lots of snow.'

It's what Luke was thinking earlier, when they were at the roadhouse, about living in a small town where the winters are bad. But he doesn't say so. Instead he lets the sentimental mood fade before he opens his mouth again.

'I've been thinking about Rick. I think... no, I know I saw him, right at the end, I turned back to look at them and he was down, covered in blood. I'm sure he was dead and if he's dead and he's here, then maybe we're all dead. It would explain Grandma Nancy being here, and all the things we keep changing.'

Matt pulls Luke's hand up to his mouth and kisses his knuckles. 'I'm not dead,' he whispers. 'And neither are you. I can taste you, smell you and feel you. You think I'd feel all this if I was dead?'

'I don't know. I've never believed in Heaven being an actual place but if this is it, I'm happy to be wrong. If we can finally have what we want it's okay with me.' He strokes Matt's shoulder, sweat-damp and hot under his hand. 'Could be that's why neither of us is freaking out. We've deliberately not done this forever. Whatever made this house and put us in it could have found this in our heads too. We fight it our whole lives, the attraction, even though there's never been anyone else around. No one else would ever know and still we never did anything about it. Then we get here and wham-bam, we can't keep our hands off each other. Really?'

The expression on his brother's face isn't what he expects after that. Matt's smiling. And out of everything Luke's said in his little speech, he chooses to pick up on just two words. 'Wham-bam?' He'd punch him if he could extricate his hand. 'We were at the centre of the apocalypse. You don't think that we deserve to stop living for others and start to live for ourselves? This is what we've wanted since we were old enough to know what it meant, you know it as well as I do. We've always belonged to each other. We sleep in ratty motels on stain covered sheets, we shower in cockroach-infested bathrooms. We spend half our waking hours on the road and the other half fighting creatures from Hell. So, yeah, when we finally find ourselves in a warm room in a great big bed with clean sheets, a bathroom with two toilets and a walk-in shower big enough we can have sex in it, the dam was bound to break because finally we're feeling safe enough to let it. It's no real surprise. Doesn't mean that we're dead and in some mythical place. So you need to present a different argument for the prosecution in the trail of we're dead vs. we just got lucky because I'm blowing that one out of the water.'

Luke stares at his brother until he gives up trying to think of something to say and finally just settles for, 'Huh.'

'What?'

'I keep forgetting how much bullshit you talk.' He gets a slap, although he has no idea how Matt's hand got to his ass. 'I swear Rick didn't make it,' he repeats himself, low and serious so that Matt doesn't take the piss again.

'Maybe he didn't, but he's here, so something saved him for a reason. Maybe it has to be the six of us.'

'But why? They're just a random group of people. You and I, I get, but them? They're four strangers we picked up along the way. We're not the bloody Avengers.'

Matt looks at him curiously. 'I don't know how you even know who they are. Emilie calls us the Scooby Gang. I'm Fred, you're Velma—'

'Hey! If anyone's Fred, it's me. You're Daphne. Besides, I never wanted any other company than you.'

'You're the one who wanted Joe to tag along.'

'I didn't think that leaving him at that motel with a dead body in our room and the rest of the guests assuming he knew us was such a great idea. That's not the same thing as wanting him along.'

Matt never wanted him to join them, and even when they weren't having sex there wasn't much Luke wouldn't do simply because Matt asked, possibly because he rarely asked for anything. But Luke couldn't leave Joe behind to deal with whatever followed, so they got a second car at the first opportunity because Matt was right, neither of them was used to having other people around. They'd been alone in their own little world for too long to share.

Alive or dead, they're still together and that's all that matters.

~..~

It's snowing. Emilie stands at the window of her bedroom and watches the flakes fall onto so much accumulation it has to have been falling heavily all night. The sky is grey with it, the ground white. It's beautiful, glistening in the empty branches of the trees, carpeting the ground, covering everything. Virgin snow. Living in California all her life she hasn't seen much of it. But one Christmas she and her Mom spent a weekend shopping in New York and it started to snow just as they arrived at the hotel. It was one of the most wondrous sights she ever saw.

The view outside the house is breathtaking.

She's dressed and downstairs before any of the others are up, opening the front door and skipping down the steps like a child. Jumping from the last one she lands flat on her feet in the deep snow, sinking until it's halfway up her shins. Already it's settling in her hair and on her shoulders. Taking a couple of difficult steps, she turns and looks at the house. It looks like the picture on the front of a Christmas card.

There are plenty of dry clothes in the closet in her room which makes it snow angel time. Lying down carefully in the wet white stuff she moves her arms up and down to make the wings and her legs together and apart to make the tail although she doesn't think angels have tails. Perhaps it's supposed to be the base of their robe. It's the first one she's ever made. She's seen people do it on television and in the movies but it's much more fun than it looks on screen and she's laughing when the front door opens and Rick steps outside, looking up.

'When did it start snowing?'

She pushes up on her elbows and smiles at him. 'Sorry, did I wake you?'

'No. I wasn't sleeping. Did you do this?'

'Me? Course not! How could I do this? Luke and Matt must have done it, but isn't it amazing?' He looks dubious. 'Not a fan of winter?'

He shakes his head but comes out to the steps, turns his face to the sky and closes his eyes, letting the flakes settle on his skin. Then he makes more tracks as he comes over to join her, staying away from her angel, lying down himself and sinking into the thick blanket. Emilie watches him for a few seconds until he disappears from view then turns her head again and looks up at the sky, at the feather-light fall coming directly at her. It's magical.

'I died,' Rick blurts out.

It takes her by surprise, takes her a couple of seconds to work out a response. 'Are you talking metaphorically?'

'No. Really. During that last fight, a guy stabbed me. He killed me and I went to Hell.'

She doesn't understand. 'But you're here.'

'I know. It doesn't make sense. But I remember Hell. When I fall asleep I dream of it, and I'm hallucinating the same things.'

She doesn't know what to say. She hasn't had any dreams for the last two nights, just sleep, deep and refreshing. Maybe her mind is too tired to construct anything or her subconscious has experienced so much weird shit recently it doesn't see the point of making more up.

'Do you remember dying?' She hopes he's imagining this, hopes he's just had a couple of nightmares as his brain deals with the same horrors hers has blocked out.

'Yes.'

'What was it like?'

She wants to know, to see if similar memories will surface in her head. She doesn't want her death theory confirmed, obviously, but eventually they're going to have to work out what's going on. She should be cold – should be freezing – but she isn't, she's just right, and that's clearly not normal.

He tells her about the dead thing in the park that was once a man, about looking down and seeing the knife sticking out of his stomach, seeing the blood, feeling the pain. He tells her about his dream of Hell that felt like a memory and about the terrible visions that are haunting him. She listens to everything he tells her and considers it carefully. She's relieved nothing like that is happening to her. The entire time he's talking, all she can see is snow. She can hear his voice but she can't see his face. She doesn't need to. He sounds very serious and very scared.

When he's finished she tries to comfort him by telling him the truth; she doesn't remember seeing him die, doesn't remember seeing him dead. But then she doesn't remember seeing him at all right at the end because she was so focused on Luke and Matt at the top of the hill. Once the attacks on them stopped she didn't take her eyes off Luke until the flash that almost blinded them.

'If you're right, can't you just stay here?'

'I don't know. We don't even know what this place is.'

Which is true, and wherever they are she can only hope they aren't going to be here indefinitely. She isn't bored yet; it'll take a lot more quiet days and long and restful nights before she's anywhere close. But contrary to her feelings when they first arrived, she doesn't want this to be the last place she sees. If she's helped to safeguard the world she would quite like to live in it for a while. She wants to see all the monuments Hollywood insists on destroying in every disaster movie since the Millennium: the Eiffel Tower, the Pyramids, the London Eye. Places she thought would be there forever and now can't be so sure.

'I can't go back. What I remember... it's worse than anything we've seen up here; way, way worse.'

She wishes she could think of something useful to say, something that will help, even if she isn't certain she believes him. 'Have you spoken to Luke and Matt?' she suggests in the end, because she just can't think of anything else. 'They seem to be capable of changing this place. They should be able to do something, shouldn't they?'

'I was thinking maybe all of us can change it if we try.'

She's highly doubtful about that, so she closes her eyes and concentrates hard on a chocolate sundae with hot chocolate sauce, whipped cream and toffee pieces. She even holds out her hand in case it appears but it doesn't.

'I don't think I can,' she admits, not the least bit surprised. 'Have you tried?'

He hesitates. 'No.'

'So try.'

He falls silent for a long few minutes, during which time she becomes aware that the snow under her has melted and there's a fresh layer settling on her. She sits up carefully, brushes it off and gets to her feet, turning around to look proudly down at her creation. It's a perfect snow angel that looks just like her in some strange way. Rick's lying still. He hasn't made an angel. But his eyes are closed and she wonders what he is trying to do.

'I don't think it's working.' He sounds worse than miserable. He sounds defeated.

'What did you try?'

'I tried to make a bird fly overheard.'

She hums. That's more beautiful than she might have thought him capable of. But still it's probably more complicated that she had in mind. 'Why don't we start with something simple? We'll try together. Imagine a snowman on the steps.'

~..~

'I see it is snowing!
Unique shapes falling to the ground
Land as virgins.'

There's a single note of joy in the landlord's otherwise flat voice. It immediately distracts Rick from concentrating on building a snowman with his mind and leaves him feeling faintly ridiculous. He's been hoping so hard to see the strange man again but now he's here and he wishes he wasn't. Opening his eyes he gets up quickly inside the Rick-shaped void in the snow, standing in the hollow of his own stomach, between the outline of his hips. The landlord is standing on the bottom step in a good foot of the stuff, the hem of his coat and his boots hidden from view. He looks as if he simply materialised there.

'I have never seen it snow here.
I suppose it could be
God's icebox.'

Rick has the distinct impression that the landlord has just tried to make a joke, perhaps his first ever, and he thinks he should laugh at it but he can't even bring himself to smile. The white flakes are sticking in the dark curly hair and on the long coat, sparkling like diamonds. But as Rick stares at him the skin starts to slide from the expressionless face, leaving behind bronze metal plates like the workings of a pocket watch, glass eyes glinting in the white light, and tiny pistons where his mouth should be. Rick blinks loose a tear and the landlord is himself again, although his big staring eyes still look as if they're made of glass and his unmoving mouth and curling lips still look mechanically controlled. He shudders. He doesn't want to be around the landlord any longer and trudges back up the steps into the house.

Emilie follows and he hears her inviting their visitor inside. In the hall he turns around and the landlord's standing in the doorway. Rick would happily bet there are only his and Emilie's footprints on the steps. With the rate at which the snow's still falling, the angel Emilie left will be filled within the hour and the bottom step will be at the same height as the rest of the yard. It's impossible that all this came down overnight. More likely it just appeared and Rick's angry that Matt and Luke wanted it to snow, of all things. It seems like a frivolous wish when what he wants is to stay out of Hell.

Joe and Gabe are up, Joe offering the landlord coffee an in off-hand way as he heads into the kitchen. He gets no reply. Instead they're treated to another of those little poems. Rick can't remember what Joe called them.

'You are all still here.
I will come back when I need
To lead the way out.'

'Out of where?' Rick approaches him. He must know what's going on if he's waiting for something to happen and when it does he could be the one to end the illusion they're all living under, the illusion Rick does not want to see behind. 'Where will you lead the way to?'

When the landlord doesn't answer, when he just continues to stare with that same vacant expression that doesn't change, Rick gets angrier. He knows it's possibly a mistake but he doesn't think he's got much to lose. If Matt and Luke saw the things he's seen, they wouldn't be fooling around, making it snow. Emilie thinks he's imagining it all and there are no shadows under Gabe or Joe's eyes so they're obviously getting some restful sleep.

Taking a step forward Rick grasps the front of that long blue coat, making fists as best he can in the rough, heavy material and pulling the tall man towards him even as he's towering over him. Immediately Joe shouts at Rick to leave him alone, but he doesn't. His knuckles are pressed tight to the landlord's body and he can feel it hard and solid, not like skin and flesh. Maybe there's nothing under it all and he's just a skeleton, Death come to reap their souls when the time is right. But he's too heavy to be made of bone. He isn't fighting back, isn't struggling or trying to get away, and for the few seconds they're locked together Rick has the impression of staring into the face of a puppet.

Strong hands on the tops of his arms yank him back and he can't miss Gabe's voice in his ear hissing at him to let go. Reluctantly he complies, dropping his hands and stepping away. Emilie's apologising to the guy but Rick isn't sorry. 'Tell me!' He leans into the landlord's face, 'Tell me what's going on! Where are you supposed to lead us?'

There's no change in the monotone voice when the reply comes.

'I cannot tell you what you are not ready
Or what is not yours
To know.'

'Why don't you make any sense?!' He's aware of how desperate he's sounding but he doesn't care because the things that are happening are making him desperate.

'Hey!' That's Luke, yelling down from upstairs, 'We're trying to sleep!'

Rick looks up, sees both he and Matt standing on the mezzanine looking over the rail. At least they're dressed. 'Make him tell us where we are!'

Luke ignores him as he stomps down the stairs, Matt at his shoulder, and stops in front of their visitor. 'You must be the guy who talks in Haiku.'

The way the landlord turns on the spot, as if he's pivoting on the soles of his feet, makes Rick think of the toy soldiers he used to play with as a child with arms that just moved up and down and legs that didn't move at all because they were carved from a single piece of wood.

'It is an honour to meet you.
The brothers who preserved
All life.'

Luke's expression is almost comical. They've never come across as the typical hero type but they would probably enjoy some kudos if they really have saved everything.

'Okay. Well, it's good to meet you too. How about you tell us what you want, where we are and why we're here?'

'Debt cannot be repaid in life.
We will repay in death
What is owed.'

'That doesn't answer any of the questions I asked, does it? How about trying again?'

'Only you can make the decision.
Once you choose to let go
It ends.'

'Let go of what? What ends?' Luke doesn't get a response to that.

Matt comes out from behind his brother, steps around him, and approaches the landlord cautiously with a question Rick doesn't expect. 'Have we met before?'

'I am made in an image you understand.
I the key
You the lock.'

That one makes even less sense than any of the others and it's accompanied by a whirring sound followed by a sequence of clicks as their visitor's arm rises in a series of staggered movements and his left index finger unfolds so he's pointing upwards at the spiral staircase on the mezzanine landing. Then he stops. He doesn't move much anyway but it's as if an off-switch has been thrown or he's broken down.

Rick can't believe it. He needs more. There must be more. 'Can we stay?' he shouts into the landlord's inanimate face but there's no sign that he's being heard. 'Shit!' He falls back, taking two heavy, blind steps and accidentally stamping on one of the wool creatures that has ventured out from under the stairs. It doesn't make a sound, just dies under his foot, wool strands coming loose from its body. Another of the creatures makes a distressed sound and runs awkwardly towards its fallen friend. Emilie bends down and scoops it up, holding it gently in one hand, rubbing its belly with one finger, actually making soothing noises.

Rick feels sick. He grabs his coat from next to the door and goes back out into the snow. It's too thick to run through, he has to take long strides, but he needs to put as much distance between himself and the mad house as he's able. He doesn't look back. He does, however, hear Matt call out to his brother that it's snowing. He hears the excitement like it's a surprise to either of them, like anything in this God-forsaken place should be a surprise to them. This is their world he's trapped in, but the alternative is worse and it'll be forever. He isn't evil, he's just an idiot! He doesn't deserve what's waiting for him! The punishment doesn't fit the crime.

Rick doesn't stop until he reaches the roadhouse.

~..~

Luke pokes the broken-down landlord in the chest. He doesn't respond, doesn't even rock back because he's too heavy to move. He turns away, back to Matt.

'In this Scooby Gang of yours, is Rick Shaggy or Scooby?'

Matt doesn't answer. He's staring out through the open door. 'Luke. It's snowing.'

Luke looks up and sees the blanket of white stuff covering everything, then glances over to see the grin on his brother's face. He's looking like all his Christmases have come at once. Matt's even putting down the mug of coffee that Joe's just handed to him to pull on boots and a jacket that are by the door even though he didn't put them there, and to run out into the snow, laughing like a hyena.

They should talk about the robot landlord, if that's what he – it – is, but he supposes that can wait and instead follows Matt's lead, dressing appropriately and stepping out into the deep snow that crunches beneath his boots. He scoops up a handful from the steps and compresses it before throwing it at Matt, an easy target as he's got his head back and his face tilted up to the sky. Luke's aim is a bit off but it hits his brother squarely in the chest.

'Ow! Bastard!'

Quick retaliation means war, but as Matt's laughing at his own direct hit on Luke's shoulder, Luke makes a dive for him, knocking him onto his ass, scooping up the top layer of powdery snow and getting it up inside Matt's white T-shirt before he knows what's happening. Unfortunately, in Luke's bid for a quick escape, he loses his balance and falls onto his back where he's instantly straddled and pinned down. They're equally matched in a hand-to-hand fight, but it's impossible to get a grip on anything except Matt for leverage and before he can work that to his advantage there's snow down his top and a freezing cold hand down the front of his jeans.

Embarrassingly, he screams like a girl and Emilie comes to his rescue, pelting Matt with snowballs. She doesn't fight dirty, Luke notices, doesn't get physical. She might have done had it been Luke on top but she won't with Matt because she doesn't know how he'll react and neither does he. They're both insanely proprietary about each other. So she throws snowballs with Joe and Gabe looking on in amusement, but that's all she does. None of them get any closer. No one interrupts what's clearly meant for them.

This is why they wanted it to snow. They once tracked an escaped Hellhound to Whistler one winter and discovered a white world in which Luke got to watch his brother laugh for real and they got to play for a little while. It's a good memory for both of them and he intends to enjoy it this time around too.

Matt's white T-shirt has turned transparent with the melting snow. As Luke follows him into the kitchen his eyes catch on the vivid pink scar that crosses Matt's back from his left shoulder blade to halfway down his spine. Something with long, sharp talons, needle-sharp teeth and reptilian eyes did that, something they've never put a name to and never caught. It was one of those rare times when he bit the bullet and took Matt to a hospital, despite his protests and whining about medical insurance. They stayed long enough for a nurse to clean, stitch and dress the wound, but got out of there before the cops arrived. They've always made it a rule to stay far away from the authorities, never sure what would happen if they caught up. For a couple of years it was easier to believe that the cops were looking for them than it was to think that they weren't. Now it's simply second nature.

That day at the hospital they got their own stash of extra-strong meds, pills which had Matt whistling folk music and seeing pink elephants for thirty-six hours until he could walk without pulling his stitches. They kept those pills for emergencies only. That attack, and the time a baby alligator bit Luke's left little toe off in Big River, were probably the worst injuries they've suffered. They've known others who've been killed doing what they do. They considered themselves extremely lucky. Now Luke isn't so sure it was luck.

In the kitchen, Joe is making more coffee and what looks like hot chocolate, frothing milk, working the espresso machine like he was born to it.

'You're a natural,' Matt tells him as he takes possession of his second steaming mug of caffeine.

'Don't leave it to go cold this time,' Joe scolds him and Matt looks suitably chastised, playing along.

Joe hands Emilie something that definitely isn't coffee and her eyes mist up like she's going to cry.

'You are the best,' she tells him from the heart, then, 'Oh, you don't have any of those....' she trails off and both she and Joe turn pointedly to look at Matt and Luke.

'What?'

'Those little coloured marshmallows they had at the diner?'

In the storage space at the back of the diner, they found huge bags of little button mallows – ice cream toppings – along with bags of freeze dried coffee for the machine and a chest freezer containing more frozen burgers and sausages than they could possibly eat before dying of heart disease.

'Second cupboard on the left,' Luke tells her, and is mildly surprised to watch Joe reach in and pull out a packet.

'That is somewhere between utterly brilliant and creepy as fuck.' But it doesn't stop her pouring as many mallows as she can into her drink before it spills over the rim of the mug.

Matt blows warm air over the surface of his coffee as Luke dusts the last of the snow from his shoulders.

Joe asks them, 'Did anything the landlord said make sense to you boys?'

Luke doesn't mean to ignore him, he never means to exclude them but sometimes it's just habit to tune out everything but Matt. He meets his brother's querying expression.

'You said he looked familiar? You think you've seen him somewhere before?'

'Yeah, but I can't get a handle on it. Something from way back.' Then Matt answers Joe's query. 'No, nothing he said meant anything.'

'So what now?' Emilie poses the question between sips of very hot chocolate given the wisps of steam rising from it.

Luke looks pointedly at her. 'We're supposed to know?'

'I mean, what do we do? I don't think I should lie around making snow angels all day.'

'I have no idea.' It's the God's honest truth but they all just look at him. 'Honestly, I can't remember ever having nothing to do. We never just sit and read a book or watch pointless TV and no—' He holds up one finger, a warning sign to Matt to keep his mouth shut. 'Cable porn doesn't count.'

'Of course not because you never just sit and watch it. You're always... doing something else at the same time.' He looks away and Luke grins at him. They spent many a post-puberty hour watching chicks with huge fake tits suck off guys who should otherwise have been so lucky.

'Maybe we should go after Rick,' Emilie suggests, but Luke's never had time for drama. The only person he's ever run after is his brother, on the very rare occasions that he's needed to.

'He just needs to calm down about whatever's got him wound up. He'll come back. Where else is there to go?'

Emilie looks as if she's got something else to say, a different opinion, but she doesn't offer it up. 'How about a board game?'

Luke glances at her with the enthusiasm of drying paint. 'How about not?'

'Come on, don't be like that! What about Scrabble?'

'We quit school at thirteen and eleven respectively. What makes you think we even know what Scrabble is?'

'Bet you're real good at Jeopardy,' Joe puts in, and Matt laughs.

Luke glares at him while admitting, 'We could probably hold our own against Zimmer Frame from Delaware and Corpse McCrumbly from Texas.'

'Thought so. The tough life of a tracker.' Joe's taking the piss and Luke lets it slide.

'Monopoly.' Emilie tries again.

This times Matt rolls his eyes. 'The most boring game ever invented. You have to spend all your time planning a bank heist because it's the only way to win!'

'Cluedo?'

Luke sighs. 'Carry on like this and it'll be me in the kitchen with the lead piping.'

But Matt's suggestion is worse than any of Emilie's. 'What about a Ouija board? Do you think we'd reach lots of people or no one?'

'I don't think having a séance in the afterlife is a spectacular idea.'

'Fair point. How about a walk?' Now Matt's doing it, excluding the others simply using the tone of his voice. It sounds like a much better option than standing here until he punches someone, so he nods and follows, leaving the rest of them presumably staring at their backs, unaware that the conversation was over until the moment they left it.

They go out again and walk around to the back of the house. The Mustang is still there and bizarrely it's free from snow, a big black patch of shining metal in the otherwise completely white landscape. The rust bucket is covered too, so that only a hint of blackened chrome is visible.

'The Chevy used to belong to Dad's friend, Bill.' Matt recalls. 'This really is all us.'

Luke nods, sitting up on the hood of their car. 'I think so.'

Matt slides up next to him, careful not to spill his coffee. Their shoulders touch, elbows jostling for a comfortable position like they're fighting over a cinema armrest but they quickly get comfortable, pressing against each other the way they've always done.

'Remember that tracker, Jess or Joan? A guy with a girl's name. Used to hang out at that ruin of a roadhouse outside of Reno; Angie's place. Drove a battered old Skyline with a fantastic engine. Used it to street race for cash.'

Luke remembers. He tilts his head to look at Matt, wondering where he's going with this. 'Jane.'

'That's it. Ridiculous name for a guy. He used to wear the T-shirt with the marshmallow sailor on it?'

In his lifetime Luke's seen enough to drive any normal person to suicide but the only thing he's ever despaired of is Matt's inability to soak up popular culture when he himself manages it simply by spending an hour or two in a public place. 'The Staypuft Marshmallow Man from *Ghostbusters*, moron.'

'Whatever.'

'How can you not know that?'

Matt shrugs like he couldn't care less. 'The point is his T-shirt had that phrase on it.'

'Quote! It's a quote from *Ghostbusters*! Zool, the demi-God says it when they're on the rooftop, 'Choose and perish.' Ray thinks of the Staypuft Marshmallow Man who appears and tries to kill them.'

His brother's staring at him. 'How do you know that?'

'How do you not know it? Everyone knows it!'

'But how do you know it?'

'When you were young I used to sneak out to the drive-in once you'd fallen asleep.'

Matt's mouth drops open, his eyes widen. 'You left me in the Airstream alone to go watch movies?'

'Yeah. So what? Nothing happened, did it? You weren't kidnapped by Old Man Paedophile and sold into slave labour. So shut your cake hole.' Matt rolls his eyes. 'So what about it?'

'What about what?'

'Jane's T-shirt, the Ghostbusters quote.'

'I was thinking, although now it's been built up too much....'

'Get on with it!'

''Choose and perish'. I think that might be what the landlord was saying, in a roundabout way. We have to make the decision to leave.'

'And then we perish?'

'I don't know.... I'm just saying, that's kinda what it reminded me of.'

'That's a stupid choice. Why would we walk away from this if we thought we were going to be dead the moment we left?'

Matt looks around them. 'Boredom?'

He has a point. They've only been here a day and they're already wondering what to do with themselves. The new facet to their relationship hasn't changed anything. It's good to finally be acquainting his dick with someone else's hand but they're too used to one another, to being around each other twenty-four-seven, for it to be a permanent distraction. Besides, they're both too exhausted, mentally and physically, to be doing it more than twice, three times a day, tops. Now they've stopped chasing things Luke thinks he can feel each and every old injury finally demanding if not attention then definitely acknowledgement.

'Anyway, we're not dead.' Matt states it with feeling, with certainty. 'We would know.'

'How would we know? We haven't died before. How can we know what it feels like?'

'What we've been doing? I don't think we'd feel that good if we were dead. Then again, if it's all in our minds and our bodies don't really exist we'd imagine sensation. It wouldn't have anything to do with our physical forms.'

Luke presses his fingers into his eyes, massaging his eyeballs behind the lids. He's tempted to nudge Matt's elbow and spill his coffee. He wonders if dead people get headaches. 'Have you always been like this and I've been too caught up in you to notice?'

He can feel Matt pouting; he doesn't need to see it. 'You're no longer caught up in me?'

'Of course I am! It's just, well, different. You know, now nothing's trying to tear you apart on a daily basis.'

Matt takes a deep breath in and lets it out slowly. 'And you were asking why we'd ever walk away from this?'

Luke's still thinking about that, about how to respond, when they both sit up in unison. Something's coming. They can hear it, shifting through the deep snow covering the path along the side of the house. Habit has them tensing for a fight but it's just Joe, striding through the white stuff with determination, hands in his coat pockets.

'Hey,' Luke calls out in greeting.

Joe stops and smiles, shouting over, 'Notice how it's warm out here even though it looks cold and there's enough snow on the ground to embarrass the Arctic?'

'I don't like being cold,' Matt explains, the reason for the weirdness.

'I keep coming out here expecting to find a Starbucks on the other side of the road.'

'You know how much I hate those chains. Besides, no one makes coffee like you do.'

'Well, I'm glad I'm good for something around here.' He hasn't come any closer. He's staying within shouting distance. Clearly there's something on his mind.

'What's up?'

'Rick's not back.'

Luke shrugs. 'I assume he's at the roadhouse cooling off from whatever got him going in the first place.'

'It's not like him to lay into someone like that. And it's only eleven in the morning.'

'Feels like the afternoon,' Luke mutters.

'Are you worried about him?' Matt calls out.

Luke watches Joe shift his weight onto his other leg. 'Maybe. Something's going on with him. Emilie says he thinks he died in the battle.'

They both know she's right. They were right. They confirm this with a single glance at one another. Here, now, it's trivial, but in the past this ability to communicate without words has saved their lives.

'I don't know what to say,' Luke responds. 'He seems the same as he's been since we picked him up.' Joe nods and obviously it's not the reason he's out here. 'Something else?'

'Emilie wants to know if there's any chance of getting something by Tess Gerritsen on the bookshelf.'

The words 'I'm not fucking Santa Claus' are right on the tip of his tongue but Luke bites down on them at the last possible moment and just nods. He's probably narrowly avoided a never-ending string of bad jokes about red velvet from his brother, the comedian.

Joe shrugs. 'I said I'd ask.'

As he turns to make his way back, Matt calls out, 'Joe? Thanks for all the coffee. I'd never dream of replacing you with a franchise.'

Joe waves back at them over his shoulder, and as walks away they hear him say, 'I wouldn't mind some culture, possibly a theatre?' It sounds like he's talking to himself. Luke hopes so, he hates the theatre.

'If we gave them everything, do you think they'd be happy?' Matt asks him idly.

He seriously doubts that and Matt already knows the answer. 'It's not that big a place. If we gave them everything, where would they put it?'

Matt smirks. 'Very funny.'

'Listen....' Luke gets serious, sliding his hand over Matt's palm and pushing his fingers up into the loose sleeve of his coat. 'I'm still so caught up in you I don't know where I end and you start. The two of us... we're all tangled up. We always have been and we always will be.' It's difficult to say this stuff but he needs Matt to know that some things won't ever change. 'You're here and that's all that matters.'

Matt's smile assures him he understands what it took to say that. His eyes promise Luke that it's all mutual, that he loves him too and won't ever leave him. But Matt's also good at knowing when a situation needs defusing. 'You're so the chick in this relationship.'

Luke sits back but doesn't retrieve his hand where it's warm inside Matt's coat. 'I'm the chick? You're the one with the long hair.'

'You need to get over my hair. I've worn it the same way for fifteen years.'

Luke hesitates, but there's still something he needs to say. 'I don't ever want to get over you. I don't ever want to be without you. If you go, I go.'

Matt turns his head but instead of another smart-assed reply, he reaches his left hand up to the back of Luke's neck and pulls him forward until their foreheads touch. 'Yeah,' is all he says before he tilts his head and slides his mouth across Luke's. It's a quick, dry touch that doesn't become anything more but feels perfect. And it's not weird, the way they both thought it would be. That's the reason they haven't tried it before but Luke wants, needs, to try it again and for longer because the possibilities are now crowding out every other thought in his mind until he's on the verge of begging for it.

Matt's eyes suddenly widen and he sits back so quickly he almost breaks Luke's nose. 'The theatre!'

Luke stares at him, somewhat disappointed and slightly confused. 'What?'

'Oh my God, that's it, that's where I've seen the landlord before!'

'What are you talking about? We haven't been to the theatre since the night....' The same memory hits him with full force, so incredibly vivid that for a moment he can't see Matt or the surrounding snow scene, he can only see the stage, the cast of actors, the two characters who were supposed to be invisible, and the man made of clockwork.

~..~

Rick pushes open the narrow door and steps inside. The bar looks the same as it did last night, right down to the same people drinking around the same tall, unstable tables and buying drinks from the same double-D barmaid in the tight Lakers T-shirt. He orders a beer and a shot of tequila and if last night was anything to go by he won't have to pay for them. He's curious as to whose memory the barmaid came from, Luke's or Matt's, or possibly both. Maybe she did them together one dark night in some seedy motel in a two-bit town as far from the interstate as it's possible to get.

He doesn't understand Matt and Luke. He's been grateful to them for saving him back in Michigan Bar but that gratitude is fading fast and with each passing hour he's starting to harbour a deep-seated regret about ever having met them, about following them to Five Points and finally leaving the relative safety of the diner for the battlefield in the park. Sure, that was the right thing to do at the time and yes, he owed them, not just Matt and Luke but all of them, and not just for Michigan Bar but for the other times in other towns since. Look where doing the right thing has got him.

He picks up the shot glass, filled to the brim with golden liquor, and tips it down his throat so he barely tastes it, just feels the burn. He soothes that with half the cold beer. There's a television over the bar playing a recording of a Lakers game. It's the first television he's seen in months with a picture on it and it's just further proof that nothing here is real. Not the drink, not the barmaid's breasts, not the other people.

The floor is sticky from spilt drinks and possibly other fluids. He doesn't know where this bar was originally or what it was like. He doesn't recognise it so it isn't somewhere they've been with him in tow and the others didn't say anything last night about it looking familiar. It's from happier times, he guesses, if Matt and Luke have such things in their past.

The pool table's free so he gets another round of drinks and takes the glasses over to the raised platform next to the window where the table's racked, ready and waiting for a game. He doesn't want company and no one asks to join him. He picks out a cue from the set on the wall, positions the white and takes a shot. The balls scatter, a stripe falling in slow motion into the far left hand pocket. Finishing the last of his first beer, he lines up the cue ball. He, like Matt, is a born hustler. Matt's advantage is that he looks like he wouldn't kick a rabid dog while Rick looks like someone who's out to make a quick buck. He didn't always look like this obviously, or he wouldn't ever have been successful in his chosen career, but in the weeks he spent on his own between the incursion of Hell on Earth and being pulled out of a dumpster by a guy with a shotgun, he let himself go, less interested in personal hygiene than in simply surviving. He's been a conman most of his life, started out taking lunch money from his classmates and ending up parting vulnerable old women from their welfare benefits. He's always considered himself very good at what he does, one of the best he thought, until he met Gabe and realised the salesman was in another league entirely. Selling two hundred grand cars to idiots who lost half the value of their new acquisition the moment all four wheels left the forecourt is a real class act. Gabe has travelled all over the world, exotic trips paid for by money he barely lifted a finger to earn. The life of a conman isn't an easy or lazy one. Gabe hasn't done a day of hard work in his life, and he's happy to admit it, but he has made more money in a single hour than

Rick's made ever. And now he's the one standing on the edge of Hell. Life isn't fair and death's no different.

He pots two more stripes and a solid, swallows his second tequila and bends over to line up his next shot. The tip of the cue sinks into the stained green baize like the edge of a knife into melting butter. He steps back, lifting the cue at the same time as he lifts his eyes from the table and looks around. Everyone in the bar is turning to stare at him. The background white noise of conversation and music has faded to a low drone, a relentless sound that starts to drill through his eardrums into his skull. He straightens slowly, feeling very much under threat. The only weapon to hand is the pool cue but as the thought enters his head the hard maple wood starts to wilt, the top half slowly drooping until it's hanging like a dead flower over his hand. Everyone's watching him, no one's approaching him, but as he glances from one unfriendly face to another their features begin to melt away. Eyeballs liquefy into viscous white goo that runs down over cheekbones, removing flesh as it goes like water washing away dirt. Lips slip to the side and down, leaving fixed skeletal grins with nicotine-stained teeth. Scalps tear away from hairlines and fall away from smooth white bone. Drinks fall from wet hands, glasses smashing in puddles of booze and flesh. Bodies melt like hot candle wax, pink and red viscous gloop draining from clothing to leave skeletons standing, still dressed, still silently staring at him from empty eye sockets. His stomach heaves in panic and he bends over, mouth open, expecting to vomit burning tequila back up onto the baize.

But nothing comes up.

His stomach doesn't hurt and the pool cue's sturdy again in his sweating hand. He snaps his head up as the bar fills with the sound of tall tales and arguments about baseball, glasses once again thump onto tabletops and darts hit the board with muted thuds.

He can't tell if these things are really happening or are just in his head. He doesn't know if he's seeing behind some invisible curtain, catching glimpses of what's really under the veil, or if his own mind is playing tricks, teasing and tormenting him.

Laying the cue gently onto the table, knocking the 8-ball with the tip, he walks deliberately to the bar and asks for a bottle of tequila, which the busty barmaid brings him with a big smile. He unscrews the cap and tips the liquor down his throat, not stopping until he's almost choking and a third of the bottle is gone. Then he thanks her and walks back to sit up on the pool table and take his time drinking the rest of the bottle. With each slug, his vision narrows and the inside of the bar blurs until he's flat on his back on the table with the cue uncomfortably under his shoulders and the smooth surface of the balls against his hand.

~..~

They're standing in the kitchen, Joe and Gabe leaning against the cupboards and Emilie next to the table shifting nervously from foot to foot, all listening to Luke tell the tale of *The Clockwork Man*.

'It's a short story by a guy called Edward Moran, written in 1969. Mom and Dad took us to see the play the night they were killed.' Luke looks at each of them before he carries on. Matt's hand is grasped in his, both of them refusing to let go. 'It's about a couple who die in a car crash but they don't realise they're dead. They go home but the sitter doesn't acknowledge them. The house starts to fill up with people, first the cops, then child services for their kid. They try to talk to people but everyone's ignoring them and they convince themselves that someone's playing a game at their expense. Then a man appears in the hall next to the door, not a real man, he's made of clockwork and he keeps telling them to go through the door but they're scared of what's beyond it.'

'You think... the landlord is the Clockwork Man?' Emilie sounds scared. 'And he's what...? Trying to get us to go to Heaven?'

'But we haven't not gone anywhere,' Joe points out. 'I haven't seen a light or a door or anything that I've neglected to walk towards.'

'So maybe it's not all of us. He said something about a choice. Maybe it's just one of us but the others are all holding on.'

'No offence,' Gabe starts, and Luke knows what's coming. 'You are the only two with a connection strong enough. The rest of us care, sure, but I don't think we care enough to do something like this.'

Matt raises his head. 'I think Rick might be right about dying in the battle. I don't remember seeing him at the end.'

'Did you see any of us?'

'I don't know. I can't remember.'

'He told me,' Emilie puts in. 'He thinks he died. He keeps seeing Hell.'

Joe shakes his head. 'But why would any of us hold on to Rick?'

Luke can't help but wonder if it would have sounded so inoffensive if he'd said it. Probably not. 'He might be holding on to us, too scared to let go.' He glances sideways at Matt, silently asking if that could be the answer, hoping to God that it is. Matt clearly isn't convinced but it's a

151

possibility, and it's better than any of the other possibilities he knows have crossed their minds. 'So we need to talk to Rick.'

'In which case you have two choices,' Joe points out. 'Go find him at the roadhouse or wait until he gets back. While you're waiting you can drink coffee, find a bottle of wine and eat what I'm preparing to feed you.'

When it's put like that, it's really not a tough choice. It's not like this requires immediate resolution and it doesn't look like their landlord's going anywhere because he's still standing exactly where he stopped, as broken as the clock next to him.

~..~

'You don't need to keep cooking for us,' Luke tells him and Joe knows he means it but if he leaves it up to them they'll be living on burgers, fries and salty snacks within one mealtime. It's a miracle the boys aren't three hundred pounds overweight with greasy hair and bad skin the way they were eating on the road. He doesn't like to think of them at the start, a thirteen and an eleven year old with no one to take care of them, no one who even cared that they hadn't been carried off by the horror that tore their parents apart.

Nuked burritos, cheeseburgers, milkshakes and pie had been their staple diet according to Luke until Matt taught himself to cook using a battered and stained old recipe book and later the Cookery Channel once they hooked up cable. Joe's tried to imagine himself as a child, having not only to look after himself but also a younger brother. He had a happy childhood. He can't imagine a childhood at all without his parents.

During the very short time Joe shared a car with them Luke was the one to tell some stories, to share what they knew about what was going on. It wasn't that Matt was unfriendly, just that he wasn't a talker, wasn't one to share. But his unconditional love for Luke was – is – obvious. He's possessive and protective and they're a tight circle of two that he and the others don't stand a chance of ever breaking into. Even after two months Joe's still an outsider, they all are, despite fighting side by side, sharing the highs and the lows of the tail end of what he now knows was a long, drawn out battle that he was only aware of right before its climax.

Emilie and possibly Rick, who still hasn't returned, have come to regard him as some sort of father figure. But the boys don't want or need one. He muses on whether they were the same before the attack on their parents, if they've always been as completely focused on one another as they are as adults. Even more so now, apparently.

The sex thing bothers him more than it should because it's forcing him to re-evaluate his own long-held set of morals. He thought from the start Matt and Luke were together in that way; boyfriends, lovers, whatever the modern term is for two guys who sleep together and who clearly love each other. It's never bothered him, he isn't homophobic. Whatever old-fashioned prejudices and outdated notions about gay men that he may have had, the sight of Matt and Luke standing holding smoking shotguns over a dead thing in the doorway of their motel room ridded him of them immediately. He had no idea what went on between them when their door finally and firmly closed at night, he just made assumptions. They all did. Admittedly during their week's hiatus at the diner there were no rooms, no doors to hide behind, and while Matt and Luke always stayed close, always reached for each other under the table before falling asleep with their long legs hanging out of the booths, they didn't do anything overt, anything that would suggest there was something more going on between them. Again, he just assumed. But apparently they all assumed wrong. Whatever happened, whatever changed when they woke in the room upstairs, it shouldn't matter. It doesn't matter. But to find out they're brothers, even if it's not by blood, has stirred something inside him that he can't name and can't pin down. They played together as children, shared beds and baths as innocents, and now that's morphed into something that's definitely R-rated. That's what he can't come to terms with. Not that it makes the slightest difference, because he knows his opinion counts for squat where the boys are concerned and there's no reason why it should.

He doubts Matt and Luke have ever looked to anyone for anything, let alone moral judgement on how they choose to live. They've tracked down and killed all kinds of things over time and now it seems they've saved the world. What they are to one another doesn't change what they've accomplished. Joe isn't their father, they're consenting adults and he has no right to judge. But it still isn't sitting well with him. He knows he should just stop dwelling on it.

He's made bacon and mushroom omelettes and the grateful looks on Matt and Luke's faces reminds him that he loves them and that isn't going to change.

'Well? Eat up before they go limp!'

Emilie and Gabe join them too, sitting on stools around the table.

'If the landlord is some sort of guide, what does that make this place?' Emilie asks with her mouth full. Joe bites back his first response and just scowls at her although she clearly isn't seeing it, but then he isn't her father either.

There's a minute or so before anyone responds, all of them too busy eating to be immediately disturbed. Finally Matt answers.

'We think we're in Limbo, the place between life and death, where souls with unfinished business hang out until something changes and they move on. If they move on. When spirits aren't actively haunting old houses and creepy towns, they're floating around in Limbo. Or so most of the texts say. Obviously it's all theory because no one who's ever actually been in Limbo has had the opportunity to come back and write about their experiences.'

'But,' Luke adds. 'Like most of this stuff, the theory's more often right than wrong.'

'So... we're all dead, all ghosts?'

Matt picks up again. 'Ghost isn't the right term. Spirit or soul is closer. And no, I don't think we're all spirits. I don't think we all belong here. I think we all ended up here because we were together at the end and whatever... power brought us here didn't have time to figure out which of us to bring.' He hesitates. 'It's just a working theory. But if we're right about the Clockwork Man then it follows that at least one of us is dead. The problem with it being Rick, or just Rick, is that the house seems to have been created out of our memories – mine and Luke's – and from our imaginations. Whatever we wish for, in a manner of speaking, seems to become reality. So it makes sense that one or both of us is involved.' The sadness in Matt's voice is heartbreaking.

'You have unfinished business?' Gabe sounds doubtful. 'Something you haven't managed to kill yet?' It's taken a while to get used to his rare sense of humour.

'No. Not that we were aware of. Not since yesterday morning, anyway.' He and Luke share a wry smile. 'We talked about it and we can't think what else there is. We both thought when we died, we'd die and that would be the end of it. We've never really believed in a life after death. But if one of us is alive and the other's dead, you might be right in that we have a connection strong enough to do this.'

'Why would you want to leave anyway?' Emilie looks bemused. 'You're building your own perfect world.'

'Perfection isn't all it's cracked up to be,' Matt assures her, and Emilie laughs.

'Who wouldn't want everything they've ever dreamt of having?'

'No one should ever have everything because it leaves nothing left to want,' Luke sounds like he's quoting something. 'It's a nice thought, a worthy pipedream, but in practice it won't work. You build Utopia but what next? If everything's the way you want it, the boredom will drive you insane. The cracks will show soon enough, and believe me, Matt and I don't cope well with boredom because we don't know how to. Before you know it, we'll be creating things to track down and kill just because we need something to do. We'll recreate our old lives here and it'll be a nightmare for everyone.'

'I don't understand.' Emilie may not but Joe does. He just doesn't know what they need to do to stop the inevitable.

'How do we find out for sure?' he asks before Emilie can question this further.

'A séance.'

Joe doesn't have chance to respond because Luke beats him to it. This is one thing they clearly haven't talked about. 'Bro, seriously? I say again, a séance in Limbo is insane. It could get really fucking busy in here and I doubt many of them will be friendly.'

Joe's with him. 'Didn't you just say that Limbo was full of souls with unfinished business? Do we really want to tap into that?'

'Yes.' There's that high level of patience he's heard in Matt's voice many times in recent weeks, almost always directed at Luke. 'But I doubt they're all in our kitchen. If we want to know if one of us is dead, we should ask the experts.'

Luke obviously isn't convinced but concedes, 'Okay. Fine. We need a Sharpie and a shot glass.'

Emilie holds out her hands. 'Where's the Sharpie?'

'In the drawer under the sink.'

Joe clears the plates, snatches a shot glass from the cupboard and watches Matt draw the numbers *1* to *10* in a sweeping curve on the surface of the table in permanent marker, writing the letters of the alphabet in two rows beneath the numbers as well as *Yes* on the left and *No* on the right.

'Are we actually going to do this?' Emilie sounds nervous. 'Is it safe?'

'Nothing we've done since he was eleven years old has been safe,' Luke points out.

'And putting it into perspective,' Matt adds, 'it's probably the safest thing you've done in the last couple of months.'

'You could just have wished for a Ouija Board.' Emilie points that out a couple of minutes too late. Joe looks from her to Matt and Luke who look back at her as if the thought had never crossed their minds.

'We've always done it this way.'

Joe takes a stool next to Gabe who's watching but keeping quiet. 'I shouldn't be surprised by that, should I?' Gabe shakes his head. 'You're okay with this?'

He just chuckles. 'I'm sitting in an ever-changing house at the end of the world after a fight to the death with things escaped from Hell. If they want to hold a séance and chat to some ghosts, that's fine with me. I've got beer. I'm happy.' He's such an easy going guy, Joe wonders what he was like before all this when he was selling fast cars to rich kids. 'You know that phrase, 'once the worst thing that can ever happen to you has already happened, there's nothing left to be scared of'?'

'No,' Joe thinks about it. 'But it makes sense.'

'Just keep that in mind.'

'So... do we all need to hold hands?' Emilie asks as they all shift their stools towards the end of the table where the hand-drawn board faces Matt and Luke.

'No.'

She frowns. 'Should we wait for Rick?'

'If Rick's right and he died....' Matt trails off. 'No.'

'What about candles? Shouldn't we have candles and incense or something?'

'It's all bullshit,' Luke explains. 'The whole thing with the candles and the incense and sage, thyme, oregano, whatever herbs people have lying around. Why should the dead care what the place smells like or how it's lit? Just put your index fingers at the base of the glass, don't touch it, and wait.'

Joe's still not certain about this but he does as he's instructed, their fingers meeting around the shot glass. He expects something to happen immediately but it doesn't. They just sit and breathe, letting a silence descend. And it is silence. Take away their movements around the house and there's nothing left to make any noise. Even the scratching in the walls has stopped. It's the first time Joe's really been aware of not being a part of civilisation anymore. It settles around them, encasing them, entrapping them. And just before it becomes too stifling, Matt speaks.

'We're trying to contact whoever's here.' His words are calm and clear. 'We just have a couple of questions, we mean you no harm.'

Joe's surprised to see the upside down glass move, just a fraction of an inch, and glances at Gabe to his left and Emilie across the table, they're looking up too.

'Is this Limbo?' Matt starts, and the glass starts to slide to the left. 'Follow it with your fingers, but don't touch it.'

They do as Matt tells them. Joe looks at the others but the surprise on all their faces is genuine, except of course for Matt and Luke. He's thought up until now that séances were pieces of theatre but he's certain that it isn't one of them moving that glass.

It stops at *Y*.

'Is there a chance they're fucking with us?' Joe whispers.

Luke frowns at him and shakes his head.

Matt goes on, 'Are we all dead?'

This time the answer comes quickly. The way the glass moves on its own really is very freaky. *N*.

Matt takes a deep breath. 'How many of us here, in this room, are dead?' There's a pause, then the glass shifts again. Joe keeps expecting the table to shake or the plates on the sideboard to suddenly fly off and smash on the floor. Nothing like that happens, just the smooth movement inside the loose circle of their fingers until the glass stops at *1*.

Matt opens his mouth to speak but Luke stops him with a glance before phrasing the next question very carefully.

'Is it one of the two of us? Matt and I. Just yes or no.'

The pause is longer this time, and Joe doesn't think they're going to get an answer. But slowly, slower than before, there's movement within their fingers as the glass shifts again to the far right hand side of the board. *Y*.

'Which one?' Emilie asks, but Luke snatches up the glass before it can move. There isn't a sudden gust of wind, a dramatic slamming of doors or a shrill scream, just more silence. They all look up at Luke except Matt who has his eyes closed.

Emilie's staring at them, her eyes watery. 'You don't want to know which one?'

'No. It doesn't matter. If one of us is dead, we're both dead. That's why we're here, we won't let go.' He turns at the same time Matt does, and they rest their foreheads together, hands coming up to grasp each other by the back of the neck.

Joe needs to say something, to break the tension. But the thought of either of them... it's not possible. He saw them, at the end, still holding hands at the top of that hill.

'Why are we all here?' He won't be surprised if the brothers don't respond, as close as they are at that moment, but Luke's turns his head just a half inch, still touching Matt's and Joe's stunned to see tears in his eyes. Not once in the last two months has he seen either of them cry, however much pain they've been in, however bad the injuries. Now though....

'Possibly because you were with us at the end; the Scooby Gang.' He manages a tight smile. 'Or they might have thought we needed company.'

That's laughable; Joe doubts they've ever needed any company other than each other.

For a long time no one speaks. Matt and Luke seem to reach a wordless agreement, sitting up, Luke kissing Matt's forehead in a way Joe finds oddly touching and not the least bit uncomfortable.

'What happens to us if this all vanishes?' Gabe murmurs.

Matt replies, 'I'm sorry, I've no idea.'

Then Emilie asks, 'What are you doing to do?'

Neither answer verbally. But Luke drops his forehead to Matt's shoulder and groans softly.

'They're going to end this,' Joe murmurs, and he can only hope there is life after death.

~..~

Rick stops at the base of the steps leading up to the house. The light's fading. The snow's melting. His gut twists as he climbs to push open the door. There's a sound, ominous and loud in the otherwise silent house. The landlord is still standing unmoving and unresponsive in the hall but the grandfather clock, the one that was stopped, is ticking; the second hand moving in smooth, circular steps, counter-clockwise, counting backwards.

'Guys,' he shouts, moving quickly towards the kitchen, the cushioning effect of the tequila all but gone. 'What have you done?'

~..~

Closing the door of their room, Luke leans back against it and watches his brother slump down on the bed. Neither speaks for a long time, neither knows what to say. Luke turns the lock and goes over to the bed, wrapping his arms around Matt as Matt's come around him and they hold on tight.

When he speaks, his voice is rough and choked with tears, 'I don't want to go on without you.'

Luke shakes his head. 'I'm not leaving you. How am I supposed to let go of you when you've been the only person in my life?'

'I don't want you to die.'

'I might already be dead. We don't know. We can't know unless we let go and I have no idea how to do that.'

'I don't want you to let go.'

The strength they take from one another is enough to ease the initial pain. Sucking in a deep breath, Luke lets his arms loosen but not fall. 'I love you.'

'I love you as well.'

Luke lifts his head and they share another kiss just like the one outside only now he deepens it, turns it into more. Strange how this is the last line to be crossed.

Matt's the one to pull away, to wipe his nose on his sleeve. 'I don't understand. You were still standing there with me. We were injured but we were alive.'

There's a long silence. 'We could stay here.' But they both know how that would turn out. The idea of just giving up the kind of lives they've led to spend their days walking nowhere, drinking and playing pool at the fake roadhouse, is just slightly insane. 'We could stop changing things, stop wishing for things.'

'Then it would always stay the same, stagnate, nothing would ever change for any of us and eventually it would happen anyway because deep down it's what we want.'

'Eventually.'

'We'd just be putting it off.'

'Or it might just happen naturally. If there wasn't the constant threat of mortal danger, we might drift apart, just slightly, just enough....'

Matt smiles. 'You think?'

No, he doesn't think. He can't imagine ever loving his brother any less, ever not needing him or feeling the pull that he's felt towards him for most of his life. His world has never not revolved around him.

'So what do we do?'

Matt looks at him, and it doesn't take long for Luke to work out what he's thinking. It's the only way, and it's been waiting for them ever since they got here. It should be terrifying but it isn't. The only terrifying thing is the thought of living without each other, but that doesn't have to happen and this is the only way it's going to end.

'The dream.'

Matt's fingers stroke his neck. 'I think it was more than that. I think it was a suggestion, for when we're ready.'

'I can't hurt you.'

'You wouldn't be hurting me, you'd be saving me. Living without you – that would hurt.' Luke takes a deep breath but he can't, won't, deny Matt anything and Matt knows it. 'There's time,' he murmurs, and reaches for Luke again.

They both get naked as quickly as they can, desperate to feel skin against skin. Luke begs Matt to kiss him and they lie together exploring what's beyond that final line until Matt asks Luke to fuck him. There's a brief argument that Matt wins, and it takes a couple of goes and some trial and error that has them alternatively laughing and wiping tears from their eyes, but eventually they work it out. Luke moves inside his brother gently, with reverence. More than can be said for Matt who takes his turn with a desperation driven by grief. They pour everything into it; years of love and fear for one another, of protection and possession, of patching each other up and stopping one another from falling apart.

It has always been just the two of them and that's the way it's always going to be.

~..~

Downstairs, Joe washes the dishes. He made pumpkin pie but he doesn't think they're going to be around long enough to eat it. It's a shame, because it's a good pie. He thinks he could have been happy here for a while, cooking and not continually looking over his shoulder. But it's not his choice to make. He doesn't think about what Matt and Luke are doing upstairs, because he knows now there are worse things than them having sex.

Gabe is outside walking in the melting snow with a bottle of Merlot. Joe can see him out of the kitchen window, getting his shoes wet and smiling at the darkening sky.

He can hear Emilie in the hall, stoking the fire in the grate. When he looks in on her, she's going through the books on the shelves. As he watches, she slides one out and starts to cry. He can see the author's name in large letters on the front – Tess Gerritsen.

~..~

Rick pours a sherry for Nancy and one for himself and sits with her for a while. He asks her about Matt and Luke, about what they were like as children. She tells him a few stories that they would probably shoot her for revealing. They were close even back then it turns out.

'Their Mom could see it,' Nancy says softly. 'She told me one afternoon that they were too absorbed in one another and that it made her feel uneasy. I remember watching them play, out in the garden, one of those games only children know the rules for. I said, only good could come out of two brothers enjoying each others' company. They would protect each other in the future, I told her, they'd look out for one another and how could that be a bad thing? Don't get me wrong, they played rough, they didn't hold back. But when one of them inevitably got hurt, the other would immediately stop and comfort him. It was odd, but it was odd in a good way.'

Rick can see it in his mind's eye; two children playing in the warm sunshine, Mom keeping watch out of the window. Kids doing what kids do best: shouting, wrestling, kicking and punching. Until Matt starts to bleed and the sight of his brother's blood brings out a side of Luke that will have him risking his life and soul for his younger sibling one day, sooner rather than later.

'Do you understand, dear?' She turns to him and he feels like he's been broken out of a spell. He's back in the dimly lit lounge in a house somewhere between Heaven and Hell, talking to a woman who has been dead for twenty years. 'I always knew something tragic would befall them. I could feel it. It was why God killed Luke's parents and delivered him to Matt, why he made them so close. So they would be there for one another when the bad things happened.'

Rick stares, wondering if she knows that for a fact. Wondering if she knows just how close they really are.

'And they were. They survived; a thirteen year old and an eleven year old out in the world, just the two of them, and eventually they saved everyone.' She casts off the toy she's just finished, and drops it to the floor. Rick watches it but nothing happens, it just lies there. 'Joe's wrong about them. They had to love each other. It's the only way the right side could win.'

She stands up, leaning heavily on one arm of the rocking chair, pushing it downwards, shaky on her feet. Rick just watches her, trying to process what she said.

'It's been very lovely talking to you, dear.' He stands too, offering her a hand which she waves away. 'I'm fine. I believe I'm going now. You look after yourself. You're a good man at heart; don't let anyone tell you any different. Try not to hate the boys for what comes next.'

'What does come next?'

'Goodbye dear.'

She's gone.

'Wait!' But the only signs that she was ever here are the empty glass of sherry, the lifeless toy on the floor and the rocking chair still moving back and forth in front of the dying fire. He stares down at the toy before tentatively picking it up. It's just wool with a felt face. It's a child's toy not a creature hungry for raw steak. Everything's changing. The inevitable is catching up with him and there's nothing he can do to stop it.

He goes out into the hall where Emilie's standing at the window clutching a book to her chest and watching the last of the snow melt away to leave wide brown patches of wet, decaying leaves. He looks into the kitchen and sees Joe hunting around in the pantry, hears him muttering something about the potatoes sprouting and the fruit turning bad. The house is shutting down. The illusion's failing, the mask is slipping and there's only one reason for it. With his heart hammering in his chest, he runs upstairs, up the spiral staircase and bangs on the door of the turret room.

~..~

Matt and Luke hear Rick and tune him out. The twin knives were mounted on the wall across from the bed, whether they were there before neither can say but they were there when they reached for them.

They're sitting cross-legged on the messy sheets, naked and facing one another. Just like in their dream, each brother has the sharp edge of a

162

blade pressed to the neck of the other. One deep slash each will kill them both.

Closing the gap between them, their mouths meet for a last, hungry kiss over the deadly steel. They've said all they need to, they know it all anyway. They're tired too, not of fighting but of sharing themselves with other people. It's time to leave.

'Think Mom and Dad will be waiting for us?' Luke grins and nods. 'Think they'll be mad?'

'Definitely. Grounded for years with only each other for company.'

'Sounds like Heaven.'

'Ready, little brother?'

'Ready.'

It doesn't hurt.

~..~

The fire goes out. Emilie watches as the sky goes black. She calls the others in. Joe's holding an empty, rusty baking tin in his hands and Gabe's hands are empty. There's no snow now but everything's still damp from it. The temperature's dropping. Right in front of their eyes, the window cracks; a web spreading from the centre to the frame. They can hear it happening to all the other windows in the house, an eerie sound; slow and deliberate.

'It's over,' Joe whispers, and a tear breaks lose, escaping over his cheek.

They go upstairs together, the three of them, and find Rick sitting at the top of the spiral stairs with his head in his heads. They step over him and Emilie turns the doorknob. The heavy door swings open. The room's empty. All that's left are two curved blades lying one on top of the other on sheets stained red with blood. She starts to cry, and behind her Joe makes a choking sound in his throat and puts his arm around her shoulders.

'They're together,' he assures her, because she wouldn't ever want Luke to be unhappy. 'Wherever they are.'

'They have to go to Heaven,' she murmurs, then tips her head back and shouts it to whoever's listening. 'They go to Heaven, you hear me? Or I swear I'll hunt you down, wherever you are!' There's no answer. She doesn't expect one, but she's certain she's been heard. She turns to Joe and sniffs. 'How do we leave?'

'I don't know. But I think we should get out while we still can.'

~..~

Rick doesn't want to go but they drag him with them and the four of them stand in the yard with their backs to the house so they don't have to watch it disintegrate. It's cold. Joe and Gabe are pulling on their coats, and Emilie is shivering. Only Rick doesn't feel it. Rick's getting hotter, as if there's a fire burning at his back.

It's only a mild surprise when the clockwork landlord appears in front of them, working again.

'If you are ready
I will lead you back to where
You were taken from.'

Joe glances at each of them. 'It's been an honour. I'll see you around.'

Gabe and Emilie hug him but Rick doesn't.

'I don't think so,' he says in a voice filled with regret. And the world ends.

~..~

~ SIX MONTHS LATER ~

Emilie's working at a diner in Queens where it snows every year. When she first arrived she was stunned at the speed with which people had slipped back into the usual routine of life and with the way groups who fought together during the horror worked together just as well to clean up.

It's a part-time job and she enjoys it, which is surprising because she's spent her whole life up until this point avoiding working as a waitress. Now she likes the constant flow of people, regulars and strangers, locals and tourists. She's good with people and the customers like her so her boss likes her too.

During quiet times she sits at the bar and listens to the stories of those who sit with her. She listens to them and never tells her own. She likes Jake who works in the kitchen. He's a couple of years older than her but she's mature for her age and they get along. They've been on a couple of dates, nothing heavy, but sometimes they steal a kiss in the walk-in cold store and one day soon she's going to take him back to her apartment and fuck his brains out.

She still wants to see the world, but for now she's happy just appreciating being alive. She's surprised at how little she needs to do that.

Gabe's landed a little closer to home, in Nevada. The mere threat of the apocalypse isn't enough to stop the roulette wheels spinning in Las Vegas. It took him a couple of days to cross the desert and by the time he stepped off the bus it was as if an army of cleaners had swept down the strip. No blood stains on the roads or the walls, smashed windows replaced, looted shops restocked, restaurants and bars back in business. Now that the crazy has passed everyone seems to have found faith in something. The casinos are running at full capacity and good staff are hard to find.

He belongs here. It's his kind of town. After five days spent learning how the politics of the casinos worked he walked into the Luxor in a bespoke Italian suit and landed a job as a croupier. Two days ago he was promoted to pit boss when the guy he was working for was caught with his hand in the cookie jar. It's still there, his hand. It's a brutal town again now in a way it hasn't been since the beginning. Some people have developed a new taste for that kind of thing. He's okay. He keeps his head down, does what he's told and no more. He dresses well and he's good with the punters. He's on first name terms with the casino manager and in a couple of years he aims to be running a casino of his own. But he's not doing this just for himself, despite loving every second of it. He's also doing it for Rick. Because he knows Rick didn't make it.

It took a couple of days after he got back to work out the meaning of those final words as they stood in the yard and said their goodbyes. He didn't believe it. He tried to find Rick, tried to contact him, using the Internet where no one can hide. But to no avail. He hopes he went to Heaven but in his heart he knows he went to Hell. He hopes it isn't the terrible place he suspects it is.

Joe's back in Alpine. He returned with some trepidation and found a place filled with people picking up the pieces of their shattered lives. Over half the town's population is dead, the other half still shell-shocked; living people moving like zombies. They don't need a garage, don't need a mechanic. So on his first night he went over to the old bar. The interior was trashed but the structure was still intact. Electricity had been lost to the town so Joe helped to get it restored quickly. He spent weeks clearing out the bar, fixing the furniture, burning what couldn't be restored. He found a truck, hood-first, in the ruin of Mick's Motors. With a little work to the engine and a couple of cans of gas he used it to make the three day round-trip to Phoenix where supplies were getting through and he could pick up all the things he needed to re-open; booze, snacks and glasses. It was basic, but it was a start.

It's a Thursday night and Joe's Bar is packed with locals enjoying a cheap drink. Joe keeps his prices down, charges wholesale plus enough to keep the place running. He's not in it to make a profit. He's got arrangements in place with a firm in Los Angeles that delivers whatever bottles, barrels and casks are available, once a week. Last week he picked up a pool table on eBay and it's going down well with the youngsters. Whenever he hears the balls rolling across the baize it reminds him of Matt and Luke, and he spares them a minute's silence every day. Only the four – three – of them will ever know the sacrifices the boys made to stop the apocalypse. All he can do is keep their memory alive in little ways.

It's a good place, a happy place. Even those who've lost loved ones, friends and colleagues can come here to have a drink in company and leave a little happier than when they arrived. It's a supportive community and Joe is proud to be at the centre of it.

~..~

Luke slams the shot glass onto the bar and declares himself the winner. Next to him, his brother rolls his eyes, leans across and kisses him, tongue reaching for the burning taste of the tequila at the back of his throat. They down the last dregs of their beer before saying goodbye to the bartender and heading out into the warm night air. It's a five minute walk along a dark, empty road to their place. But it's a safe walk, because whenever something with teeth starts to sniff around they set out, track it down and kill it.

Their place is a sprawling ranch with empty stables and lots of land, set back from the road; quiet and lonely. They have an orchard filled with fruit trees and a garden where Matt grows everything from strawberries to oregano. Next to the house there's a garage where Luke keeps the Mustang running smoothly. Once a week they head out and just drive down a road that goes on forever but always brings them home. They haven't met up with their parents yet, they're not ready to. They might never be.

On the first day a tall man with dark curly hair knocked on their door just to check that everything was good for them. They haven't seen him since. They won't see him again. This is their time now, and while they think about Emilie and Gabe and Joe and Rick, they don't worry about them, and while they sometimes reminisce about old times, they don't miss them. They've got each other, just the way it's always been.

It's all they've ever wanted. It's Heaven.

THE END

Thank you for reading

For information and updates on books by Madeleine Marsh, and for free short stories based on the characters in this book, please go to www.madeleine-marsh.com

For news, you can follow Madeleine on Facebook at www.facebook.com/realMadeleineMarsh
    Or on Twitter @MadeleineMarsh

Printed in Great Britain
by Amazon.co.uk, Ltd.,
Marston Gate.